About the Author

Born in Austria in 1936, the second eldest of eleven siblings, Percy Mark grew up in a small village in the Austrian Alps before coming to England at the age of fourteen. Shortly after qualifying as an architect in 1959, he designed a cathedral for Monrovia in Liberia before spending eighteen months in Nigeria, completing his professional practice. He then spent six months with Dr Albert Schweitzer at his hospital in Lambarene, Gabon, in 1962 – 1963, where he met and got engaged to his life-long partner, Vreni Mark Burkhalter.

Back in the UK, as a partner of the architectural practice of Melvin Lansley and Mark during the 1970s and 80s, he engaged in private research into the application of the theory of harmonics in musical and visual proportions, leading to a period of lecturing on this subject in schools and universities in England and South Africa.

In 1995, he took over the chairmanship of the UK charity: Dr Schweitzer's Hospital Fund, visiting and supporting charitable projects managed in the spirit of Reverence for Life, both in India and Tanzania, as well as in the UK. He initiated the 'Next Evolutionary Step' (NESt) project aimed at exploring the potential contribution the philosophy of Reverence for Life can make towards meeting the challenges of the global environmental crisis and began introducing this to schools in the UK.

In 2016, his son, James, succeeded Percy Mark as chairman of the charity, now called 'Reverence for Life UK', allowing him to devote himself more fully, as part of the NESt Initiative, to the task of translating essential parts of Albert Schweitzer's third volume of his *Philosophy of Civilisation*. This resulted in 2020 in the publication, via NESt Publications, of two books under the titles *The World View of Reverence for Life* and *My Path with Albert Schweitzer*.

Conversations with his granddaughter, Emilie, inspired various small publications and essays, resulting in the current work under the name of *Lanya – Four Exploratory Journeys*.

LANYA

FOUR EXPLORATORY JOURNEYS

Percy Mark

LANYA

FOUR EXPLORATORY JOURNEYS

Olympia Publishers
London

www.olympiapublishers.com
OLYMPIA PAPERBACK EDITION

Copyright © Percy Mark 2024

The right of Percy Mark to be identified as author of
this work has been asserted in accordance with sections 77 and 78 of
the Copyright, Designs and Patents Act 1988.

All Rights Reserved

No reproduction, copy or transmission of this publication
may be made without written permission.
No paragraph of this publication may be reproduced,
copied or transmitted save with the written permission of the publisher,
or in accordance with the provisions
of the Copyright Act 1956 (as amended).

Any person who commits any unauthorised act in relation to
this publication may be liable to criminal
prosecution and civil claims for damage.

A CIP catalogue record for this title is
available from the British Library.

ISBN: 978-1-80439-633-9

This is a work of fiction.
Names, characters, places and incidents originate from the writer's imagination. Any resemblance to actual persons, living or dead, is purely coincidental.

First Published in 2024

Olympia Publishers
Tallis House
2 Tallis Street
London
EC4Y 0AB

Printed in Great Britain

Dedication

To my children and grandchildren, and to enquiring minds and open hearts of all ages.

Acknowledgements

I am deeply indebted to my granddaughter, Emilie Papantoniou, for her invaluable inspiration and help throughout the early stages of this book's development.

Her probing questions during our many conversations since well before she was in her teens, gave the initial impetus.

When she was a student at university, she edited my first attempts at retelling our conversations in preparation for the printing of the early chapters (in a limited edition for distribution amongst family and friends), and again when an expanded version, to which she contributed whole passages of her own, was self-published via NESt Publications.

And it was she, yet again, who has edited early versions of this much expanded edition, contributing further texts of her own and continuing to be my constant inspiration. This book could not have happened without her!

But my sincere thanks also go to my brother, George, for reading drafts, commenting and making suggestions throughout the many stages which have brought the book to its present form.

And not least, my deepest gratitude goes to my dear wife, Vreni, who has supported me throughout, fed, clothed and cared for me, and never failed to encourage, correct and advise me.

Contents

Preface 15

STORY ONE
BY TRAIN TO VIENNA AND BACK

INTRODUCTION 19
Chapter One - The Conversation Begins 20
Chapter Two - Religions 23
Chapter Three - Truth 27
Chapter Four - Belief 31
Chapter Five – The Purpose of Life 42
Chapter Six – The Afterlife 49
Chapter Seven – Free Will 53

THE RETURN JOURNEY

Chapter Eight – Concerns for Life on Earth 59
Chapter Nine - Prayer 68
Chapter Ten - Faith 77
Chapter Eleven - Gratitude 83
Chapter Twelve - Greed 87
Chapter Thirteen – Hope and Courage 96
EPILOGUE 104

STORY TWO
IN SEARCH FOR SOUL - In a Car

Introduction 107

Chapter One – Searching for Soul in the Bible and in the Airwaves 108

Chapter Two – Where Does Inspiration Come From 116

Chapter Three – How Can I Actually Feel my Soul 125

Chapter Four – Grandpa's Favourite Image of Existence 128

Chapter Five – Tuning into Your Soul 134

STORY THREE
OTHER SEARCHING QUESTIONS - On Garden Benches

Introduction 138

Chapter One – On a Bench at the Top of the Garden 139

Chapter Two – More About the Lord's Prayer 143

Chapter Three – A New Line of Enquiry 147

Chapter Four - 7,874,965,825 HUMANS, The Total Global Population in 2021 150

STORY FOUR
QUESTING VIA EMAIL

Introduction - How can we Humans best co-operate with Mother Earth? (Explored via Email during a pandemic) 164

Chapter One - NESt and the Age of Aquarius 166

Chapter Two – The Quest is Defined 177
Chapter Three - Honing the Parameters of the Quest 182
Chapter Four – Casting About for Inspiration 188
Chapter Five – Taking Stock 206
Chapter Six – Sharpening the Focus 219
Chapter Seven – Final Preparations 227
Chapter Eight – At the Threshold 244
Epilogue 276
APPENDIX 'A' 278
Comments by interested readers 280

Preface

Lanya and her grandfather, Frederick, now in his mid-eighties, are fictional characters but their relationship is inspired by real-life events. In the first story, as a birthday treat, Frederick takes the fifteen-year-old Lanya on a train journey to his birthplace, Vienna, and five days later they return to London. Their conversation on these train journeys explores what the young Lanya calls 'God and religion and all that'.

Between then and the following two stories, Lanya has been to university, from where she emerges with a First-Class Honours Degree and a husband-to-be. She then tried and rejected a career in the commercial art world, became an artisan baker and is now trying her hand at becoming a professional editor.

The second and third stories are set during the time of the COVID-19 virus pandemic. The sudden disruption of settled routines created open spaces for unusual thoughts – gaps for glimpses into unfamiliar territory offering potential for exploration, opportunities for journeying into the deeper regions of our being. These two later stories give expression to this, with probing questions delving behind outward appearances, and digging deep in search for meaning, understanding and purpose – first during a car journey, then on garden benches and finally – COVID-restriction compliant – via email.

Whilst Lanya's inner journey in the company of her grandfather actually began when she was four years old, we now meet them both on a train going to Vienna.

STORY ONE

BY TRAIN TO VIENNA AND BACK

INTRODUCTION

This train journey is set in a time before the coronavirus was even dreamt of.

As train journeys go, few will have left a more profound and far-reaching impact on the lives of these two travellers than this one, even though outward appearances would give no clue of this.

They are perhaps an unlikely couple of travel companions: an elderly grandfather, wearing his favourite hand knitted jumper, and his young granddaughter in a smart navy blue dress. They sit opposite each other in an empty train compartment leaving St Pancras Station. Lanya is one of Frederick's six grandchildren and has recently turned fifteen. In fact, this is the very reason for their trip. As a birthday treat, Frederick had promised Lanya a train journey to a destination of her choosing, and without hesitation she had chosen Vienna. She knew her grandfather had been born there and from overheard conversations had gained the impression that it must be a very beautiful place.

Chapter One

THE CONVERSATION BEGINS

Whilst the train was speeding through London's suburbs, Lanya had been chatting excitedly about the scenery whizzing past their window. Now, having left suburbia behind, and the sensation of travelling at great speed was fading in the open countryside, Lanya became quiet. She sat with her forehead resting against the window glass, dreamily savouring the novelty of embarking on such a long journey. For a while she was deep in thought. Suddenly, she turned to her grandfather with the question, "You know God and religion and all that, Grandpa?"

He had been relaxing in his seat, head back against the headrest, also gazing out of the window. Now he sat up, quite taken aback by such a question coming out of nowhere. Of course he did not know that she had been planning to ask him this question ever since this train journey together was first mentioned.

"Well, I'm not so sure I *know* God, but I have heard and read descriptions of what some people like to call God. I do know a bit about various religions, though. But why do you ask?"

"Because I find it all so confusing. What we are told in school and what they say in church, and then what is on the news about religions fighting each other – it just doesn't make any sense, any of it. And I thought you could help me to understand."

He was astonished, to say the least. To be sure, he had

wondered what they would talk about on this long journey... but straight in – just like that... how to respond?

"Well," he said, a teasing twinkle in his eyes, "I can tell you, that the word 'religion' comes from the Latin word *'religare'*, which means: 'to bind again' or 'to re-unite'. Although some people say it comes from the word *'religio'*, which means 'obligation' or 'reverence' or 'bond'..." But then he hesitated, knowing only too well that a discussion of semantics was not what his granddaughter was after.

"Be serious, Grandpa," she said anxiously. "I mean... I've got to make some sense of this. Is there a god? Some people say there is no such thing. If there is a god why are there so many different religions and why do they keep fighting each other? And where do fairies and elves and those creatures fit in – which you know are important to me?"

Frederick knew Lanya too well not to expect some serious conversations – but this was right in at the deep end. He realised, of course, that Lanya was in complete earnest and wasn't going to let him get away with smart, clever responses. These were big questions which weren't going to be answered in a few sentences. And to be sure, he knew only too well that there were no simple answers to such questions. But in his heart of hearts, these had been the *real* questions for as long as he could remember – the most important questions for anyone to ask. Lanya now wanted to talk about them seriously. He had to rise to the challenge!

"We are coming into the last station on English soil now," he said, looking out of the window. "Soon we will be entering the tunnel and then we'll be under the sea. This is a good place to be thinking about such things because the sea is the mother of life and life is God's creation, the most sacred thing we have here on earth."

Lanya was looking at her grandfather expectantly.

"I think we'll come back to God later," he said. "Let's talk about religions first. Let's begin by considering your question as to why there are so many different ones and then think about what they have in common, and where *truth* might fit in. This is going to be a big challenge which might take us quite a while. But after all, we have a long journey in front of us – and what are grandfathers for, after all?"

As the train dived down into the dark tunnel and the lights came on, they braced themselves to talk about these questions which had preoccupied theologians and philosophers for thousands of years.

Chapter Two

RELIGIONS

"The train we are on," Frederick began, "will be travelling a distance of a thousand miles from London to Vienna and our travel time on this journey is about eighteen hours. When Christ was born, Romans did this same journey on horseback in several weeks. To travel to China might have taken several years – which people did do at that time. But it was only during the last century that it became possible to travel around the earth in a matter of hours and to speak to someone on the other side of the globe in a matter of seconds."

He paused for a moment, so Lanya added:

"And we can easily see what is happening on the other side of the world on our televisions or use the internet to send messages or emails all around the globe."

"Exactly," he agreed. "We take it for granted that we can be in touch with people nearly anywhere on earth and see all parts of the Earth's surface from our satellites."

"Yes, let's not forget space," she said enthusiastically, gesturing up at the roof of the carriage. "We now have lots of wonderful pictures of Earth taken from space."

It was strange to think of space whilst travelling in a dark tunnel under the sea.

"Yes, we now know," he went on, "how really small the Earth is as part of our solar system and our galaxy and all the rest out there. Thousands of years ago, people living in one part of the Earth had no knowledge of other parts and other people's lives far away. Yet each of the different groups of people had thoughts, quite independently of each other, about the great powers they experienced around them, and about the relationship they felt between their inner lives and the outside world. All cultures felt the need to have something to worship and to believe in, whilst contact between different groups was extremely restricted compared to nowadays. So each group developed its own ways of communicating amongst themselves about these unseen powers, or beings, which they called *spirits*, and of worshiping them, and somehow coping with these mysteries. There are no doubt many reasons, but I think this is one practical reason why there are so many different religions and traditions."

Lanya leaned forward, resting her arms on the table between them, absorbing what he had said. After a few moments she said, "How many different religions are there actually? I know about Christianity, the Jews and the Muslims. And I know someone who is a Buddhist, so that makes four."

"I don't really know how many there are," he said hesitatingly. "There must be hundreds, if not thousands, if you count all the different tribes in the rainforests and the savannahs in Africa, South America and Asia, and the First Nations of America and Canada, Australia's First Peoples, and the Maoris of New Zealand…" He paused, scratching his head. "Perhaps we should decide which to name as the main religions," he continued, as if to himself. "Could we say that the main religions are those that have written texts as their basis, you know, like the Bible and the Qur'an. And of those I can only think of three more that are currently practised, to add to the ones you have already mentioned, namely: Hinduism, Jainism and the Chinese Thinkers."

"Who are the Chinese Thinkers?" Lanya asked immediately. "And what about Catholics and Baptists and all those?"

"Well yes, it gets a lot more complicated because each of what are called the World Religions is split into dozens of different denominations, sects and groups. But let's not go into all of that now, it would get very involved and we can tackle that at some other time if you like. As to the Chinese Thinkers: during the 6th century BC – about the same time Pythagoras lived in Greece and Sicily – two great philosophers lived in China and their legacy has been handed down to us in two schools of thought – the Taoists and the Confucianists. But again, I think we should leave these for another day, don't you think?"

Lanya was content with this and pressed on with her earlier question, "So why do they fight each other?"

"Yes, that is indeed a very important and vexed question for us these days. Of course, religion is not the only reason why people fight each other. Often religion is used as a pretext when it is actually about land, money and power."

Lanya looked troubled and asked, "You'd think that religions would try to stop this fighting – at least the Christian religion. It is supposed to be about love, isn't it?"

"You would have thought so. But for many people, their own religion has to be the only one – the right one. All the others have to be wrong. In religious language 'wrong' tends to be the same as 'evil', so for many people, the evil of others has to be stamped out at all costs. For these people, theirs is the only true God and their way is the only true way of approaching Him. Sometimes, extremist believers feel the need to persuade everyone, by force if necessary, to believe exactly what they and their group believes. And when two such groups come up against each other, the sparks fly and often blood flows." Frederick took a deep breath – this subject troubled him deeply.

Lanya sighed and covered her face with her hands, warding off the heaviness she felt at her grandfather's words. "I don't understand," she said slowly. "If all these different religions grew up from way back, when people were not in touch with each other as they are now, then these religions surely are just like all the different languages. People don't have to kill each other just because they speak a different language?"

"That's a very good way of putting it," he agreed with enthusiasm, "If only more people could see it like that."

"So why don't they?"

This wasn't easy. He took another deep breath and said, "Because, contrary to how people think about their language, they think that their religion is *The Truth ordained by God* and that therefore they own THE TRUTH. But the thing about truth is: that you cannot own it. It is not something that you can have. You can only be it. You can be truthful, but you cannot hold it in your hand and say: 'This is the truth, I have it'. As soon as you do that, it has already disappeared, vanished into thin air like a moonbeam. How does that song go?"

She knew immediately, and sang it out loud and clear, "How do you hold a moonbeam in your hand?"

Chapter Three

TRUTH

By now they had left the tunnel and were out in open countryside again, traversing the vast open spaces of northern France. Lanya sat facing the direction of travel and as they were looking out at the view, a hazy September sun was travelling with them behind the trees. The effect of the flickering beams through the trees bathed the compartment in a soft but restless sunlight. Frederick was wondering what more could be said about truth.

Dreamily, Lanya remembered how, when she was younger, fairies had played an important part in her imagination. After a while, she asked, "You haven't said anything about fairies yet and how they fit into the picture? I used to think a lot about fairies – now I'm not so sure about them. Is there anything you can tell me about them?"

Glad to be distracted away from his heavy thoughts about truth, he replied cheerfully:

"Well, I'll try. But first, tell me how you learnt about them?"

"From fairy stories, of course," she said quickly. "Where else?"

"Of course, and fairy stories are made up by grownups for children, aren't they?" he said with a twinkly smile.

She nodded, looking at him intently.

"Well, there are many things which grownups have difficulty explaining; things which don't fit easily into their usual way of seeing the world. So they hint at these for the benefit of their children in the form of fairytales. Children are much more willing to accept things without a logical explanation or scientific proof because they still have a vivid sense of mystery and imagination."

"Are you saying that they aren't really true, that grownups just pretend they are?" There was a touch of anxiety in her voice.

"You remember what I said about truth being something that *is*, something you can *be* and not something you can *have* or lock up in a box – or even lock up in words?"

"Yes – so? Are fairies true or not?" she insisted.

"Well, let's think about what we know about them. Have you ever seen one?"

"No; have you?" There was challenge in her voice.

"I may have done," he said quietly. "I'm not really sure. Maybe we should try and determine what kind of being a fairy would be, if it did exist. What other names for similar beings do we know?"

"Well, there are goblins and elves and pixies," Lanya said, thinking back to all the books she had read.

"What about ghosts and spirits and angels?" he asked.

"Oh yes! And there are demons and devils and auks."

"So there seem to be whole populations of these creatures! Perhaps this shows that people vaguely sense that something exists which they can't be sure about and they have made up names and stories to be able to talk about whatever it is." After a pause, he went on, "For instance, Lanya, have you ever looked at the curtains when the sun is shining through them and seen animals or faces appear in the patterns? Or in an abstract picture. We have an abstract painting hanging in our house – just colourful shapes – and when I look at it without focusing on any particular part, then sometimes I see all sorts of weird faces, and whole creatures even appear out of the brushstrokes. But if I focus my eyes, they are just blotches of colour again."

"Yes, that happens to me too," she said eagerly. "When I stare at the tiles on our bathroom floor, which have a sort of 'mottled' pattern, I also see faces, but rarely the same face twice."

"I thought you might. So, can we get any leads from this?"

"Are you saying that what we see in the curtains or the tiles are fairies?" she asked, looking dubious.

"Perhaps," he said with a shrug. "Imagine yourself living thousands of years ago. There is no television, no radio, and no cities as we know them. Most people live very close to nature. Now imagine yourself sitting on a fallen log at the edge of a forest overlooking a valley with a little stream below you. Behind you is the mysterious darkness of dense woodland. It is evening. You are relaxing at the end of the day. Dusk is creeping in. There is a very gentle breeze from the east. Your eye rests vacantly on an old, gnarled oak tree a little way off to the right. Suddenly there is a face in the small bush beside the tree's trunk. And then, what you thought was the root of the tree transforms into the figure of a little person with a pointed hat. You are spellbound. You hold your breath. The little figure seems to be scratching at something in the bark of the trunk. The face in the bush is watching it. The small ball at the tip of its pointed hat is bobbing up and down. You watch, motionless. Eventually, you can bear it no longer and get up to have a closer look, but they are both gone. There is only the little bush at the side of the bottom of the trunk.

"Then, as you slowly walk back towards the village and come to a bridge across the little stream, your eye is caught by something else. As the evening mists are rising from under the willow trees you see the gentlest, most delicate of creatures gliding from branch to branch. You watch them floating off, and others follow. You can hardly believe your eyes and stand, mesmerised, for a long while, in amazement. A last ray of the setting sun breaks through a gap in the crimson clouds making the floating creatures glow in changing colours… The sun sets and all is changed. Darkness descends over the valley. You hurry home. But how are you going to tell others what you have seen?"

The subtle rhythm of the train accompanied their thoughts as they sat for a while in silence. Frederick had his right hand resting on the little table between them. Lanya leaned forward and laid both her hands on his. "I see what you mean: the truth is in the experience, and the experience is in the imagination, and you have to find words to describe and share your experience."

Wrapping his fingers around hers, he said, "I don't mean to imply that I don't allow the possibility – or even the likelihood – that there are disembodied beings: beings that only interact with us on a mental or spiritual level, which can't be seen or heard on the physical plane. There is such a lot we don't know and can't explain. Where do the ideas which arise in our imagination come from? Who is to say that they are any less real or true than the hard facts of physics and chemistry?"

Chapter Four

BELIEF

The train arrived in Paris. On their way from the Gare du Nord they had a quick lunch at a pavement café on the Place de la Republique and then dashed across the Place de la Bastille and down the Rue de Lyon so as not to miss their connecting train leaving from the Gare de Lyon. Once more, they found an empty compartment and sat panting – relieved that they had made it. The high-speed train hurtled through the southern outskirts of Paris.

Lanya re-started the conversation, "So what is it you actually believe in, yourself?"

"They say that seeing is believing," he said, tongue in cheek. "People used to believe that the Earth was flat and that the Sun went around the Earth because that is what their eyes told them. But, it is not as simple as that now, is it? We are asked to believe many things we can't see. For instance, astronomers have conjured up a whole picture of outer space for us. Should we believe all they tell us about that, even though we can't see it with our own eyes? I, for one, have never believed this business about the Big Bang as the beginning of everything. Have you heard of the theory of the Big Bang?"

"They talk about it in school, but I didn't pay much attention."

"It just doesn't make any sense to me," he said in his

'challenge the scientists' voice. "It might have been the beginning of the bit of the universe we happen to be in. But what was before that Bang? And *in what* did it take place?"

"I don't really know much about all that," admitted Lanya casually.

"Well, there is no need to trouble yourself with it, because quite soon they are going to ask us to believe quite a different theory about how everything began. That's the odd thing about how the achievements of science are communicated to us. Every time they come up with a new theory, although the scientists themselves know very well that it is only a theory, we're told by the media that it is the finally discovered answer to everything. Then, ten years later it happens all over again!"

"Now you are being sarcastic," said Lanya with a smile, "and it doesn't suit you."

"You are quite right, Lanya, I should restrain myself and behave. But, you see, I can't help thinking that with our obsession with science to the exclusion of other ways of seeing things, we are losing our way. Don't get me wrong. During the last few centuries science has come up with amazing things and we have benefited hugely in our physical comforts and our possibilities of movement and communication. And this was no doubt necessary for the ongoing evolution of the human race but now it seems to me that it's time to turn back."

"What do you mean – 'turn back'?" she interjected, "Surely we can't turn back the clock?"

"No, I don't mean we should repeat the past, but to change direction. Think of it this way: we can look at human development as being like the ascent up a mountain whose sides are too steep to go straight up. So our path takes a zigzag course. It goes across the slope in one direction and then turns back in the other direction. The times when turns are made, are usually the most creative but also the most challenging periods in human history. Each period in civilisation has to tackle its own challenges. For example, in the Middle Ages in Europe, it was all about belief, the soul and the inner qualities of valour and devotion. But that ended up in the burning of witches and the Spanish Inquisition and people being driven from their homes in thousands because of what they believed. Then some people thought there must be another way, and they began to seek truth in the natural world around them. And thus, what we call modern science was born. As I said, this has resulted in some huge benefits in technology and general affluence, but it has also brought us to an abyss with regard to climate change and pollution. So I think we are due for another 'turn'. That's what I mean by 'losing our way'."

"That's all very interesting, but what has this got to do with our discussion about what to believe?" Lanya enquired slightly impatiently.

"What I'm trying to show you," he continued, "is that on this zigzag path, what people tell you to believe, continues to change. Leaders of religious organisations and scientists are always out to tell us what to believe, pretending that they know. But if you keep an open mind about things which you hear from other people, or things you read, then perhaps you will start to find answers to your questions from inside yourself. And those are the answers you can believe with confidence. I can't tell you where they come from but if you start listening out for them, you will soon recognise them."

"Have you had any such 'answers' you can tell me about?" she asked, intrigued.

"Well yes, I can," he said. "As long as you remember it's

just something else somebody has told you."

"But you are not just *somebody*," she said indignantly.

"Oh yes I am – especially as far as this is concerned."

"All right, but tell me anyway. You know I won't accept it if it makes no sense to me."

"Well then, when I was a student, I would cycle to college through London's Regents Park every week-day. I used to think all sorts of thoughts on those bike rides, mostly about a girl with flaxen hair in the year above me! But there was a time, when I thought a lot about how the world worked and tried to make sense of things, much as you are doing now. One day it came to me out of the blue: that we always tend to think of things in opposites, but that these opposites are in fact connected, linked together by something on which they are suspended, like beads on a thread. I called these threads 'Qualities'. It seemed to me that these 'Qualities' are like the warp on a weaver's loom, setting the framework for the weaving of the fabric of the universe."

She looked puzzled.

"Take hot and cold for instance," he continued. "We call them opposites don't we?"

"Yes!" she exclaimed, "and they are linked on the thread of temperature!"

"You've got it straight away, Lanya. So, let's play a game to see how many opposites and threads we can find. I'll call out the opposites and you tell me the threads. Near and far?"

"Distance," she said.

"Fast and slow?"

"Speed, or velocity," she replied.

So they went on like this until he said, "Ugly and beautiful?"

"Looks," she replied after a moment's thought.

"Yes, or appearance," he added.

Lanya realised that they had entered a different category and suggested, "What about 'good and bad' then? – or 'love and hate', or 'kindness and cruelty'?"

"Yes, you are quite right. These are the important opposites as far as our conversation is concerned. However, our language does not have good words for all the threads in this category. And by the way, I would say that the opposite of hate is perhaps 'fondness' or 'liking' rather than love. Love is a much abused word. I think it may not have an opposite and may belong to yet another different category altogether. The importance of my realisation," he went on, "was that, whilst we usually see so many things in pairs, in reality these things come in threes. If we can see and recognise the third element in these things, we come closer to experiencing unity in our world and we approach the essence which lies buried in all religions…" He hesitated and thought for a moment, before continuing: "The thing is, I then secretly practised this for years – always finding the common thread between opposites as I came across them in daily life. And looking back, I see now that this probably was the beginning of my own inner journey. I remember thinking that I had found the essence of this particular exercise when I discovered that whenever an 'either-or' situation presented itself, and I had difficulty in choosing, I would find a way out of the dilemma by looking at it through the lens of 'as-well-as'."

He stopped again and took a deep breath, whilst Lanya asked, "How do you mean? – I don't understand."

"You have to try it for yourself to see how it works," he said. "You see, this is what I meant when I said… 'you will start to receive answers to your questions from inside yourself, and those are the answers you can believe with confidence'… This was something I discovered for myself and I trusted it, and it stood me in good stead. When you are faced with opposing options and you say to yourself: 'as-well-as', instead of 'either-or', you choose a different path, you create a bond, you create unity, and a new situation arises, a new direction opens up. But you have to experience this in practice."

"I see. I will certainly try it," she said somewhat hesitatingly, "so when I can't make up my mind about which of two dresses I should put on I say 'as-well-as'… and wear both?" she added tongue in cheek. But at that moment he was taking himself too seriously to take a joke, and he reacted with a wry smile.

"Fair enough," he said, "If you're going to be silly, we can talk about something else."

"No, no. I'm sorry, don't be upset!" she said quickly. "But what has this to do with my question about 'what to believe'?"

"I'm not going to tell you what to believe," he said firmly, "If you look around, there are plenty of people doing that. I have told you of one instance, where a realisation came up from inside myself and I trusted it and tried it and it worked well for me. Then I learnt much, much later that this connects with what philosophers call the 'Law of Three', which describes how, in this world of perceived dualities, opposites can be brought into relationship with a third factor, giving stability and harmony and creating unity – with far reaching implications. As for instance: if any one of these trinities which we just created in our little game earlier, is represented as a triangle, and we reduce the distances between the three corners, they will gradually merge – for our naked eye – into a single point. If you then look at it through a microscope, you will be able to go on reducing the distances – depending on the strength of your instrument – until eventually you will be faced with the question of infinity, which is where the search for what to believe has to begin, because that is where 'All will be one – and zero'." His voice, usually mild and diffident, had become firm and authoritative, and Lanya listened intently.

But now she burst in with, "How can it be one and zero at the same time?"

"Yes, exactly! That was one of the questions which I then had to face when I was a student. Of course, then these things were all just vague feelings – fleeting images. Now some things have become a little clearer – but only a little." He took another deep breath. In truth this was still a total mystery to him and on the very rare occasion that he had to try to put it into words, he found it hard.

"The concept of 'zero' is a difficult one to grasp," he began again, squinting at her with a furrowed brow. "It's a bit like that moonbeam – when you think you have it – there's nothing there."

"Well, there wouldn't be, would there – it's zero!" she interjected, cheekily.

"Well yes, 'zero' is a slippery customer. It keeps appearing to change places with 'one' – or should I say – disguising itself as 'one'. Yet it is there all the time. In everything. Behind everything – everywhere. When it's one – it's somewhere. When it's zero, it's everywhere. But for our brain – for our thoughts – even everywhere has to be somewhere. That's the puzzle."

"You are teasing me! Can we get to the point?" she said with a slightly impatient smile.

"The 'point' is indeed where it's at! As I said: if you pursue a point – a dot – to infinity, it disappears out of our field of vision. That is, it becomes infinitely small until it switches to zero; though never ever completely. This is the great mystery with which we have to learn to live, if we want to gain some clarity about what to believe. The mystery of 'All' and 'Nothing'."

There was a long pause. They both looked vacantly out of the window at the passing landscape, deep in thought. Eventually, Lanya said with a deep sigh, "Oh dear, this is all far beyond me. You have to bring this back to earth for me."

"To approach this conundrum, let's consider what we might mean by this 'All'? What I mean by it is 'all that we experience by being here in this life' – our existence in this three dimensional world of our senses. The world in which we have our 'being'. We have five physical senses, don't we? And in ancient Greek philosophy these are matched up with the five 'elements' from which, in their view, the physical world is constituted. The ancient Indians had a similar scheme. As did the ancient Chinese, although theirs had some significant differences we won't go into now." He started counting with the fingers of his left hand. "Earth & smell; water & taste; air & touch; fire & sight; and ether & hearing. They represent a progression towards ever greater subtlety. You will note that there are five elements here, whilst in school they probably only talked about the first four. You may also know, that the first three have been subdivided by scientists into up to a hundred and eighteen chemical elements with more being discovered all the time."

"You are not going to give me a chemistry lesson now, are you?"

"I wouldn't dare – you probably know much more about chemistry than I ever will. But I had to set the scene by sketching out this 'scheme', because what interests us here is the fifth element, *ether*, which in modern scientific culture has gone missing. It seems to have disappeared. What the Greeks called 'ether' we now call 'space', but although ether fills all space the two are not synonymous, as sub-atomic research is discovering, and it is these various misconceptions surrounding ether and space which we have to unravel in order to gain some insight into the relationship between zero and one. Are you with me on this? Do you want us to go on with it?" He was worried that this was taking too long.

"But of course! Let's get to the bottom of this riddle with which you are teasing me," she exclaimed, smiling broadly at him.

"Okay then," he said, "imagine I am holding a vase." His hands mimed holding a vase out towards her. "Here's the key question: if I take the vase away, what is left in its place?"

"Well," she replied, "the space from all around it flows into… except?… oh, I see!… flows into what?"

"Oh you clever girl, you've got it at once!" He was so proud of his granddaughter.

"Yes – 'into what?' That's the question," he continued. "That space was there all the time, was it not? The air will have flowed in and filled the volume where the vase had been, but the 'space' has not changed one bit. That 'space' is everywhere, and is what the ancients meant by the 'ether'. It is not between *things* but all *things* exist 'in it' and are permeated by it. We can't do anything to it. Our five senses can't affect it, they just perform in it. It is the background to all we do – to all existence and to all of life. And here we are back to what we said earlier: 'this space is everywhere; in the created, three-dimensional world it is the '*ether*', the 'All' and the 'One is one and all alone and everywhere shall be so', to adapt the words of a very old song. However, there is a *beyond* even that, where pure space is '*Zero*'. On the zigzag path up the mountain we mentioned earlier, this is the main thrust of our 'turning back' – the acknowledgement of this 'space/ether'; its rediscovery and its reintroduction into our picture of the world. We are picking it up off the floor, where it had fallen – slipped off the edge of the scientific table, quite unnoticed – and we are putting it back on the table, as part of the overall picture – our world-view."

Wide-eyed, Lanya sat, stunned, gazing into space. They both did. After a while he said, speaking more quietly than he had done in his earlier excitement, "For the ancients, this space, this ether, was the threshold between the physical and the spiritual aspects of life. This can be experienced, as we have just experienced it now, in what has been called the 'here and now', where it is neither too hot nor too cold, neither too far nor too near, neither good nor bad. Everything is just as it is and has the qualities that it has. That moment is neither too early nor too late, because it will be the point in time which links to eternity, just as every physical point links to infinity."

He knew he had got carried away and was just about to apologise when her question showed that she had been following very closely, "Why do we feel hot and cold and all those opposites then? And whatever do you mean by the 'here and now'?"

"Of course, at one level the experience of hot and cold, etcetera, is for our protection, to keep us within the limits of what our bodies can withstand. But if we can be fully 'present' – in the present moment – a state of stillness through which time flows like a current – which is what some call the 'here and now' – then we are aware of the temperature, the location and the light of whatever condition we are in. We accept them as they are and do not make judgements about them. We take the appropriate action to protect ourselves if necessary. We only feel too hot or too cold because we always want to be somewhere other than where we actually are."

"I see. I think I do follow you," she said hesitatingly. "When

I am at my dancing class, I forget everything else. I just dance, and everything seems to be in its proper place."

"Just so!" he whispered, nodding.

"When you talk about the law of three," Lanya asked after a while, "does that apply to the Father, Son and Holy Spirit?"

"Absolutely, it does. That is how Christianity expresses the essence of that law. In Hinduism there are three main gods called Brahma, Vishnu, and Shiva. They also talk about three powers or energies, which they call the 'Three Gunas': Rajas, Tamas and Sattva. These can be translated into our language as Activity, Sleep and Stillness. These three, according to the Hindu view of things, permeate the whole of creation. You can see that our 'triangle' which we conjured up earlier, would have Rajas and Tamas at the bottom corners and Sattva at the top."

"What I can see," Lanya said dreamily, "is that what you believe is not as simple a matter as I thought."

For a while they both sat in comfortable, silent contemplation of the momentous conversation that had just taken place. What Hindus would call a 'satvic' moment.

Chapter Five

THE PURPOSE OF LIFE

The train had been climbing up into the foothills of the French Alps and had passed into Switzerland. For a long time they just sat looking out of the window, absorbed in the beautiful Swiss landscape, and neither of them wanted to talk. It was late afternoon now. The deep blue sky was cloudless. The setting sun was casting long shadows in the direction of the train's destination across rich green meadows. Eventually, it was Lanya who once more broke the silence.

"You said that Hindus have three main gods, but we Christians only have one god, don't we?"

The answer to this question, on the face of it, was a simple 'yes'. But Frederick sensed that this was the opening to a much larger discussion about the concept of God. He closed his eyes for a moment to order his thoughts; he wanted to tread carefully.

"That goes right back to the beginning of our conversation and your very first question, doesn't it?" he began. "When communication was much more laborious than it is now, people's imagination developed in various and different ways to interpret the unseen world. Some cultures called the inhabitants of that world 'nature spirits', some populated it with many different gods, and arranged them in well-structured hierarchies of the spirit world. Yet others put the emphasis on one god supported by archangels and angels and other such spirits. But, Lanya, isn't the real question: what can we actually know about God?"

Lanya nodded, urging her grandfather to continue.

"Scientists have now provided us with some sense of the enormity of our universe in comparison to the minuscule size of an atom. Could you imagine that our solar system is the equivalent of a tiny atom in the body of an enormously larger being? To that being, life on earth could be like life on an electron of an atom inside your body."

Seeing the puzzled look on Lanya's face he reached into his leather bag and took out a pen and paper and drew a diagram of an atom. He passed the paper to her. Pointing with his pen he said, "This is an atom, which consists of a nucleus in the centre and electrons circling around it, similar to our solar system with its sun and the planets."

Looking at the drawing Lanya said, "I've never thought about it like that. Do you mean that the inside of an atom is just the same as our solar system?"

"Not exactly the same, but scientists are telling us that there are similarities. And I think that we could also compare our galaxy to a cell in our bodies. This would be in line with the ancient wisdom which says: 'As above, so below'. In today's scientific language, what I am suggesting is that the structure of the world is fractal, meaning: that every part is organised on the same principle as the whole. In religious language we say that God is everywhere and in everything. Jesus made the same point when he taught us to pray: 'Thy will be done in earth as it is in heaven'. As I endeavour to make the atoms in my body obey my will, so God expects us to obey His will – not forgetting of course, the experiment with 'free will', but we'll come to that later, perhaps."

Lanya was relieved to hear some familiar words and the

slightest of smiles lit up her bewildered face. She recognised the line from the prayer and it made her feel that she was again beginning to make some sense of what he was talking about; and she asked, "So are you saying then, that this enormously large *being* could be, as it were, our god – the god of our scientific age?"

"You remember," he continued, "when we talked about 'answers' coming from inside yourself? Well, let me tell you of another time, when such an 'answer' came to me. One morning when I was in my early forties, I had just parked my car in the office car park and happened to glance down at the thumb of my hand holding the car key. In that moment, suddenly, I saw myself standing on an electron, part of an atom inside the tip of my thumb – to which my body was an unimaginably huge organism. At the same time, I knew that I was standing on this Earth, which is part of a solar system inside the thumb of some vast imaginary entity, to whom I was infinitesimally small. It was a kind of double vision. And I assure you, this wasn't just an idea. At that moment this was for real – 'a *realisation*' you might say. It was an inner conviction which has remained a reality for me and shaped my thinking ever since."

Amazement was written all over her face as the scale of the mental picture struggled to take shape in her mind. One of those rare moments of infinite stillness and unity enveloped them both. Passing time seemed to stand still, as if in an interval.

"What I am tentatively suggesting," he eventually continued, "is that this human body, living on planet earth, inhabited by a consciousness we call 'I' (as in 'I am the way…'), is the embodiment of God for a creature living on an electron in an atom of this body. Similarly, an unimaginably large being – which some call the universe – is the embodiment of God for me.

This for me has become a reality. For you this is, of course, just an idea which somebody – your grandfather – is telling you. All the different religions describe their own ideas about God and what He is like in their own way, as we have already said. And they may of course all be right. If a group of children sit in a circle around a tree and each child makes a careful drawing of that tree from his or her perspective, no two drawings will be the same. But they will all be an image of the same tree."

"Yes, I get that," Lanya said. "Each of your children represents a different religion, and they all are drawing their representation of the same god as seen from their perspective. But are you therefore saying that you don't believe in the Christian ideas about God? Don't they claim to be the only true religion?" Lanya asked hesitantly.

"Well, I obviously don't believe that last bit, which is why we are having this conversation, isn't it?" he replied, wondering how he could explain this. "We are speaking English together now. When we get to Vienna, most people are going to be speaking German. At the station in Paris everyone was speaking French. Of course English is easiest for us, because we know it best; but when we hear other languages – as you said this morning – we don't condemn them as stupid or wrong just because we don't understand them. I think it is the same with religions. Just because a religion is different from ours and we are not familiar with it, doesn't mean it is wrong. It just means we don't understand it yet. And of course Christians aren't the only ones who make that claim of being the only true religion."

"Yes, I like that analogy," Lanya said earnestly, "and just as we can learn another language, so we can also learn another religion if we want to."

Nodding, he added, "And if we do learn another religion, we

may well find that the way it expresses some things makes more sense to us than certain aspects of our own native religion; and we may then find that we disagree with the way some parts of *the tree* have been drawn in our own religion. Then we have the option to try and look at *the tree* itself – in our hearts – and to make up our own mind about what we see there."

"I see," she said with some relief. "Just because we find some things in the religion in which we were brought up difficult to accept, doesn't mean we have to reject or condemn the whole religion."

"That's exactly what I'm saying." He nodded and went on, "But then there are those who refuse to learn or practice any religion at all, saying that there is no such thing as God. They claim religious belief is just a figment of our imagination – just wishful thinking. And some boast that they have no need of a god – that they can manage very well without."

"And you think they are wrong, don't you?" she asked challengingly.

"Well, they are fully entitled to their way of seeing things. But I have not managed to make sense of my life without allocating a high degree of probability to – as Goethe puts it: '… everybody's willing is but a wanting, because in fact, we should; and faced with That Will capricious whimsy is silenced'. What Goethe means by '*That Will*' is in our language variously called 'destiny', 'fate', or 'God'; and I have a need to communicate with, and clarify my relationship with, whatever '*That Will*' may be."

"Whoever is Goethe, who speaks in such riddles?" she asked, but went straight on, "Though I think I get what he means: that behind what seem to us to be whimsical, arbitrary chance-happenings, there is in fact some sort of intension, however mysterious and unfathomable this intention may be to us."

"Goethe is a German poet who lived from 1749 to 1832, and I hope you will learn a lot more about him when you are a bit older; and your interpretation of my attempt at a translation of a line in one of his poems is exactly how I read that riddle."

"So – what then can we really know about God?" she asked, repeating his earlier question with emphasis.

He leaned slightly towards her across the little table and asked slowly, "In fact, how do we *really* know anything about anything?"

They were both perplexed for a moment, looking at each other in silence, before he continued, "I would say that in order to be able to answer these questions, we have to undertake an inner journey to that part of ourselves which knows. And when we find that, then we may know the truth. And people say that God *is* the Truth. Hindus call this 'Tat Tvam Asi'. In English: 'That Thou Art'. And inscribed over the entrance to the ancient Greek temple of Apollo at Delphi are the words: 'Know thy Self!'"

She came across and sat next to her grandfather and lent her head on his arm. He smiled. After a while he said slowly, "Well there you have it. I got carried away again. I tried to catch that moonbeam and give it to you in a few words. I tried to say to you, 'That is the truth!' And what happened? They were just words – empty shells waiting to be filled." He shrugged his shoulders, and added, "And yet, that is probably the best that we can do. Poetry, drama, stories, and other works of art can sometimes do better, because they deal in analogies and appeal to our emotions, touching and awakening our deepest feelings. That is probably why Jesus spoke in parables."

"Oh dear, how will I ever find the answer?" she sighed.

"The answer? You may stumble across the answer anywhere, at any time, but it is unlikely to be told to you by somebody. There will be many little answers. Some of them may seem like big answers at the time and then turn out to just be signposts on the path of your inner journey."

"Is that the purpose of life then, this inner journey you talk about?" she said, not so much as a question but more as a realisation. Her head still rested on his arm and was gradually getting heavier. He was going to reply 'Well yes…' but she had drifted off to sleep.

Chapter Six

THE AFTERLIFE

They spent the night in a hotel in Zurich. The journey had been planned so that they could see the Alps in the evening as well as in the morning light. This meant an early start, rising with the sun to catch the early morning train. Mist lay over the waters as their train passed smoothly along the edges of lakes, through villages and meadows, glistening with morning dew. Ochre and white cows were standing in the grass chewing cud. The wooded slopes under a soft pink sky stood black and motionless under wisps of thin mist rising in the early sunlight.

They were in an open carriage now, without compartments, but they managed to get a window seat with a small table between them and nobody was sitting next to them. For a long time they just gazed out of the window taking in the magical morning atmosphere. Eventually Lanya looked around shyly, checking that no one would overhear her question.

"There are still lots of things I want to ask you."

"Well, I'm glad," he said, smiling, "I hope you never run out of questions, because as long as you have questions, you'll keep on travelling with an open mind. Unless of course you find 'the answer', then that would be a different matter – that would be called 'enlightenment'. But what did you want to ask next?"

"I wanted to ask you about dying and what happens afterwards?" she said in a low voice.

"So many people are hesitant to talk about that," he said, looking at her calmly, "but I think we should talk about death a lot more. I don't mean about killing – there's far too much talk about that – but dying, which is the one thing about which we can all be quite certain. Not what happens afterwards, that is very *un*certain. But death will come to all of us eventually, of that there is no doubt."

"Have you ever seen a dead person? I mean, not just on television but in real life?" There was a certain excitement in her voice.

"Yes, I have," he replied simply, wanting to dispel the mystery surrounding the subject and be matter of fact about it.

"Many?"

"No, not as many as you might expect a person of my age to have seen. But then, I have not been in any war or disaster area. The first funeral I attended was that of my elder brother, when I was twenty-three and he had been twenty-five. He had had a skiing accident and his body was brought to my parents' house and I remember noticing how peaceful his face looked."

"Were you very sad?" she asked.

"Not really. We had not been very close. I liked and respected him a lot. However the paths of our lives went very different ways. His funeral was a big public occasion. He was something of a hero – a ski champion – in his part of the world. He would have felt very honoured by the occasion, if he was watching, which he might well have been."

"So you *do* believe in a life after death!" she whispered eagerly.

"There are certain things we cannot know for sure and this is one of them. There may be sages in places like India and Tibet, who do profess to know about this – but I don't, though I like to keep an open mind about it. I have read books about people who claim to know, or claim to have been told by spirits what happens. I have gained the impression that those who might really know, won't talk about it, perhaps because we would not understand, nor would we know what to do with the information if they did tell us. For me, this is where faith comes into our conversation. Faith affects our attitude towards death and dying because it gives you the conviction that in the end all will be well. Faith is the thread on which the beads of optimism and pessimism are strung." As he said this he once again drew a triangle in the air with his fingers referring back to their earlier conversation.

"Isn't death a terrible thing, however you might look at it?" Lanya asked.

"Is being born a good thing?" Frederick quickly asked back.

With a bemused smile Lanya said, "Well of course it is. We wouldn't be here otherwise, would we?"

"In spite of all the pain and suffering life imposes on so many creatures?"

She hesitated for a moment. But then she said forcefully, "Yes! Despite that."

"That shows your faith is healthy and strong," her grandfather answered, patting her hand. "So the next question is: 'Is death part of life?' Could creatures be born and live forever without dying?"

"I suppose not," she said. "I suppose everything is born, has its life, grows old and dies. Barring accidents and wars and that. I suppose that *is* life. So death must necessarily be part of life," she conceded.

"So why should death necessarily be terrible? We don't find dropping off to sleep so terrible."

"But when you fall asleep, you expect to wake up again and

go on living, don't you?"

"Why shouldn't it be similar when we die? When you are in deep sleep, or even when you are dreaming, you don't know what will happen when you wake up, do you? You have faith that all will be well. Do you recall the ancient words of wisdom I mentioned earlier: 'As above, so below'? I think they could also apply here. You could say perhaps, that 'being alive in this world actually is dreaming in the next'."

"Do you mean that when we die, it might be like waking up from a dream, and we would then be in a different life altogether?"

"Exactly," Frederick agreed. "Now, if we go with this assumption, the next question would then be, 'Who lives, or, who is the dreamer?' This is the ultimate question, and they say that when you discover the answer to this question, you have completed your path; you know all that is worth knowing. Life provides the opportunity to find that answer and faith provides the sustaining energy for the journey."

Lanya was content with that and there didn't seem anything more that could be said on the subject after that. So after a while they settled into chatting about other things and eventually went to have some lunch in the dining car.

Chapter Seven

FREE WILL

When they got back to their seats after lunch they both had a doze and now they felt rested and cheerful. Lanya was checking her phone and Frederick had got out a little Sudoku booklet and was playing with numbers. They had left Switzerland a while ago and were now speeding through the Austrian Tirol. The valleys here were narrow and the mountains so close that it seemed they could touch the deeply shadowed rocks flicking past the window.

Suddenly Lanya started again. "If there *is* a God, why does He let so many bad things happen to people?"

Frederick looked at her with raised eyebrows. "Why only to people?" he said eventually. "What about the animals, sea creatures, birds and insects?" Then he laughed. "Evading your question again, aren't I? Actually, I've been asked this question many times. It's one that bothers lots of people and I've never been quite sure how to respond, because it's not a question I've had to ask myself, so I must have already answered it somehow."

Lanya smiled and settled herself more comfortably in her seat as she watched her grandfather consider the question. After a while he said, "Let's see whether we can find our way to an answer. Perhaps there are two categories to consider here: bad things that we humans do to each other and to other creatures, and bad things that happen outside our control."

He leant back in his seat waiting for inspiration, and she said,

"Yes, that makes sense. Let's start with the first one."

"OK," he said, sitting up again with enthusiasm. "But where to start – there are so many aspects to this. Who decides what is '*bad*'? What motivates people?" He hesitated for a moment with wrinkled brow. But then his face lit up and he continued, "What do you think is the one thing that has to be completely freely given in order to exist at all?"

Wondering what that had to do with her question, she said slightly testily, "I don't know."

"Think for a moment," he said, "It's not a trick question but a very serious one."

There was a silence. Then suddenly her eyes lit up and she all but shouted, "Love of course! Unless love is given completely freely it's not true love, is it?"

"You are absolutely right," he said with a big smile. "If there is any thought of gain involved, or any pressure, coercion or fear, then it cannot be true love. So, to bring true love into existence – and for it to be freely given, there has to be free will. And if there is to be free will, then there has to be the option not to love and to be nasty and harmful and all those other negative things. Do you follow me?"

"Yes, I think so."

"Now, if you were in charge of the world and you had to decide whether to risk harm being done, in order to permit free will and bring the possibility of true love into existence, would you do it?"

"I suppose I would," she replied tentatively, "or would I?"

"That is the question you have to ask yourself, if you accuse God of allowing people to do 'bad' things. But before you make up your mind, consider how much 'good' there is in the world. Think about how much beauty there is in the world, and how much love? Sometimes people concentrate too much on the awful things and take all the rest for granted. But when you think about it, you may agree with me, that the good vastly outweighs the bad. And that out of every *bad,* a *good* comes eventually, however long it may take."

"Do you really think so?"

"Yes, I really do think that there is no cloud without a silver lining and that all things will be well in the end – and that if they are not well, it's not the end. That is not to say that I don't often forget it, and have to keep reminding myself."

"I shall always remember this now," Lanya said enthusiastically, "because I quite agree with you. It is when we forget this, that we become afraid and all the good in life gets forgotten."

They smiled at each other and for a while they sat in silence.

"What about the second part of your question, then?" Frederick asked eventually, realising that this was the far more difficult part for him.

"Yes, what about all the natural disasters: earthquakes, tsunamis, deluges, hurricanes, droughts and floods and that kind of thing; and what about diseases, illnesses and deformities, that are nobody's fault?" Her voice was getting agitated.

"And what about the fact that all creatures have to eat other creatures in order to survive?" he added.

But she was quick to point out, "Although this is no longer true for humans, is it? The rise in the popularity of vegetarianism and veganism is proving that."

"Very true – and high time too," he conceded, "but it still applies to the whole of the rest of the animated world. And who says that plants are not creatures? However, I'm thinking that, perhaps, before we address the question of the plight of casualties, be they of natural disasters or of predation, we should be clear about who is asking this question. Let's imagine a small ant which has got into your salad, or perhaps a flea whom you have just caught biting your arm, is asking the question. What would you say to them? You are like a god to them – you hold their fate in your power?"

"Yes, what would I say to them?" she said thoughtfully, but soon continued, " If I had not heard about 'Reverence for Life', I would probably just squash them to death without a second thought. As it is, I would say 'sorry, chums, you are in the wrong place – off you go and annoy someone else'."

"But that wouldn't really answer their question, would it? They are asking why God allows so many bad things to happen to them?"

"Well, that's above my pay grade – I'm only a little junior god. I didn't set up this creation."

"Fair point," he said with a big grin, "but the point of this little diversion was to draw attention to the fact that in the big scheme of things – at the scale of our solar system or our galaxy – we humans are far more insignificant than an ant or a flea is to us. So how are we going to find out how the creator of this universe would answer this second part of your question for all of us?"

"Yes, absolutely! That *was* my original question."

He thought for a long moment – looking out of the window, where the first signs of a suburbia were whizzing past, indicating that they were approaching Vienna. He turned back to Lanya, "Perhaps, what God has in mind for us within this creation is not at all what we normally think it is all about? Perhaps the point of living in this creation – for all of us, from microbes to planets – is not creature-comfort: i.e. – happiness, long healthy lives, good food, good sex, fame and fortune, etc... perhaps it is something completely different?"

"Is that really what we normally think life is all about?" she asked. "What about scholarship, art, literature, scientific and technological achievements? Aren't these more important than the things you've listed?"

"Maybe," he said, "but maybe both our lists are just vehicles for yet another much deeper purpose?"

"You mean, like the things we talked about earlier, like free will and love and the purpose of life?" she asked.

"Yes, that is exactly what I mean. And I have a feeling that we will have to take this earlier conversation much further in order to find a plausible answer to your last question. But that will be for another day, because this train journey is coming to its end very soon," he said, pointing out of the windows at the tall buildings on either side.

And indeed, a flurry of conversations had begun to fill their carriage and the hustle and bustle of everyday life began to invade their intimate space. Frederick started helping Lanya gather her things and lifting their suitcases off the luggage rack. The train slowed right down and finally stopped in the Westbahnhof station in central Vienna. As they waited in the queue to step onto the platform Lanya turned to her grandfather and whispered, "Was this the beginning of my inner journey then?"

Frederick's hand squeezed her shoulder. "It certainly felt like that to me," he whispered, "and we can explore the next lap of *that* journey on our return trip," he said with a broad smile. They heaved their cases off the train and, with a spring in their step, they walked down the platform into the arms of a cheerful welcoming party.

THE RETURN JOURNEY

Chapter Eight

CONCERNS FOR LIFE ON EARTH

They stayed with Frederick's sister, who lived in a rooftop flat a twenty minute tram ride from Vienna's ring-road encircling the old city centre. The days were filled with a tight schedule of family visits, sightseeing, gallery visits, tram rides and walks in the lovely parks and woods of Vienna. Each evening there was a musical event: either a visit to the opera or a recital by one of Frederick's musically gifted nieces and nephews. Lanya felt at ease with everyone and enjoyed meeting the extended family.

All too soon, some of the younger members of the family were escorting the pair back to the station. There were hugs and farewells and promises to keep in touch, and last minute exchanges of email addresses before a whistle sounded and Lanya and her grandfather were heaving their luggage on board their train back to London. Having waved vigorously from the window until the little group on the platform had receded from view, they flopped into their seats which, this time, were next to each other in a full carriage, with Lanya sitting next to the window.

It had been an exhilarating few days, packed full of new experiences and jolly chat. As it had neared its end, both Lanya and Frederick each secretly began to look forward to their return journey and a continuation of their conversation, which they both knew to have been of great significance but still left many more unanswered questions in Lanya's mind.

Looking at each other as the train gathered speed, they smiled and heaved a deep sigh, as Frederick said, "That was a pretty full week we've just had. Was it not all a bit much for you?"

"Yes, there was a lot to take in," she replied, "but I loved it all. Especially the evenings at the opera! To experience that wonderful performance of *The Magic Flute* in the town where it was composed and first performed!" She sighed again, but contentedly, and continued, "I also very much enjoyed talking with cousin Stephan, you know, the mountaineer – he is so interesting. He told me all about geology and his adventures climbing high up in the mountains studying the rock formations and looking for crystals and gemstones. Now, when I look at the mountains, I'll always be reminded of how earnestly and caringly he talked about them."

Frederick gazed out of the window with nostalgia. "I remember," he recalled, "that when I was just a year or two younger than you are now, my parents took two of my younger brothers and me up the mountains – sometimes on three or four day tours. I still recall the overpowering experiences of seeing the earth, when standing on those peaks, looking at the far horizons, feeling the grandeur and vastness of it all. I do hope you'll get a chance to experience that high and rarefied mountaintop world one day too, Lanya."

"So do I!" she said and braced herself to voice something that had been worrying her for the past few days, "but you know, Stephan said that up on many of the high plateaus, where there had always been permanent snow all year round, there was now no snow to be seen anywhere in summer. And where there are still real glaciers, you can see where the permanent snow-line had been in your father's time. Now the surface of the glaciers is some fifty to one hundred metres below that line. He said that it drives it home for him, like nothing else, that climate change is for real, and the effects are there to be seen in full view! It made me wonder why people don't take this more seriously. Don't they realise it is our future – the lives of my generation – they are messing with?"

As usual, she wasn't pulling her punches. Frederick felt a slight shudder down his spine at the magnitude of the accusation.

"We need to be careful when we point the finger," he began. "The *they* you accuse includes all of us. The actions necessary to do anything really effective will mess with all our lives so radically that *they* prefer to ignore it, hoping it will go away, or that someone else will deal with it."

"But it won't go away, will it? And the longer it's left, the worse it will get! Isn't that so?" she fired back.

"Yes, of course you are right," he admitted, "so what are you and I going to do about it? Why don't we have a go now? We've got plenty of time in front of us," he challenged.

"Yes, let's discuss this properly. How can someone like me cope with this? Some people say that it is too late already anyway?"

"Who can know that? Certainly I don't." He shrugged his shoulders. "But I have read that scientists say there is a twenty to twenty-five year delay between our actions and the resultant full effect on the climate. So that global climatic conditions being measured now, are the result of actions of people in the early 1980s. There were obviously a lot less polluting and climate-damaging activities then, compared to now. What we are doing now will be felt by you in the 2040s – when I will be long gone. How old will you be then?"

"Well, I'm fifteen now so I'll be forty years old in 2042,"

she replied after a moment of calculation, "so I can expect to feel the full effect of whatever damage we do today."

"That is certainly a sobering thought," he said hesitatingly, "but we have to be careful here, I think this delay only applies to the effect of carbon dioxide emissions on the climate, and the whole picture is much more complicated. But let's not get bogged down. That's the trouble with this subject, as soon as you start on it, you can so easily get bogged down in the detail. Let's stick to the broad brush. And we have to accept the situation as it is now – whatever it is."

"OK then, what can be said about it now, and what can we do?" she said eagerly.

"We are doing something by making this journey by train instead of flying. Trains are more environmentally friendly," he said. "But there is a catch here already, because the first response of most politicians, when they began to acknowledge that there was a problem, was to bat it away onto the shoulders of the general public, asking us to recycle and use public transport. At first, people accepted that responsibility but now, more and more of us realise that without political action and the cooperative involvement of industry and commerce there is no chance of having any decisive impact. The people in power, at the top of commerce and industry as well as government, must come to realise that this is the number one problem facing us. In recent months, some progress has begun to be made in that direction, but much of it is still what they call *greenwash* – nice words, not only not backed up with action, but distracting the attention from the real action."

"Don't we live in a democracy?" she challenged, "So why don't we put people in charge who do accept the real urgency of the problem and are determined to do something about it?"

"Well now you *are* opening the real can of worms," he responded. "The problem with our democracies is that, free and open as they are claimed to be, not only do the people who are voted into office of government not wield the ultimate power, but they are put there by the people who do; namely, the people who own and control most of the money and can therefore manipulate the outcome of elections."

Lanya, realising that this was going to be a long answer, settled herself into her seat, whilst he continued, "There have always been people who had a lot more wealth than others. In previous centuries, in our part of the world, there were kings and lords at the head of an aristocracy of wealth and power. In the last three centuries there have been revolutions aimed at dismantling that social structure. You know – the French Revolution and the Russian or Communist Revolution, and also to some extent, the Industrial Revolution. But they have not been very successful – revolutions never are – which is why I recommend concentrating on 'evolution' – but that is another story. Within a few years of the French Revolution, France had an Emperor – Napoleon; the Russians had a dictator – Stalin; and the Industrial Revolution, now aided and abetted by the Digital Revolution, has resulted in a new elite with a wealth gap incomparably greater than anything any previous centuries have known."

"How do you mean?" she interrupted, "Surely the wealth of kings and bishops and dukes was vastly greater than anybody's today!"

"You would have thought so – and you are meant to think so – as I certainly did, until I started looking into it and found that the reality is very different."

"How?" she asked eagerly.

"This is a big subject. Big books are being written about it, because some people are very concerned and think this lies at the core of much of our troubles. Let me give you just a couple of examples: for instance, they say that in 1688 a cardinal's income would have been about eight hundred times that of a beggar. Today a hedge fund manager can earn a hundred thousand times what someone on benefits gets. To help you visualise this: if you imagine the person on benefits as being thirty centimetres tall, then the hedge fund manager would be thirty kilometres tall. A high flying plane would pass by his hips and his head would be in the stratosphere. Someone in the developing world, say somewhere in Africa, who lives on one pound fifty pence a day, would be about half a millimetre tall. Your seventeenth century cardinal would be less tall than the Eiffel Tower."

"Whaou! That's amazing! Mind-blowing, in fact."

"And what's even more incredible is that the hedge fund managers are not even the real owners of wealth today, they are just their minions. The really wealthy are even richer than that. It is claimed that the eight richest individuals on earth today own as much as the poorer half of the total human population put together, that is, their wealth is equal to that of the three and a half billion of the poorer people day."

"What? Eight people own an equal amount as billions of people put together? That's horrendous!" she exclaimed indignantly. "That can't be true, surely?"

"The fact is that unbelievable amounts of money – quite inconceivable sums of it – are in the hands of very few individuals. And these individuals know how to operate the present system so that it constantly increases the money in their proverbial – or should I say 'digital' *coffers*. Thus, they are not interested in changing a system which they know how to manipulate so well to their own advantage."

He took a deep breath and they both sat in silence for some moments whilst Lanya was trying to digest what he had said. Just then, the train had stopped at Linz and many people had got off, leaving the seats opposite them empty, so that Lanya could move across and allow Frederick to slide up to the window. When they had re-settled themselves, Lanya said, "This is all very hard to grasp, but I think I get it. These few super-wealthy people have the real power and they are not interested in change. They don't want an upset to the system which they control, and certainly not for the sake of something like climate change. But aren't they being a bit stupid and ostrich-like, considering that climate-change looks now inevitable, that its signs are there to be seen and are already being experienced by large sections of the global population and will eventually upset everything?"

"It looks exactly like that from our viewpoint," he agreed, "but as long as everything is going so swimmingly for them, why should they worry? After all, with all that money at their disposal, they live in the belief that they can fix anything."

"We'll just have to convince them somehow!" she said, her voice full of determination. "Just imagine what could be done if these super-rich people became convinced that this thing was actually happening and would inevitably destroy their world. They would soon put their money to work to prevent it, wouldn't they?"

"And there are signs that this might be beginning to happen. The large insurance companies are beginning to flag up risk assessments with some quite horrendous costs attached to them, and this is causing some raised eyebrows at least. But you know, I'm not at all convinced that this would actually lead towards a solution. These people operate according to a certain mindset which taints everything they do and think. And whilst effective in piling money into big mountains, it also causes a lot of collateral damage on the way. In fact, all the problems we are talking about now – climate change, the problems with our democratic system and of course the gap between rich and poor, could be regarded as collateral damage – unintended consequences – of the activities perpetrated by this mindset. The danger is, that if they were to set about solving the climate problem and they began throwing serious money at it, they would soon be causing so many other problems which they had not intended, that the situation would only get worse – though it might in the short-term still improve their own make-believe, fairytale, billionaire world." Frederick could not completely conceal his deep anxiety.

Lanya's facial expression darkened as the enormity of the problem they were discussing began to build in front of her. She felt fear rising in the pit of her stomach. Frederick, who was long used to living with the theoretical possibility that there would be no way around the hiatus for which climate change had become the catchphrase, recognised the signs of comprehension on Lanya's face and was suddenly struck with a heavy pang of conscience for having brought a fifteen year old girl to this point.

"Never say never!" he began again, leaning forward and putting a hand on her shoulder. "There are many very caring and genuinely committed people working on possible solutions to at least mitigate and limit the effects of climate change. Much progress is already being made on at least slowing the increase of emissions, on accelerating alternative energy generating technologies and so on. The environmental movement has by no means given up, and there is no reason for us to succumb to despair. As you know, school children are taking to the streets, realising that their future is at stake. The media is finally coming round to treating the subject with some commitment. There are signs that some industry-bosses are taking '*going green*' seriously and making it an integral part of their real agenda."

"You are obviously used to living with these thoughts," she said quietly, "but I need some time to come to terms with it, now that I feel the enormity of it as never before."

"It has become increasingly clear to me," he said with a touch of resignation in his voice, "that living through climate change – whatever that will finally turn out to mean – is now the inevitable challenge which all life on earth will have to cope with."

"In that case, we will just have to make the best of it, won't we?" she said with determination.

What a brave little fighter she is, he thought. He wanted to take her in his arms and give her a good long hug. Instead he said, "I think you're right, Lanya, we have taken this far enough for now. Let's have a break and see what we can find to tempt us in the dining car. What do you think?"

She was on her feet before he had finished the sentence. Lanya had noted the location of the dining car as they got on the train and now led the way towards the middle of the train. After their intense conversation, they enjoyed the atmosphere in the restaurant which was full of life and happy conviviality. The meal was good and they sat chatting in the comfortable chairs of the dining car whilst Frederick sipped his coffee.

Back in their own carriage, both were soon fast asleep.

Lanya woke first. She gently nudged her grandfather, because dusk had descended over the landscape and lights began to flicker outside as their train rolled through the outskirts of St Gallen, where they had planned to break their journey. Leaving the station, they soon found their hotel, and after a light snack, they were both happy to turn in for an early night.

Chapter Nine

PRAYER

Once again it was an early start. They rushed and caught their train in the nick of time. These days, Frederick was not too good in the early mornings! They were surprised, but glad, that this train had proper compartments, because in Switzerland nearly all trains now had open carriages and there was little of this older rolling stock left. They even found an empty compartment and eagerly took possession of it.

Smoothly, the train started to glide away. They sat in amazement, watching the peculiarly Swiss phenomenon of railway graffiti covering walls, roofs, whole houses, bridges and tunnels on both sides of the tracks. As they emerged into the countryside, Frederick sensed that Lanya was struggling to formulate her next question. She seemed unsure how to start. So for a while he gave himself over to the gentle rhythmic movement of the train on the smooth Swiss tracks.

Finally it burst out of her.

"You know, there are several loose ends which now need sorting out for me. First of all, you remember that at the very beginning of our train journey, when I asked you about God and religion, you suggested we talk about religion first and that we'd come back to God later. Well, we talked about all sorts of things and God did come into it, but you never really talked about what God means to you. Perhaps you don't really want to talk about that, but after yesterday's conversation I couldn't help thinking about this during the night. And to be honest, I got really scared and that made me begin to think about prayer."

Frederick was struggling with his emotions as she was speaking. On the one hand, he was sorry and worried that he had scared his granddaughter. On the other hand, he was so deeply touched that she should confide in him in this way. But above all, he was astonished and – if truth be told – awestruck that in this agnostic, atheistic age, this young girl, when faced with the stark reality of the present predicament facing the world, should find herself seeking refuge in something to call God.

"Oh my darling," he said taking both her hands in his, "I'm so sorry to have scared you, but in spite of your young age, I think you are strong enough to look at our global situation without rose-tinted spectacles. We all have to experience and learn how to handle fear in our lives in one form or another. Out of fear grows courage, and courage leads us towards God, whatever we might mean by that word." He let go her hands, but the steady gaze into each other's eyes, full of trust and shared understanding, continued for a while as she spoke, "Yes, thinking about how someone like me can cope with all this, I had an inkling of what you have just said about fear and courage. It made me wonder about prayer and made me want to ask you whether you yourself actually ever pray?"

"Yes I do, as a matter of fact," he responded.

"Oh do describe to me how and when?" she pleaded eagerly.

"As I expect you know, I was brought up in a Christian household. My parents were members of a Protestant congregation in a predominantly Catholic area in Austria. When I came to England at the age of fourteen, I stayed with a couple who were agnostics. Even then, I was not comfortable with much of the language used by the Christian Church, and in my youth I developed a strong interest and leaning towards Eastern religions. Now, as you know from our earlier conversation, I regard the different religions rather like different languages which express fundamentally similar things in different words. Recently, I have found the Lord's Prayer a good vehicle for me, but with modifications, as you will see, if you want to go there... But I can imagine myself praying equally well in the language of a number of other religions, and with similar difficulties. In fact, there was a time in my life, many years ago, when I did pray in the terminology of the Hindu religion, and I still mix Hindu and Buddhist ideas into my prayers now."

"I suppose you pray before you go to sleep? Isn't that when many people pray – other than when they are in church?"

"Very often these days, and for many years now, I wake up at three or four in the morning. I have long given up trying to turn over and go back to sleep. I get fed up with hours of frustrated tossing and turning and counting sheep. So now I get up, put on my dressing gown and walk about a bit, just concentrating on putting one foot in front of the other and breathing rhythmically. Then I sit down to meditate. When I was in my late twenties, not long after I married your grandmother, we were both introduced to a method of mantra-meditation and I still keep that up fairly regularly now. During daylight hours I usually meditate for about half an hour, but time feels different at night and I never look at the clock then. I just stop when it feels right, lie down in bed without opening my eyes, fold my hands on my chest and pray my version of the Lord's Prayer."

"What's a mantra-meditation," she asked.

"There are many different methods of meditation. What I practice originates from a Hindu background in Northern India.

But maybe that story is better left for another time."

"Oh, OK," she said, nodding in acquiescence and continued, "I do know what you mean by the Lord's Prayer, though. We learnt it at school. Do you pray it aloud?"

"No, I pray it silently, in my head. And I am constantly adapting it. In fact each time I pray, I am working on trying to understand what it might really mean. Therefore it keeps changing a little as things open up to me."

"Oh do tell where you're at with it now – if you want to, that is."

"Well, this *is* all very personal, to be sure," he said, realising suddenly what he was getting into, "and it is very much a work-in-progress – so you'll have to bear with me – it's just me trying to make sense of things. To many people I am probably being totally heretical, but maybe it will mean something to you and it might well help me clarify some things by talking about it. So, let's see where it takes us."

"Yes, let's," she said eagerly.

"Well, first of all I should say that I don't usually use prayer to ask for things. I assume God, or whatever it is I pray to, knows better than I do what is good for me, or for any of us. Though that is not to say that there haven't been occasions when I felt desperate and cried out for help. But usually, I use prayer to think deeply about things, and the Lord's Prayer has turned out to be the best vehicle for me to do that. Anyway – you learnt it at school – so how does it start?"

"*Our Father,*" she began to recite, and he immediately interrupted:

"You see, there is my first difficulty already!"

"Why? What's wrong with that?"

"Is God male? Why not female? Why have any gender? If

God is Spirit and is everywhere – in all created things – and is eternal, having no beginning and no end – all attributes of God which I find essential – then why should he be a 'father figure'?"

"I never thought about that. I suppose a father figure makes you feel safe and secure. And since prayer is often a response to fear – as you said – doesn't that make a lot of sense?"

This girl is a lot older than her fifteen years on this earth, Frederick thought, and after a brief moment replied, "You probably know that at the time when Jesus is said to have given this prayer to his followers, he was part of a male-dominated, paternal culture already thousands of years old. Since then we've had another two thousand years of male domination. But now this is changing, and I feel caught up in this change. However, this is not at all straightforward. It is not a case of simply saying: let's pray to a female God. '*Our Mother, Who art in heaven*' – because that doesn't work for me either. Of course the Roman Catholic Church has prayed for centuries '*Holy Mother of God*', but I can't do that. There is a mountain of imagery associated with this phrase which I cannot cope with."

"What about using the word 'parent' then? That includes both genders. '*Our Parent, Who art in Heaven*'; have you tried that?" she suggested.

"No I haven't. I suppose by implication it still evokes the idea of a 'single parent' and then you're right back in the gender issue." He paused with a sigh, looking vacantly into the distance. Lanya waited, sensing that he hadn't finished the point.

"For me," he eventually continued in a firm voice, "the concept of '*God*'*,* if it has any attributes, must be eternal and without beginning. The best I have come up with for the time being is '*Our Creator*'. That is how I start these days. It still has masculine connotations but I turn a blind eye… for now. It's a mystery to me, why, in our culture, we seem to be unable to address a genderless spirit. The Buddhists try to manage without a God altogether. The Hindus manage this better – as far as I'm concerned – with their 'Atman' and 'Param-Atman', or 'Brahman'. Anyway, learning to live with mystery is fundamental to my concept of prayer, so I try and cope with *not-knowing*," he said with a sense of finality.

"All right then," she continued, "'*Our Creator*' it is. Let's go on: '*Who art in heaven*'."

He interrupted again. "Sorry, but there I already have the next problem: where or what is *heaven*? Why place God somewhere? In some location? Isn't God everywhere? However, here my experience of 'living inside my thumb' is of some help."

"You mean *heaven* is your version of *space*?" she suggested.

"Well nearly, yet not quite," he said hesitatingly. "I'm still really struggling with this. A creator must predate the creation. It is clear to me that everything that is created has its *being* in space and is penetrated by space. Thus, the world of S*pirit* would seem to transcend space, and space is the interface between the created world and Spirit. It is interesting that all the ancient religions seem to talk about *heaven and earth.* But I have not ever really understood this properly. It does however confront us directly with the challenging concepts of infinity and eternity." He uttered another big sigh.

Lanya was baffled but she was determined to press on. "OK then. So far we have: '*Our Creator, who art beyond Space*'. Are you happy with that?"

"Well, let's say '*in and beyond Space*', otherwise it creates an image of space as a kind of bubble floating in something else, which is also impossible, because this space is also infinite, isn't it?"

"If you say so. This is all beyond me. All right then, '*...in and beyond Space, hallowed be thy name*'. Any problems with that?"

"I feel the need for a name here. And the name I have come up with for myself is, '*One-in-All*'. That unifies the microcosm and the macrocosm for me."

"What are they?" she asked.

"For me they are names given to the minuscule world, inside the atoms of my thumb, and the huge world inside the thumb of that other, unimaginably enormous Being I mentioned earlier."

"All right, I get that. So now we have, '*Our Creator, Who art in and beyond Space; thy name, One-in-All, be hallowed; Thy Kingdom come*'," she summarised, and added, "Now you're going to query '*Thy Kingdom*', aren't you?"

"Well, aren't *you*?" he asked, "Do you know what is meant by the 'Kingdom of God' or the 'Kingdom of Heaven'?"

"When I hear those phrases I always think of angels and archangels and the things that the paintings and sculptures in churches are full of. But I'm sure you have some other ideas about it," she responded.

"Indeed I have," he said, "but they don't necessarily rule out your ideas. Yours and mine wouldn't necessarily contradict each other. After years of drawing a complete blank in my own mind, as to what the Kingdom of God might refer to, an idea did come to me, and I'm quite pleased with it. We speak of the 'animal kingdom' and the 'plant kingdom', etcetera. Well, in that sense, biologically, humans are part of the animal kingdom, aren't they? But with the human species a new factor comes into play: the crystallisation of consciousness into self-consciousness. We are, each of us, aware that we exist as an individual being. We don't necessarily know who or what we really are, but we know *that* we are."

She leaned back in her seat, settling herself for another lecture. Her grandfather was in full flow now.

"I think there is consciousness in the animal kingdom, varying in degree with different species and with different individual creatures. If you have ever had a cat or a dog, you will not disagree. But the human species, I believe, is in the process of evolving self-consciousness. This is the ability to be aware of the workings of your mind; that part of you that can observe the activity of your own thoughts and can respond consciously to inspiration and to imagination. It can observe and control your physical desires, your likes and dislikes, and can hear and respond to the voice of your conscience. This ability is not yet fully developed in humankind, but I think our evolution takes us in that direction, and it may well be that there we can encounter entities, spiritual beings with a self-consciousness much more fully developed than ours, and these could be what the ancients called angels." He again took a deep breath.

"That is a pretty big idea!" she interjected. "Are you saying that, if we pray, '*Thy Kingdom come*', we are asking for the full development of our self-consciousness to be completed. Is that what you mean?"

"Exactly so. You may know that for the last fifteen or more years I have been working on a project which I call the 'NESt Initiative', which stands for the 'Next Evolutionary Step' for humankind. Working towards that kingdom is exactly what this initiative is about. In this context you might say that NESt is trying to hasten the coming of the Kingdom of God. And it seems to me increasingly, that if humankind does not take this 'next evolutionary step' soon, it may be game over for us. We may wipe ourselves out as a failed experiment; and a lot more than just us humans may disappear. We are already driving a huge numbers of other creatures to extinction."

"This is a big ask then when you pray these words."

"Well yes, it is rather. In fact, this and the next phrase are the ones I retain as petitions in my Lord's Prayer. All the others I convert, but we'll come to that."

There was a pause. Lanya took a bar of chocolate out of her bag and offered some to her grandfather. He took it, relieved to have a break. They both munched away for a while, looking out of the window. The train was gliding along with barely a sound, past beautiful lakes and rolling hills – the snow-covered high mountains on the far horizon.

Chapter Ten

FAITH

After about ten minutes, Lanya was back on the case. "So what about the next phrase: '*Thy will be done*'?"

"Yes, that can also stand," he said, "and it is perhaps the most important of all the phrases for me. But the complete phrase is, '*Thy Will be done in Earth as it is in Heaven*'. It was my father who told me years ago, that it ought to have been translated from the Greek as *in* Earth rather than *on* Earth, the point being that it refers to the substance of earth, i.e. to physical matter, not to the planet."

"So the whole thing so far goes like this," she summarised once more, "'*Our Creator, Who art in and beyond Space, Thy name, One-in-All, be hallowed, Thy Kingdom come, Thy Will be done in Earth as it is in Space and beyond*'."

"All right," he said, satisfied, and went straight on to ask, "But now, what about the '*Will of God*'? What do we make of that? Do we agree that God is everywhere and all-powerful?"

"Yes, that is how I would imagine God."

"Then, everything that happens must be in accordance with God's Will. Otherwise it would surely be prevented, would it not?"

"I suppose that must follow – logically," she replied with some hesitation, sensing that it might not be as simple as that.

"I'm glad," he said, "that you added the word: 'logically',

because here's the rub this time: logically, if God doesn't stop all the bad things in the world, then they must all be God's Will as well as the good ones. When we pray, '*Thy Will be done*' we acknowledge that it includes all the 'bad things' as well. This is a great mystery, and I am reminded of it every time I pray."

"Yes, I see," she said dubiously, "but that can't be right, surely? God can't want bad things to happen?" But then, before he could answer she added, "Hold on a moment: are we not now back to the question I put to you at the end of our journey *to* Vienna – which was, if I remember rightly:… '*if there is a God, why does he let so many bad things happen to people?*' And I remember, we dealt with half of it then. So perhaps we can address the other half now?"

"How clever of you to make the connection; well-remembered!" he said with a broad smile, "Can you also remind me of what the half we dealt with was about?"

"Well – I remember, you split my question into two parts: those bad things which we do to each other and to other creatures, and those bad things which happen to us through no fault of our own. The first category you justified by linking it to the freedom we are given to *love*, which inevitably necessitates us having the freedom *not to love.* I get that, and I think I agreed that, on the whole, it was worth it. The amount of love there is in the world – and I assume that includes goodness and kindness and all the other associated *good* qualities – outweighs the lack of it and all the opposites. We did start to look at the second part of my question, and you started saying something like: '…that perhaps, what God had in mind for us within this creation is not at all what we normally think it is all about…' but we ran out of time because the train arrived in Vienna."

Lanya's expression was full of expectation whilst Frederick

had sunk back in his seat, deep in thought. When he finally sat up again and leant forward onto the little table between them, there was a sparkle in his eyes.

"Well, I can think of a few things to consider here, which might help us," he began. "First, let's clear away some of the undergrowth before we tackle the *big stuff*. We often think something is bad just because it is not what we planned, or because we just like or don't like something. Or we have been taught to think a certain way about something. There are any number of events that fall into this category."

"Where we may wish for, or want something, you mean, and are disappointed when we don't get it," she completed his thought, and added, "and how often do we find that what we actually got was much better for us? Or where we realise later, that something we thought would be bad actually turns out to be for the best? Like, when I was ill and missed school and then realised how much I wanted to not fail the year, which taught me how to work really hard to catch up."

"Exactly so," he said with a smile, "that's a perfect example. This happens all the time, and these instances just need a bit of humility on our part to recognise that we don't always know best."

"All right then," she said, "but what about the bigger events which have nothing to do with our own wishes or prejudices, like natural disasters, accidents or illnesses? How can we cope with the idea of regarding these as also being part of God's Will?"

"Yes, I think now we are back to where we were at the end of our last conversation before arriving in Vienna. And this is where we ask once more: What is the purpose of life? What have we really come here for – unto this earth – into this life? Why are we here? What is our task here?"

"And the answer to these questions is what you meant when you suggested that God has something quite different in mind for us than we normally think, isn't it?" she asked with a sense of recognition in her eyes.

"Absolutely," he nodded. "But the thing is: I don't think I can answer these questions for myself in the context of only one life-span. But as soon as we broaden the context into a wider setting which includes the possibility of a sequence of lives, both on this earth and perhaps elsewhere altogether, then many plausible answers come into view. The most obvious one for me is the idea, that we come here to learn things as part of a much longer journey of development and evolution. The experiences of hardship, pain and suffering, and even death take on a totally different significance when seen as learning and growing opportunities. Unfortunately though, for some reason, we are reluctant learners, and the lessons we have come here to learn don't come easily to us. So we have to be pushed and cudgelled. Therefore the fact that we live here in a world fraught with danger can be accepted as intrinsic to its purpose. This is how I would like to understand and interpret this aspect of the Will of God. And thus, even with big events, involving thousands of casualties, we have to remember that valuable lessons can be learnt and good can come out of them in the end. These fateful events and destined situations challenge us to accept them and to make the best out of them. That is how our souls grow, mature and develop towards their final destination – union with God."

"Oh dear, Grandpa, this is hard!" she said with a big sigh.

"Don't forget," he added, "this interpretation is only possible, if the tally is not taken in this life alone, and is not applied to the fortunes of this single body we inhabit here, now."

"I do see that," she said, pensively, "but it is still hard to see the really bad things in this way – evil things, like murder, wars, cruelty to animals and people. Can they really be the Will of God?"

"Remember, we said these fall into the other category, where we have to accept the bad for the sake of the good. But it does become very hard with the really big questions facing us now, like climate change, mass extinctions and the possibility of the end of life on Earth, even." There was tension and a tremor in his voice now.

"Oh, my goodness!" she sighed. "Where are you taking me with this? The end of life on Earth! Do we really have to think about that?"

"Now, now, Lanya, let's calm down; we are only considering theoretical possibilities," he said soothingly. "But God is a big concept, a lot bigger than our universe, as the experience inside my thumb has taught me. We must not belittle God. God, for me, is plenty big enough for this universe to just be a speck in his little finger – or should I say: 'Thumb'? So, if we think about the Earth in relationship to the Will of God, we have to recognise that it is most probably one of many – maybe countless – planets where there is life. Even in our solar system, where so far no life as we know it – organic life – has been found other than here on Earth, we are told that there is convincing evidence that there may well have been organic life in the past, elsewhere, on other planets. And are we not told that at some point, our sun will burn itself out, explode and turn into a supernova – of which there are apparently plenty observable examples in our galaxy – and will that not be the end of our solar system? So, we cannot talk about the '*Will of God in Earth as it is in and beyond Space*' without including all those possibilities, can we?"

"Of course not. I can see that. Truly, I can! But it is scary none the less."

"To be sure, this is not easy to take in all at once, but you are strong, and bright, and can cope with it," he said, reassuringly. "Our earth and the events on it are just a small part of the Will of God. Even the end of life on Earth, although a huge event for humanity, would be just a minuscule blip in the vastness of the universe. But that does not mean that life has no purpose. It is not a question of how long we spend here on Earth that matters. It is what we experience and learn from that experience that matters."

Lanya sat for a moment twisting a strand of her hair around her finger and taking several deep breaths. Then she asked, "So is this why we pray: '*Thy Will be done*'? Because we believe that the Will of God presents us with the opportunities to have those experiences which we need in order to learn the lessons we have come here to learn?"

"Exactly so, Lanya, and by doing so, we confirm to ourselves that we are ready to accept whatever these opportunities and challenges might be. And this is the essence of faith. It is the surrender of our will, of our understanding, of our aspirations, desires and dreams – of all we are and have – to the Will of God." He was filled with emotion and admiration that his granddaughter seemed to cope with this.

Lanya sat up a little straighter, inspired by the gravity of her grandfather's words. And for a while, they sat in silence, immersed in the ideas that had just emerged between them. Suddenly, Lanya leant back again in her seat and said, "So in this line of reasoning, you are telling me that it is the act of faith that gives sense and purpose to this existence on earth and to our lives, and basically – helps us to cope. And that each of us can see our individual life here as but one chapter in a book, or one term – or even one week or one day – in the course of a long educational journey? That is what you are saying, isn't it?"

Frederick just nodded and smiled.

Chapter Eleven

GRATITUDE

They had not noticed that Switzerland had been left behind a while ago. Looking out of the window, they now realised that the French Alps were passing them by unnoticed and they sat in silence with their faces pressed against the glass, enjoying the dramatic view.

After a while, Lanya asked cheerfully, "Ready to move on to the next phrase, which I think would be: *'give us this day our daily bread'*? But I must say, talking of bread, I wouldn't mind having some of that right now. What do you think?"

"I think that's a very good idea," he said with a broad smile, and once again, they set off to find the dining car.

A couple of hours later, on their way back, Frederick was concluding an anecdote from the hitchhiking days of his youth as they settled back into their seats. "…that was when I first learnt something that has remained true for me ever since," he was saying, "that, very often, I only find what I am looking for, after I have given up looking for it."

Lanya had not been giving his story her full attention, and now, looking out of the window, she asked, "Do you feel like continuing with your version of the Lord's Prayer? Or are you too sleepy now? I know you like to have your little nap after lunch."

"Yes, of course," he said. "After that coffee, I feel quite

awake and ready for anything."

"I think we were considering: '*give us this day our daily bread*', which we have just had in abundance," she joked.

"Quite," he said matter-of-factly, "And the first thing to note here, is that this does not only refer to physical nourishment. And, secondly, I have changed that as well. In fact, I have changed the next four requests into confirmations for myself. This started with the thought that I have all I need and more, much more, so do I really need to ask for bread? And then I realised that this applies to all these four requests. So I have rephrased them for myself as follows:

'*Thou givest us this day our daily bread;*'

'*And forgivest us our trespasses as we forgive those who trespass against us;*'

'*And leadest us in temptation;*'

'*And deliverest us from evil.*'

I find that works well for me and reinforces my feeling of gratitude for all I have been given and am given every day."

"I really like that," she responded enthusiastically. Then she asked, "Do you think of anyone in particular when you pray, '*as we forgive those who trespass against us*'?"

"That's a really good question, because I often can't think of anyone I know personally who has done me any harm. Then I think of all the greed and the lying and cheating that goes on, particularly in politics, but in business as well; and all the resultant exploitation, violence and warmongering which make our lives more complicated and dangerous than they need be. And I often consider how I can forgive them? Do I even want to forgive them?"

"But then, if you think of what we were saying about the Will of God, don't we *have* to forgive them? Doesn't God forgive them, if it is all God's Will?"

"You are so right!" he acknowledged, "But, I still don't find this easy. Sometimes I think I can, and at other times, not. There are other interesting aspects to this phrase. In the German Bible, it has been translated as: '…forgive us our debt…' or '…our fault…' and debt-forgiveness has become a very real question for us these days in connection with debts which poor countries owe to rich countries."

"OK, I can see that this is too complicated for me," she said, "so shall we move on? '…*and leadest us in temptation*' comes next. What is there to say about that?"

"Don't you find that life is full of temptation?"

"It's not something I think a lot about," she replied.

"Well, have a go now. You must be able to think of one temptation which you find a challenge to resist?"

After a small pause, she said, "Well, I suppose – on Facebook I am sometimes tempted to make an unfriendly comment, and then I delete it again. But, I am not sure why I need to feel grateful for the temptation to write something unkind; but is that the sort of thing you mean?"

"That's exactly the sort of thing I mean," he said. "In that instance there was something in you, the voice of conscience, your better judgement, that led you to pull back from that action. So you were '*led in temptation*'. It is that guidance for which I feel grateful, and the increasing ability to hear it which I acknowledge. The question now arises: 'would you rather live a problem-free life or be faced with temptations and grow strong in your ability to resist them – within limits of course?"

"I can see," she said, "that for someone addicted to alcohol or drugs, or who suffers from obesity, it could be a very big issue. But they might prefer not to be faced with such temptations."

"That brings us back to what you think the purpose of your life is – as we have discussed earlier. If you think that you are here to get from birth to death in the most comfortable, easy, luxurious, trouble-free way, that's one thing – and it has its consequences, as we have seen. But if you think you are here to grow and become strong and wise and good, then, like an athlete who sets challenges for himself in order to build up his strength and endurance, you can use the temptations which life presents to you, to build up your resistance to them and learn from the consequences if you give in to them."

"So, I can be grateful for challenges and temptations because they make me a stronger person, especially if I listen to the guidance," she repeated. "Yes, OK, I can make sense of that."

The outskirts of Paris had been whizzing past the window for a while and now the train was pulling into the station. The change of stations went without incident and they caught their next train in good time, and were soon settled into their seats opposite each other for the last leg of their journey.

Chapter Twelve

GREED

"We were nearly at the end of the Lord's Prayer, weren't we?" Lanya asked as the train started to roll again and the now so familiar sound and rhythm of the wheels on the tracks began to beat the background rhythm again.

Looking round to scan the half empty carriage Frederick said absentmindedly, "Who would have thought that the Lord's Prayer would keep us occupied for nearly a whole day's train journey?"

"The next line for us to consider, I think, is, '*and deliverest us from evil*'," Lanya said, ignoring his question.

"Yes," he said with a sigh, "and this is the most difficult one for me."

"Why? Don't you think we are being delivered from evil?" she asked.

"Well, there is that," he said with a wry smile, "but it's more a case of understanding what the word 'evil' might actually mean and what might be the root cause of it. It is not fashionable to talk about evil these days. Best not mentioned, you know… could be uncomfortable…"

"But I don't see what the problem is? Evil is evil! There's plenty of it and we badly need to be delivered from it, don't we?"

"Long live the innocence of youth! Perhaps we should leave it at that – keep it simple. It will get complicated for you soon enough." He would gladly have left it at that. He didn't really know where the rub lay for him with this; he glossed over it every time he prayed.

But she replied, "Oh no, you can't leave it there. I now need to know what your problem is; you've raised my curiosity!"

"You want to beware of being too interested in evil," he said jokingly. "But, I suppose, having started this, we now have to see where it takes us. In centuries past, in our Christian civilisation, evil was personified and given various names, like Satan or the Devil. Mythology has it that he was once one of the archangels in heaven. But he rebelled against God and was sent to preside over another place called hell, or the underworld, populated by demons. After death, people who had decided to serve – or had fallen victim – to the devil in their lives, would be sent there, or to an intermediate place called purgatory, where those who hadn't been good enough to be destined for heaven nor quite bad enough to go straight to hell, would be given a chance to redeem themselves through suffering and contrition. If they felt sufficiently sorry, they would go to heaven; if not, then everlasting hell-fire awaited them, from which there was no escape, ever. Is that what you have been taught about this?"

"I have never been taught anything about any of this," she replied. "I have heard some of the words mentioned in conversation and have seen them in books, though not 'purga… something'."

"I don't think, really, that we have to bother too much about that historical stuff," he said, scratching his head pensively, "except that, perhaps to mention that some people in the Roman Catholic Church still believe in heaven, purgatory and hell literally, but mostly now they are taken to be allegorical, having deeper meanings for which they stand as analogies – like the idea that when Satan rebelled, God allowed him to retain a certain amount of power and to act as tempter or seducer in order to test humankind, which also links to what we said about *temptation*. But I'm more interested in how we might perceive evil nowadays in today's language, and where its essence might lie."

"I don't think I can help you there," she said, looking puzzled.

"Yes, I realise that. But you wanted me to go into this, and I'm trying to do my best. So the subject area which deals with good and evil is called ethics – and if I want to mean it when I pray, '*and deliverest us from evil*' I will have to delve into ethics. But there's one more general point I want to establish before we go there." Frederick was pushing on regardless now. *Evil* is something only humans are capable of committing. We do not accuse animals of evil actions. If a hawk hacks at the flesh of a living blackbird, as I had to watch through our kitchen window the other day, awful as that is to see, we don't call it evil. Or if a cat plays with a mouse until it dies of exhaustion, we may not like to watch, but we don't call it evil; would you agree?"

"I suppose I would," she said diffidently, and after a moment's pause, continued, "But if humans did such things we *would* call it cruel and evil. Although, actually, come to think of it, not all humans would. Some people don't think that bull fighting, cock fighting and fox hunting are evil and these sports are certainly cruel to animals. Also, what about cruelty to other humans? I saw a medieval torture chamber on a school trip once and those instruments looked very cruel and evil."

"Thankfully," he said with a sigh, "I think torture has now been outlawed by all Western countries, even though that is no guarantee that it doesn't still happen. At least it is regarded as illegal. This raises the interesting point, that there is an evolution taking place which is pushing the boundaries of what is regarded as evil. Perhaps we can detect a development here. Actions which were quite acceptable in earlier times, may be regarded as evil and quite intolerable now?"

"Isn't the rise in vegetarianism a sign of that?" she volunteered, "Even veganism is becoming more popular. Aren't these motivated by a rebellion against the cruelty of the meat and dairy industries? Mind you, there seems to be no lessening of the cruelty of war when you listen to the news and see the pictures on television."

Frederick took a deep breath, worried that they were getting way out of their depth, but she continued, "So, let's summarise where we have got to: we agree that evil – and good, I suppose – are solely human attributes and therefore constitute a significant difference between us and other members of the animal kingdom. There appears to be an evolution which is shifting the boundaries of what is regarded as evil. And this is all part of a subject called *ethics*. But how can we approach the question of what might be regarded as the *essence* of evil in our time, as you said?"

She paused momentarily and they both sat deep in thought. Then suddenly she had an idea, "Hold on – doesn't Albert Schweitzer have something to say about that? Surely, he must have thought about this?"

"Yes, of course. Well done for reminding me," he said. "Schweitzer, defining ethics, wrote that 'whatever helps to support and encourage life to reach its highest potential is good, and whatever harms or destroys life is evil'. But he also acknowledged that it is not possible for any creature to live without destroying other life in order to sustain itself. He maintained that for humans, ethics require that they reduce that necessity of killing for nourishment to its feasible minimum and to carry the inherent burden of responsibility with the utmost seriousness. What do you think? Does that help us with our present question?"

After a short while she replied, "I'm not sure it does, really. If I understand this correctly: we are trying to find out what motivates people to do evil rather than good things, when they have the choice. Because surely, if you do something because you have no choice to do otherwise, like killing an animal for nourishment, or self-defence, it can hardly be regarded as evil, can it?"

"What an excellent point, Lanya," he said, "substantiated by the fact that an executioner is not regarded as a murderer. Neither is a soldier, who would be court marshalled if he did not do his duty by killing the enemy. So there has to be an element of choice involved in opting for an evil act. So what would cause a person of sound mind to make that choice?"

"This must be taking us close to the core of the question now!" she said. "What if we try to apply this to what we called *'the really big questions of our time'*, earlier – I mean climate change, mass extinctions and so on."

"And the possibility of the end of life on Earth as we know it," he added.

"Yes, quite. Are these not the result of the actions of people who consider themselves to be 'of sound mind'? Rational, powerful people making what they regard as rational choices?"

"Yes, this might be the crux of what we are looking for," he said, aware of the significance of the moment. "What motivates people to act in ways that can produce such devastating cumulative effects? This must take us to the essence of how evil manifests in our time."

"I think it is greed," she said, after a pause. "All the little and big acts of selfish greed put together have this effect."

"You are so right!" he said, "Yes, greed! Greed and uninhibited self-interest have not only been thoroughly legitimised today, but have been glorified as providing the effective driving force and energy behind our systems of commerce, economics and politics. Indeed, our so-called 'growth' in affluence during the last couple of centuries has been attributed to the free rein given to these attitudes."

"So – what is greed?" There was a finality in her voice.

Attempting a definition, he said, "I think it is the desire for possession. And it becomes evil when exercised at any price regardless of the common good and only for one's own advantage. It is natural to want enough food and shelter but, as Gandhi said, 'there is enough on this earth for everybody's need, but not for everybody's greed'. Interesting to note, that animals don't seem to ever bother to accumulate more than they perceive as their need. So this is another specifically human attribute. And I think that greed is a response to a certain kind of fear – the fear of the human ego that there might not be enough to satisfy all its likes and whims and fancies. When this is coupled with a thirst for power, it can drive us to become utterly ruthless and destructive."

"I agree," she said. "When people only think of themselves and of their own advantage, their own profit, their own wellbeing, regardless of what harm is caused to others, that's when greed becomes positively evil. And you say this is generated by the ego. Is it then the ego that is the essence of evil today?"

"I think it is what the ego has been encouraged to become in today's society. However, I think that it is a misguided view of the function of the ego. Do you remember me talking about the

NESt Initiative earlier?" he asked.

"Yes, of course I do," she replied slightly indignantly.

"Well, as part of that project I developed the idea that the next step in human evolution will have to be in the psychological sphere. I suggest that the human ego – as the sense in us which gives us the feeling of our individual identity, the feeling of 'I' – 'Ahamkara' as the Indians call it – has been going through its teens, so to speak. It has been acting like a 'teenager' during the last few centuries, or even millennia, and what turbulent and terrifying times they have been. But now it is time for the ego to grow up and become responsible and sensible, and to learn to play its proper part in helping to care and protect all forms of life on our Mother Earth. That is what I think Albert Schweitzer ushered in with his phrase: *Reverence for Life*. Does that make any sense to you?"

"I think I understand," she said. "You are using the language that describes the growing-up process of an individual human being and applying it to the human race as a whole, yes?"

"Well – to large parts of the human race, the currently dominant parts, which are the ones we happen to live amongst, and which we call *civilised* and *developed*. There are parts of the human race scattered around the globe that are well ahead of us in this respect, even though we routinely call them primitive, savage, uneducated and *developing*."

"How do you imagine that this next step in human evolution is going to come about?" she asked.

"There are many signs that this evolution is already happening all around us. We have already mentioned the increased interest in vegetarianism and veganism. The whole organic food movement is part of this. The work of Greenpeace, the World Wildlife Fund, David Attenborough, and hundreds of other organisations and bodies working on the climate change issues… they are all part of this – the antidote to the evil of today. Yes! that is what I am thankful for when I pray: *Thou deliverest us from evil.* This makes a lot more sense to me now, after our conversation, than it did before, and I am really grateful for that too!"

"It is certainly a very hopeful place to end our discussion about evil," she said with a sigh of relief. "I was a bit worried earlier on, but I so agree with you that there are many people out there doing good things and working against the negative impact of all that greed. I think it is a wonderful thing to be grateful for." Her face was lit up by a big smile and she truly did feel a sense of having worked through something very difficult, as did he.

There was a pause. They were both letting their minds drift over what they had been discussing. Then both opened their mouths to speak at the same moment.

"After you," Frederick said.

"I was going to say, this just leaves the last few lines of the prayer. Do you include them?"

"Yes I do," he said, "they do round it off. The only thing I change is that I say: '*For Thine are the Kingdoms*', in the plural, because it reminds me of all the different kingdoms of living creatures and I want to include them all. Otherwise I leave it unchanged and end with: '*for ever and ever, amen*'."

"Now let me see whether I can remember it correctly," she said and began to recite:

'*Our Creator,*
Who art in and beyond Space,
Thy name – One-in-All – be hallowed,
Thy Kingdom come,
Thy Will be done in Earth as it is in and beyond Space.

Thou givest us this day our daily bread,
And forgivest us our trespasses as we forgive those who trespass against us,
And leadest us in temptation,
And deliverest us from evil.
For Thine are the Kingdoms, the power and the glory,
For ever and ever,
Amen.'

Have I got it right?" she then asked.

"Well, as I said at the beginning of this conversation, this is a work in progress, and we have given it a good go. Quite a few things have clarified themselves for me during our conversation. I shall have to think some more about various aspects like the word *trespasses* and whether I should replace it with *debt* or *fault*; we shall see. But now I am rather tired and wouldn't mind a little nap," he said, leaning back in his seat with droopy eyes.

Smiling at him kindly, Lanya got out her iPhone to check for any messages, and he was gone as soon as his eyes were shut.

Chapter Thirteen

HOPE AND COURAGE

When Frederick woke up, the train had emerged from the tunnel and they were hurtling through the Kent countryside. Lanya offered him some chocolate from the little supply she still had in her bag. They were both conscious that this journey would soon be at an end. After a while Frederick felt there was one more point to make, to bring their conversation to a close.

"I would just add one more comment to our mega-conversation," he started. "It is something I think is particularly relevant to the conditions of our time. When civilisations are young and full of creative energy, thrusting outwards into empire building, power games, the creative arts and material progress, there is generally not much time and energy left for introspection and philosophising. People are caught up in the momentum of the general enthusiasm of going forward. Courage, fortitude, ingenuity and a general sense of adventure are qualities which come to the fore. However, when a civilisation is past the peak of its life-cycle and it goes into decline, people in somewhat privileged positions tend to have time on their hands. The opportunity for introspection and for asking searching questions about meaning and purpose opens up for some. In past civilisations at this stage of the cycle there have been people who have made the most valuable contributions to the treasure trove of human wisdom, by being willing to ask the deepest and last questions the human mind is capable of formulating and to go in search for answers to these questions. I believe that the civilisation in which we are both embedded, is at such a stage of decline. And you and I have been using this train journey to do just that: searching for answers to some of life's big questions."

"You are not suggesting," she responded to his soliloquy, "that we have been making a contribution to the font of human wisdom? Aren't you getting a bit carried away?"

"There are no answers without there first being questions," he said. "It is as a result of your earnest and genuine questions, that some answers have arisen between us during our conversation. They are as new to me, near the end of my journey, as they may be to you at the beginning of yours. This is how wisdom comes about – living wisdom – as opposed to book knowledge."

He felt that he was a lot clearer about many of his own thoughts, having spent this journey exploring and explaining them with his granddaughter, and he wondered what she might be feeling about what she was taking away with her from their journey. So he enquired, "May I now ask you one last question: can you summarise what you feel you have learnt from our conversation on this trip?"

"Yes, actually I did think about this whilst you were asleep. We have covered a lot of ground!" she exclaimed. "I am not quite sure what I was expecting when I began with my questions. I was keen to learn about religion and God – I had planned that. But I do feel I got a lot more than I bargained for. Actually, can I tell you a story, to illustrate how I feel? Because all I have learned over the past week has made me remember a story I once read about a hummingbird."

"Oh do please! I love stories," he said eagerly.

And she cleared her throat and began, "Once upon a time, a little hummingbird lived in a forest. One day a huge fire broke out and engulfed all the trees in flames. All the animals were forced out of their homes and everyone thought that there was nothing they could do – except for one small hummingbird. Without wasting any time, this hummingbird flew to the nearest stream and filled its tiny beak with a drop of water. Again and again it flew back to the stream and dropped the beads of water, one by one, into the flames. The other animals in the forest mocked the hummingbird's efforts as they stood and watched the fire burning down their homes.

"'You are too little! - you can't put out this fire!' one of the animals called out.

"'What do you think you are doing?' said another.

"'I am doing what I can,' the hummingbird replied simply.

"That's my story. I think you have shown me how to be like that hummingbird," she said with shining eyes. "We have said many times that our universe is huge. To me, that is like the huge forest that the hummingbird lives in. Somehow within our massive world we have to make our tiny life mean something. I think what I will take away from our conversation are values that will help me to live a meaningful life."

"Values?" he inquired.

"Yes, values!" she said with emphasis. "We learnt about values at school and each answer you gave to my questions seemed to highlight a different value for me."

Frederick was intrigued. "We began by talking about religion. Can you explain which value it was you learnt about from that part of our conversation?" he asked.

"Well, when we talked about religion, you explained that there are many different religions because humans have an innate desire to connect with things beyond themselves. All religions are an expression of this innate spiritual quality so there cannot be one true or right religion. This has taught me the value of openness. To be open-minded and accepting of people's differences and to be open to new ideas."

"Yes, I see," he said.

"And then, when we talked about fairies, it showed me that humans have come up with many ways to explain the world. Truth does not necessarily have to be a proven scientific fact, it can be something one believes in. I think I will call this the value of imagination. It is important to feel comfortable with the unknown and use imagination to make sense of the world. This is how we can connect to things that are bigger than ourselves and grow our understanding."

"Yes, wonderful, the value of imagination! And the next value?" he asked.

"Next I asked you what you believe and you explained your theory of the 'qualities' and about 'space'. Although I found this quite difficult to understand, what I take away from this part of our conversation is the value of peace. Although, I know you didn't call it peace."

"No, I called it the here and now or the current moment," he remembered.

"But, you see, to me that sounds like peace. Within our busy lives, like the hummingbird flying to and from the stream, we must also take the time to notice the present moment and find inner stillness."

He nodded his acceptance of her interpretation and asked, "Are there more examples?"

"After that, you told me about your realisation of being within your thumb. This was an example of when an answer came from within you to help explain the world. That is the purpose of life, isn't it, to figure out what you believe and go on an inner journey to find the answers. I think this is the value of trust. I must have trust in my own thoughts and not be easily swayed by the opinions of others."

"A very important value indeed," he agreed. "And the next question you asked me was about death, wasn't it?"

"Yes, if the purpose of life is the inner journey then what is the purpose of death? You shared with me your idea about the afterlife being like waking up from a long dream. Death is not something to be afraid of. It is a natural part of life. For me, this is the value of improvement. I want to keep improving myself and my life, so that when the dreamer wakes up she remembers a beautiful dream, full of happiness, love and learning."

"What a wonderfully positive way to see it," he said, smiling at his granddaughter.

"You then explained that we have been given the gift of free will so that we can love. Because love can only be given freely and so this is our great reward for having free will. But we must accept that some people choose to do bad things with their free will. Simply, this is the value of love. We must choose to use our free will to be kind and give love."

She paused, trying to remember the next part of their conversation.

"I believe our discussion took a darker turn then when we talked about climate change," he prompted.

"Oh yes, you said that it is inevitable that climate change is going to have a massive effect on our world and the super-rich and powerful people who could stop it cannot be convinced to change as this would affect the very structure of the system that keeps them rich and powerful. This means that the only way to survive climate change is to live through it. This then is the value of skilfulness. It is going to be important to prepare to survive climate change. We need to learn skills that will help us to live in a world that is very different from our world today."

She continued straight on. "And one way we talked about preparing is through prayer. Prayer can be a way to seek comfort and refuge when things are scary, like the prospect of the world ending. I think this is the value of courage. It is all right to feel fear as long as you have a way to deal with it so you can carry on. When you pray, you don't ask to be saved or protected. Instead you express gratitude for the help we are already getting. We need to be brave and courageous so we can accept whatever comes."

Gaining momentum now, she said, "And this linked to our discussion of God's Will. You said that the essence of faith is to be humble and surrender our will to God. This is the value of hope. We have to have faith that everything will be all right in the end. You use prayer to be thankful for what we have. This is the value of optimism. We have to believe that this world is the best of all possible worlds and feel gratitude, even for the difficult and challenging things we experience. Even temptations are an opportunity to learn and to exercise to become a stronger person."

"Exactly," he said. "And the last thing we talked about was how to define evil in today's world. What values do you take away from that part of the conversation?"

"Yes, we defined the essence of evil in our time as greed. So, an action that puts self-interest before the common good is an evil act. This is the value of responsibility. We have to take responsibility for our actions and make sure they do not harm life unnecessarily. We have to show empathy towards other creatures and respect the whole of life on our planet.

"You see, each value is like the drop of water carried in the beak of the hummingbird. They are the tools we can use to make small differences in the world. If this world is going to end because of climate change, like the forest in the fire, then I want to be like the hummingbird. I am not going to sit back and watch it happen. I think there are things that can be done. I am going to use my drops of water, my set of values, to do what I can."

The train had been rolling through the London suburbs as Lanya finished her recollection and interpretation of their momentous conversation.

Her grandfather was both delighted with Lanya's summary and amazed at her grasp of all that had been discussed. He was only too aware that his memory was no longer as good as it once was, so he asked, "Do you think you could make a list for me of all the values you have identified during our momentous conversation on this memorable journey?"

"Yes of course," she replied eagerly, "I'll write them down for you straight away. It will help me to remember the main points of what we discussed as well," and she took a notebook from her bag and began to write:

To live a good and meaningful life we must live with the values of:

Openness
Imagination
Peace
Trust
Improvement
Love
Skilfulness
Courage

Responsibility
Optimism

As the train pulled slowly into St Pancras Station, Lanya had finished writing and her grandfather carefully folded the piece of paper and put it safely in his leather bag.

Whilst they were putting on their coats he remarked, "I think neither of us are returning as quite the same persons that left here not ten days ago."

"I think you are right," she said. "You have set me a great challenge to go on and live a good and meaningful life. I hope that I can rise to the occasion. I shall carry our words deep in my heart for the rest of my life, of that I am sure."

They gathered up their belongings and got off the train. Walking down the platform they suddenly stopped and gave each other a big hug.

EPILOGUE

A day later, Lanya found this on her phone:

"My dear Lanya,
this happened early this morning.
I thought you might like it as a memento."

IN AN INSTANT

It was a perfectly ordinary day,
To the office, bright'n early, I was wending my way.
The car was parked under the cedar tree
and locked – as normal as can be.

I stood a moment, key in hand
And turned my head, surveying the land.
My eye was caught by the tip of my thumb
And I stood perplexed, quite still and numb:

"What 'I' is this?"

Conscious of itself in three worlds as one?
In our universe – part of the body of an immensity,
As well as inside an atom of my thumb – simultaneously,
Whilst in my body – on this Earth, spinning around our Sun.

"As above – so below!"

A being, whose body is my universe,
Is relying on my loving obedience,
As I am counting on my thumb's compliance,
Whilst my body is its atoms' universe.

Under that tree next to my car
On that very ordinary day,
My mind went all that way,
The same 'I' stretching that far.

In an instant!

STORY TWO

IN SEARCH FOR SOUL
In a Car

Introduction

By July 2020, the Covid restrictions had been somewhat relaxed as the numbers of infections each day were gradually coming down and a tentative feeling of optimism was given voice by government spokespeople and media commentators. In the summer sunshine pent-up yearnings for 'liberation' from restrictions could no longer be resisted. In vain, more cautious scientists were sounding warnings and expressing concern.

In this atmosphere, Lanya, now twenty-six years old, married and working in a bakery, seized an opportunity to take her grandfather on a journey towards Birmingham, driving in her car up the motorways into the Midlands. And we join their conversation on this journey.

An earlier version of this conversation in a car, entitled 'Lanya's Search for Soul' was first published in 2021, as the first of eighteen essays in a collection entitled: 'The Human Soul – Essays in honour of Nalin Ranasinghe' edited by Predrag Cicovacki of the College of the Holy Cross as part of a 'Series in Philosophy' published by Vernon Press.

Chapter One

SEARCHING FOR SOUL IN THE BIBLE AND IN THE AIRWAVES

It was early in the morning for Frederick, Lanya's Grandpa, now in his eighties, when Lanya pulled up in her car at the thatched cottage where he lived, to invite him to join her on a trip to the Midlands, where she had business to transact. He did not take long to be ready, and off they went.

After the initial exchange of news and general chat they had fallen silent – a comfortable silence that was quite natural between them. Their relationship was such, that they did not need to see each other often to feel close and connected at some deeper level than that on which normal family relationships or casual friendships thrive. So far apart in age, these two, when they had time alone with each other, did not take long to delve deep below the surface of things. This morning was to be no exception. As soon as they were on the motorway, Lanya broke the silence with, "Do you think, Grandpa, that we have such a thing as a soul; and, if you do, can we talk about it, like – is it immortal?"

The question rang in Frederick's ear for a few moments before he could answer, "Whoa, Lanya – straight in at the deep end again. Where does that come from all of a sudden?"

"Well, you remember you lent me your New Testament before my wedding, so that we could choose a piece for you to read in the church?" she began, "Well, I got to reading the whole of the Gospel according to Mathew one evening – it's quite a good read, you know, when you read it like any other book, not in bits and pieces but in one go. I don't know why, but I was particularly struck by the verse – I can even remember the number: 16 – 26: '*For what profit is it to a man if he gains the whole world and loses his soul? Or what will a man give in exchange for his soul?*' Because I don't really know what is meant by the word 'soul', I hoped the gospel would enlighten me further. But the word is only mentioned two more times. Once in the famous saying: '*You shall love the Lord your God with all your heart, with all your soul, and with all your mind,*' and once, when Jesus leaves his disciples in Gethsemane and says: '*My soul is exceedingly sorrowful. Even unto death. Stay here and watch with me*'. These sentences made me even more intrigued but they didn't really help my understanding any further. You can see what an impression this made on me – that I can still remember the words exactly."

She paused and he asked, "Did you read any of the other gospels?"

"No," she said, "but I did look up 'Soul in the Bible' on Wikipedia and learnt that, according to them, the writers of the Old Testament did not consider humans to have an immortal soul, but the writers of the New Testament, influenced by ancient Greek thought, did. So that's where I am now with this, and hence my question. What do you think? I'm sure you can help me."

Whilst Frederick was still wondering how to respond, Lanya suggested that they stop for a drink or something as they were just approaching a service station.

The place was virtually empty and whilst he chose a table and settled himself into a chair, Lanya already came with his black coffee and a glass of water for herself. She sat down opposite him, switched her phone onto silent and put it away in her bag.

They sat for a little while sipping their drinks. Then Lanya, who often came out with extraordinary facts, asked casually, "Did you know that there are one hundred trillion bacteria in your gut?"

"Really?" he responded astonished. "Where did you find that titbit of information? I'm not sure I can visualise one trillion of anything, let alone one hundred trillion?"

"That's what I recently read in a pamphlet from a company selling health supplements; and I thought of it now because I was thinking about all the bits of information hanging around in the air waiting to be picked up by some computer or telephone or iPad anywhere on the globe. Just think of the numbers! All the people talking to each other, researching, surfing, watching things on the internet! Whole films and concerts, streaming from some database to untold numbers of different receptors located anywhere and everywhere? It's just mind-blowing! And just four decades ago there was none of that. And yet we don't see, feel, hear, taste or smell any of it. We don't actually know whether it affects our bodies in some way. We are certainly not aware of it. Unless you have the right kind of receptor you just don't know it exists. Doesn't all that blow your mind?"

"It certainly does," he replied. "I often think about that as well. And about what might be out there that escapes all our receptors or for which we have no receptors at all. Also, it is not only the vastness of the numbers that goes beyond the capacity of my mind to comprehend, but the strangely blinkered, compartmentalised way in which we cope with this sort of thing."

"How do you mean?"

"Well, as you say, the air is filled with all that information which our five senses cannot access unless it is processed by receptors which convert it into pictures and sounds which our physical senses can pick up. We are quite happy to engage with all that and grateful that it works, whilst ignoring how it works. But when it comes to the soul, or the spirit, we say that, unless we can prove its existence by measuring it and perceiving it with our five senses, it doesn't exist."

Lanya pondered this for a moment, sipping her water, before responding with, "But there are lots of things we accept as having existence which are outside the range of our sense-perception. We know that there are sound waves which we can't hear, but animals can; similarly with lightwaves, like ultra-violet or x-ray, where we have built receptors which can translate them into readings and measurements which we can interpret. As you say, it all hinges on having the right receptors."

"Exactly!" he retorted in a slightly superior tone.

"Why is it," she asked, slightly narked, "that when I talk with you, I so often end up feeling that I have to defend science; that science comes under attack in our conversations?"

"That's because I do attack the common, popularly held scientific viewpoint, which is created not so much by scientists but by the media. And I admit that I often get carried away and attack scientists unjustly for things that aren't at all down to them. I do apologise for that."

"So, what are you blaming them for now? I was just expressing my wonder and awe at the incredible numbers of things and you turn it into an issue about receptors and insinuate that science is somehow at fault here?"

"Quite true," he admitted. "You know me too well; but perhaps there is an issue about receptors which really is worth looking at."

"All right, let's look at receptors then," she said consolingly with the faintest of smiles. "It might lead us smoothly back to my question about the soul. But do we need another drink and perhaps even a biscuit for this? Another black coffee?" she asked over her shoulder – already on her way to the counter.

Whilst she was gone, he pondered the fact that his conversations with Lanya always seemed to go into the depths of things. She was so quick to read his subtler thoughts, and her open and enquiring mind always led him on into more profound territory. He didn't really know anybody else quite like her in that way. When she returned with a tray of goodies, he was ready with another tack. It was very quiet, and they were quite undisturbed. Anyway, the tables had been arranged with wide spaces between them on account of the 'social distancing rules' which made the place look spacious and calm. As soon as she began placing the cup, her glass and the nibbles on the table, he started, "You were saying earlier how less than four decades ago we didn't yet have any inkling of the digital world which now envelops us. Well, I've just been thinking of another aspect of our lives which has changed quite considerably in that time, partly as a result of the digital revolution. I still remember how, as a teenager, I needed to take my bicycle apart and put it together again in order to fully understand how it worked. The same with my first motor scooter and even with my first car – I knew how to take the carburettor apart, clean the points, clean the spark plugs and generally mend and service things myself. I also remember even as a small boy, I would take my toys apart to see how they were put together. It was just part of understanding the world I lived in.

"But then, when I had children of my own, I noticed that they had no such desires or interest. They just needed to be able to operate the objects and gadgets around them. They saw no need to understand how they worked. There also came a point when I realised that I myself was surrounded by things of which I had no clue how they worked, and that I had stopped making any attempt to understand how my car worked. This happened in a relatively short time – maybe a decade or so – and during the same period things began to be made so that you couldn't take them apart. People lost interest in mending things. If something stopped working you just threw it away. Nevertheless, there was still a general understanding of mechanical processes. And then the computer arrived on the scene as a domestic item in people's homes."

"Can you really remember when that was?" she interrupted him.

"Not exactly, but it must have been in the early 1980s. I do know that Tim Berners-Lee invented the World Wide Web in 1989, and your uncle, Ben, had his first BBC PC in his bedroom before that. It all happened so amazingly quickly. It gathered real momentum just about when you were born – now there's a thought…"

"So I'm well and truly of the internet generation!" she exclaimed.

"You are indeed – though I would say not at all a typical member of it. Anyway, the point I'm trying to make here is this: with the advent of computer technology as an everyday item in people's homes, I think, any last vestige of understanding – or even wanting to understand how things worked went out of the window for the general public. People generally are satisfied if they manage to master the operation of these 'magical' machines."

"But, for my generation there's nothing magical about it,"

she interjected. "We take all that for granted."

"Precisely," he said emphatically, "that's how magic works. Because we take things for granted we miss what's really going on. With that comes a certain gullibility, a willingness to be manipulated, an acceptance to take someone else's word for it – in short – a reliance on someone else's receptors and a neglect of our own."

"I wondered how all this was going to come around to your problem with receptors," she said with a big smile. "But I'm not sure I get your point."

"There are lots of peripheral issues arising from this, but for me the central one is the effect this is having on the human soul."

"Ah – you see – here we are back at my original question. What do people actually mean when they talk about 'soul'? Ever since I read the gospel according to Mathew I've been quite confused about this. We didn't really touch on the concept of 'soul' on our trip to Vienna, or since, did we? But the word is now haunting me and I don't seem to be able to make sense of it."

"Yes, this is indeed a very serious – a very real question! But you are opening up a very wide landscape here," he said thoughtfully. "Shall we get back on the road and see how far we can get with it in the car? Otherwise you'll never get to your assignment."

They filled up with petrol and re-joined the motorway. As soon as they were out in the second lane Lanya re-opened the conversation with, "So where were we?"

"I think I would quite like to finish the point I was trying to make earlier, before we tackle the concept of 'soul' – if you agree?"

"Of course. From what you were saying, one will lead nicely into the other in any event."

Frederick briefly looked out of the window to collect his

thoughts.

"I think, in essence, we were considering," he began, "how the advent of digital communication was affecting the human soul, and in particular, how reliance on external receptors was taking us away from paying attention to our own internal receptors of things beyond the scope of our five physical senses, the existence of which some sectors of society deny and others ridicule."

"We hadn't quite got that far, but I get what you are saying," she interrupted. "You were pointing out – if I understood you correctly – that we were quite happy to accept the existence of unseen waves of energy carrying messages sent out by computers and picked up by receptors anywhere on the globe – or in outer space for that matter – but were inclined to deny the existence of other unseen waves or energies not originating from fabricated machines. And now you are saying that this is because we have become disconnected from our own internal receptors for such waves or impulses and this disconnection is increasing – due to our obsession with these new external receptors – to the point of no longer being able to tune in to our own receptors at all, and we therefore deny or disown the existence of such waves. Have I got that right?"

"I could not have summarised it better. But do you see what I mean? And do you agree?"

"I'd like to get a little more specific about these other waves, energies and impulses and our receptors for them, before I answer that. What can be said about them?"

"Yes, fair point! And indeed, that is the crux of what we are discussing, which we need to clarify before we can seriously consider questions like 'the immortality of the soul' and venture out into that wide landscape I referred to earlier."

"Come on then, I'm eager to do this," she encouraged him.

Chapter Two

WHERE DOES INSPIRATION COME FROM

"OK then!" he said, sitting up and uncrossing his legs. "Imagine you are walking along a path in a wood. A bird is singing its heart out overhead. The bees are humming in the trees – if only – (well, they used to). You are at peace and a feeling of elated contentment flows through you... and there! – as from nowhere – is the answer to a question you have been struggling with for weeks. No drum-roll, no fireworks, but suddenly inspiration strikes: all of a sudden you know what you are going to do – perhaps to help a friend, or something in your work, or with the rest of your life! I'm sure you've been there?"

"I certainly have! Quite a few times. Not always in a wood, but nearly always somewhere in a beautiful landscape or by the sea." She glanced across at him with shining eyes.

"Where do we think that such dearly sought insights come from?"

"Yes, I have often wondered? I suppose certain cells inside our brain aligned themselves to let the information come through to our consciousness."

"Yes, all right; but that's like saying the radio got tuned into the right wavelength to allow the music to come out nice and clear. Or the connection between your laptop and the router was re-established and allowed an email through. We use these analogies because this is now our everyday experience. We don't have the language to explain it in other ways. So, staying within that analogy: we don't expect either the router or the laptop to make up the information themselves, do we? It has to come from somewhere – at least so far. Some say that Artificial Intelligence will change things in this regard," he said with a provocative smile.

Lanya sensed the danger of being side-tracked into a cynical tirade about AI and quickly asked, "So how would this question have been answered before we had computers?"

"Poets used to talk about being inspired by the muses of a particular place. Composers talked about responding to the 'genie' of a place. Painters talked about capturing the 'spirit' of a place. Sculptors talked about working in harmony with the quality of a piece of rock or wood and being inspired by the spirit of the material. People could be lured, seduced or beguiled by sirens in certain places; or they could be enchanted, enraptured and transported by elves or guiding spirits or guardian angels. Architects would talk about a 'sense of place' and letting that inspire and guide their designs. These are the analogies people used to use to express their experience of receiving ideas, inspiration and feelings – what we would now call 'input' – through receptors which they had trained and refined in particular fields of the arts. Is that making any sense to you?"

"Absolutely!" she nodded enthusiastically. "And you are suggesting that there is a parallel to be drawn between the waves that now fill the air with digital information and the energies which people experienced in certain places and from which they gained inspiration?"

"Well, I think, people saw themselves, much more than we do now, as part of a community of spirits which interact and cross-influence each other. In other words, the idea of the human soul could be more easily seen as integrated into the larger picture of natural creativity."

"So, would I be right in thinking that all this is still there," she interjected excitedly, "but it tends to be drowned out by the noise of our life, like bird song is drowned out by motor engine noise along motorways?"

"Oh, I do like that analogy!" he said, nodding, and looking out of the side window into the trees whizzing by, he was suddenly intensely aware of the humming of the engine and the tires. She was quite right, he thought – it was all still there, just obliterated by the noise of modern life. It was still possible to connect with all of that, but it just was so much harder to find the times and the places.

He turned back to Lanya. "Of course this is a vast field, and what we are looking at now is only one tiny corner of it. I said it would be a wide landscape to cross. For instance, in many cultures in the past, there was active engagement and communication with the ancestors. The indigenous peoples of North America talk about communication not only with ancestors, but with the Wind, with the Fire of the Sun, with Mother Earth, and with the trees of the forest, the rivers and lakes, with mountains, clouds and rain. Their receptors were open to communication with all of these. We know this from their stories, their songs and their sayings." He paused, overcome by a longing to be more actively part of that world again, which he remembered vividly from his childhood.

"Did they not have members of their communities who were specially trained and experienced in this kind of communication?" she asked after a pause.

"You mean shamans or medicine men and women?"

"Yes, exactly. Have you had much experience of their fields

of activity?"

"No, not really," he said, "no actual direct experience, but I have read some accounts of such direct experiences, and they were very illuminating. Particularly, one I can remember is of a young Canadian called Jeremy Narby who wrote a book called 'the Cosmic Serpent', in which he describes his experiences in South America – it might have been in Peru, I'm not quite sure. He went there as a young lawyer, under the auspices of a Swiss organisation called Nouvelle Planete, who were helping indigenous tribes living in the Amazon rainforest to establish legal rights to their territories. This was in the 1990s. I found his account especially interesting because he was a very 'down-to-earth' and scientifically inclined young man. Towards the end of his stay in a particular village, the elders arranged for him to take part in a carefully managed session of taking hallucinatory substances and he describes in great detail the experience of having this quite amazing conversation with two huge snakes. It's quite a while ago that I read this book, so I can't really tell you too much details, but it left a deep impression on me, and I can thoroughly recommend it to you."

"One hears and reads quite a lot of dubious, negative and critical stuff about shamans, witch-doctors and ancestor-worship," she interjected. "It has not had a very good press, has it? So, I'd like to read something positive about it."

"The bad press which still lingers, is the tail end of centuries during which Europeans have gone out into other parts of the globe, systematically destroying the cultures for whom this kind of connectedness to nature was an intrinsic part of their normal way of life. Our ancestors confiscated their lands and all but exterminated their communities. And the Christian Church with its missionary zeal went about ruthlessly maligning and obliterating the knowledge and deep insight which lay behind the rituals and practices of these peoples. Insights which, on the whole, with only a very few exceptions, completely eluded the European invaders, because they were simply blind to them. Not a happy aspect of our history. Anyway, this blindness goes back quite a long way in our culture. If anything, we can find more openness towards it now than we could for a long time."

"I obviously touched a nerve there," she interjected in response to the combative tone in his voice.

"Well, I have been saying this for years now. Unless we Europeans come clean and acknowledge honestly and openly what our ancestors of some twenty generations ago were doing – largely in the name of Christianity – how are we ever going to become fully reconciled in this era of globalisation? How can we have a genuine peace on this earth? But perhaps we are getting somewhat drawn away from our subject?"

"But I can see what you're saying, and how this is very relevant to our peace of mind and well-being," she said with emphasis.

"I'm glad of that," he said, taking a deep breath, "but I shouldn't get so heated. The trouble is: we are not at all free yet of the underlying attitudes that allowed these things to happen – even now. But let's leave that. We can come back to it at some other time – which we probably will, because the subject is not going to go away any time soon. Let's get back to considering what might be available to us if we can rediscover, reactivate and properly tune our natural, built-in human receptors."

"Yes let's," she nodded and asked, "What about that place we talked about the other day up in the north of Scotland? Don't the people there have something to say on this subject?"

"You mean the Findhorn Community," he said, his

expression brightening. "You are so right, they do indeed! For your grandmother and I, the conferences we took part in up there around the turn of the millennium – at the birth of the Eco-Village Movement – were highly significant in helping us to clean out and re-tune our receptors for the subtler energies which were being smothered by the noise – the rush and tumble of our lives. And actually, just a few days ago, I looked at their website and watched a Ted-Talk recorded there by Michael Lindfield on 'interspecies communication' in which he re-tells how Dorothy Maclean discovered how to communicate with the spirits of the vegetables they were growing for their survival, in the salty sand dunes there. The sand on the beach was the only place available to them, and they learnt to co-operate with the plants in such a way that even on that beach they were able to grow huge specimens of various vegetables and to produce enough to sustain themselves during those early days. Their website quotes Dorothy, who died only recently – just three months after her one hundredth birthday – as saying: '*What nature says to us awakens something deep within our hearts*', and when *she* says that, it is meant literally, not metaphorically."

"You mean she was able to communicate directly with the plants?" Lanya asked, a bit incredulously.

"As far as I remember, she used to get quite specific messages which she used to interpret and relay to the other members of the community. This is all recorded quite meticulously in books. In the Ted-Talk to which I listened, Michael Lindfield told a rather nice story which I remember well: '*When I was a child*' he said, '*they told me that God sleeps in the stones, dreams in the plants, stirs in the animals and wakes up in humans*'. And he went on to say that this lists four kingdoms, but that the musical scale had seven steps and the rainbow had seven colours, so he asked: '*what about the other three kingdoms?*' I like his inference, but don't quite agree with his numbers: the musical scale does have seven intervals, but in music we talk about the octave as having eight notes, and if the analogy is to work, I should expect there to be eight kingdoms."

"Oh, let's see what they might be called!" she exclaimed excitedly, and plunged straight in with, "The elves, obviously, which belong to the nature spirits, like the genies of a place you mentioned earlier; then the muses you mentioned, would – I think – already be of a higher order, from where the great artists get their inspiration; then we would have the great spiritually inspired individuals like Jesus and Buddha and other fully realised humans, and finally, God. And there you have seven steps and eight kingdoms. How about that?" she called out triumphantly.

"Very good," he responded, a little guardedly, "but it may be slightly more complicated and involved than that. However, as a broad-brush concept – not bad."

"What's wrong with it?" She had expected more enthusiasm from him than that.

"We would not be the first to have a go at this. There have been many attempts before. The Catholic Church has talked for centuries about angels, guardian angels, archangels and the Son of Man. The ancient Greeks had very complicated hierarchies amongst their gods – as there must surely also be amongst the thirty-three million gods of the Hindus. I suspect the ancient Egyptians also had hierarchies amongst their gods."

"All that is too convoluted for me," she interrupted impatiently. "What do you yourself think about it?"

"As you know, an ongoing hobby of mine is to adapt the Lord's Prayer to my needs. That has brought me to wonder about what to make of 'Thy kingdom come...'? You also know that another preoccupation of mine is to speculate what the next step in the evolution of humankind might entail and whether it may be possible to have any conscious influence on this evolutionary process, which I have called the NESt Initiative. In the context of both these projects I have seen homo sapiens as being in transition from the animal kingdom to a fully self-conscious, fully ethical creature on the level of the great religious leaders you have already mentioned. This could then be called the fifth kingdom. But I wouldn't venture to be specific beyond that. On the other hand, on a different level, at a much larger scale, I would want to visualise several octaves, both below and above the one we experience as our physical world in which we have the four kingdoms we all know. On the micro-scale we would talk about bacteria, viruses, cells, molecules, atoms etc. down to the infinitely small. On the macro-scale there would be solar systems, galaxies, clusters of galaxies etc. on the way to the infinitely large."

He paused and appeared to have lost the thread. So she came to his rescue with, "Oh you, with your big ideas – that's all way beyond me. Let's get back to more familiar territory. In fact, I think we are due for another stop. I need a break from driving in any event. Actually, if you look into that compartment, you'll find some biscuits. I wouldn't mind a nibble until we come to the next service station."

They had a biscuit and drove along in silence for a while until she pulled off the motorway and parked the car. It was a pleasant, sunny day and they could sit comfortably outside with their lunch.

"We should really have made this journey by train – as we did when we went to Vienna," Lanya commented at one point, "but with you in the most vulnerable group – virus-wise – I thought it would be safer this way – and it's proving to be so, sitting out here in the open rather than having to eat in a confined dining car, or munching sandwiches in a possibly quite full carriage."

Chapter Three

HOW CAN I ACTUALLY FEEL MY SOUL

Whilst Lanya checked her phone after they had eaten, Frederick had a bit of a doze. But soon Lanya was keen to push on. The motorway was even less busy now, and as soon as they were settled back into cruising mode, it more or less burst out of Lanya. "I'm sorry, Grandpa, but I have to go back to the beginning," she said with deep feeling in her voice. He sat up to listen carefully as she continued, "because ever since that time when I read St Mathew's gospel, I have been grappling with the question of how I could actually feel my soul? – how I could sense it? It seems to me that the concept of the human soul is something vague, intangible, elusive. So how do I know if I have sensed my own soul?" She paused for a moment, but before he could attempt a reply she continued, "There was a day when this feeling – this longing to understand and be in touch with my soul was particularly strong. It was a day I spent on an organic farm in Cambridge. I spent it with the farmer, learning to sickle wheat, to thresh the grain by hand and mill it in a small solar powered mill. Then with the fresh flour we made bread and baked it in a wood fired oven.

"As I stood in the wheat field, the sun shone down on me. I could see the slight breeze making the golden field shimmer as the ears of ripe wheat bobbed and bowed. I bent down and carefully performed the slicing action – the sharp blade of the sickle cutting through the straw at just the right angle to form it into a wheat sheaf. In that moment, I could feel a bond with the thousands of farmers who had done that exact same movement. It is such an ancient, traditional way to harvest wheat, it was as if the movement itself connected me to a long line of souls before me.

"As I worked my way up the fifty-metre plot of wheat I found myself thinking about my soul. Could I sense it here in this field? I think I did. It wasn't a loud, confident feeling, more a tentative whisper. But it was there. A feeling of happiness, contentedness, a sense that I was in the right place and doing the right thing. I felt part of something bigger, connected with past farmers and bakers and even to the wheat itself, which has been growing for millennia, intrinsically entwined with human history. My eyes were wide open to appreciate nature and its beauty. Was this my mind tuning out from the business of everyday life and tuning in to the quiet voice of my soul?

"Since then I began wondering: what if I lived a life that allowed me to sense my soul more often and more clearly? What if I actively tried to nourish my soul so that it could flourish? What would that be like? …I think if I did that, I would more often find myself standing in a field of wheat, surrounded by nature, sickle in hand, the sun in my eyes, and envisioning how to turn the beautiful harvest into a delicious dinner…"

He was looking at her in amazement; her shining eyes glowing, her face radiant; a young woman finding her role in life – finding her proper part to play upon the stage of life – and rejoicing in her discovery and recognition. She glanced over at him and asked, "Do you have such a memory of tuning in to your soul?"

He mumbled something about, "I will have to give that some

thought." But then he found his composure and said, "If you weren't driving and if we weren't in a COVID-19 pandemic I would take you in my arms and hold you very tight. If that was not your soul speaking just now, I don't know what would be! I doubt that I could add anything worthwhile to this moment."

They drove along in silence; not so much lost in thought as floating in a contented peace. Eventually Lanya said, "That's all very well, but there must be more that can be said about the soul – about how the concept fits into the bigger picture philosophically?"

"Well indeed there is," he replied, "but I'm afraid it might blur the beautiful picture you have just created."

"Yes, but I need to understand more about the theory, intellectually, as well as experiencing it emotionally – I'm sure you agree, knowing you – and I'm sure there's more you can say. For instance, the second time the soul is mentioned in Matthew, it is listed as one of three: the heart, the soul and the mind. So how does that work? How do they relate to each other?"

"Well, you know, there are so many different ways that people have divided up the totality of the human experience," he started diffidently, but she interjected immediately, with a big grin on her face.

"I don't want the full range, just your favourite one, please!"

Chapter Four

GRANDPA'S FAVOURITE IMAGE OF EXISTENCE

"All right then, my favourite picture of the human experience of existence - let's have a go:

We can divide the totality up into four identifiable worlds: The physical or gross; the energetic or subtle; the creative or causal; the infinitely eternal or spiritual.

The physical or gross world is perceived as the five physical elements linked to our five physical senses: earth to smell; water to taste; fire to sight; air to touch; and space or ether to hearing.

The energetic or subtle world consists of subtle equivalents of these five elements, perceived as part of what we call the mind. But to explain this I have to refer to Hindu Advaita terminology because we in the 'West' do not have an adequate vocabulary for the make-up of the mind - not for this picture anyway.

The Advaita tradition divides the structure of our mental world into four sections:

Manas: the office boy - the ordinary, continuous mental activity and constant chatter in our heads;

Buddhi: the powerhouse - the creative, discerning, discriminating part of the mind;

Chitta: the storehouse - the memory and centre of cognition, insight and understanding;

Ahamkara: the feeling of "I" - the sense of being an individual - the Ego; (not to be confused with the 'Self')

I place Manas as part of the subtle, energetic world, whilst the other three, Buddhi, Citta and Ahamkara, make up the creative, causal world, where fundamental causes originate.

There is not much I can say about the eternal, infinite, spiritual world, except that we know it is there – not least because we have the words, and something inside us knows what we mean by them, however vaguely."

"That's quite a lot to take in, Grandpa; you will have to write all that down for me to ponder," she interrupted in a thoughtful voice. "But where does the soul fit into this picture of yours?"

"Before we can come to that," he continued, "I have to say something about 'ether' or space. The ancient Greeks regarded the ether as the fifth element. I'm sure you remember that we did touch on this on our trip to Vienna some years ago, but it needs to be a clearly understood part of this picture. I like to think of it as the threshold between the phenomenal world – the world in which distance and the passage of time can be measured and therefore, everything has limits and is constantly changing – and the transcendental world which lies beyond limits and change. I therefore see it as the interface between the three worlds – gross, subtle and causal – and the spiritual world. However, we need to remember that when we divide into compartments, what is in reality a fluid continuum, we are doing so only in order to be able to give these compartments names with which to refer to them in our thinking and in our discussions. There are no such sharp divisions in reality.

"Now, as for the soul, I would like to think that the whole of what I have defined just now as the phenomenal world, is like a set of clothes which the soul can wear, or like a house with many rooms in which the soul can live when she visits this earth. In other words: the three worlds – gross, subtle and causal – are the soul's habitat, into which she is incarnated. I believe that when a person – or any creature – dies, the soul leaves all that behind and returns – as it were naked, or disembodied – to where she came from, and she wakes up there, as from a dream. Some people believe that they survive after death as the personality they think they are here, but I rather doubt that. They believe they go to a heaven (or hell or purgatory, as we said earlier), where things are much as they are here, only incomparably better or worse. Both these images may of course be right, depending on a soul's stage of development. As to names: I find the Hindu term Atman and Param-atman most straightforward and easily accessible to me. Atman stands for what I call the human soul – the spark of the Divine in us. Param-atman stands for the collective entity of all Divine sparks in all of creation – the Absolute. But don't forget: all this is speculation, and largely dismissed as nonsense by a majority of the scientific community, except perhaps by those studying the sub-atomic world, where similarities with what I have just described are beginning to appear. But then: where would science be without speculation, proposition, hypothesis and experimentation?"

"Oh please, let's leave science out of this for now," she interrupted. "I understand that this is your picture of how these things might be arranged – which is what I asked for – and I think I get it; and I like it. Anyway, you clearly think that the soul comes from somewhere and is here on a visit?"

"Well yes. I think that souls come here to learn something, and that this world is a school for souls."

"I see," she said enthusiastically, "so then, like in a school, souls are at different stages of development, depending on what they are here to learn and how far they have got in their lessons – I like it a lot. Do you believe in reincarnation then? Like coming back next year/next life into a different year-group?"

"Yes, I do – sort of..." he said somewhat guardedly, "I haven't come across any other idea that makes nearly as much sense, but like every analogy, it has its limits – 'to be handled with care', I should say."

"And what about animals: surely they must have souls too!" She was very excited now.

"In my picture," he took a deep breath, "as I see it, every single creature, every living entity – and there are no entities which are not alive – including every cell in our bodies, every atom even, every solar system and galaxy, has soul at its innermost core. We are so used to seeing things as separate objects with hard boundaries and divided from one another. But that is all just appearance. In reality, below the surface, everything is fluid and connected. All entities take on form, have their time of existence and dissolve, but whilst they have existence, they have soul at their core."

"I'm not sure I follow," she said with a worried expression, "Is what you are describing another way of saying that 'God is everywhere – not just in church on Sundays' – is that what you mean?"

"That is exactly what I mean. Let me try an analogy to demonstrate what I mean by fluidity: Take a snowflake: water-vapour in a cloud condenses, falls into colder air and turns into a snowflake – a beautiful, unique, six-pointed star, drifting gently down on the slight breeze with millions of others – each a different version on the same theme, eventually coming to rest on a roof, making a thick blanket of snow during the night. When the sun rises in the morning, its first rays make our flake sparkle and shine in all the colours of the rainbow. Then, at noon, on this glorious day, the full blast of the sun makes our flake melt and seep through the blanket of snow, trickling down to the edge of the roof, where now, in the evening, the dropped temperature makes it freeze on a long icicle hanging there. The next day the sun is even hotter, and the icicle breaks off and falls to the ground where a child picks it up and sucks on it, pretending it is a lollypop. The ice that was our flake ends up in the child's lungs and re-emerges in the evening as vapour when the child, now indoors looking out of the window, makes it condense on the glass. During the night the vapour freezes into a beautiful design of ice-flowers on the glass, which twinkle and glow in the first rays of the following morning's sun when the child opens the curtains and with its finger draws a heart into the melting flowers. The water that was our snowflake now runs out of the bottom of the heart, down the glass, onto the windowsill, through a drain-hole in the sill to the outside and then falls onto the snow-covered ground below where it freezes and melts several times before, eventually, in Spring, it flows with the little stream into the big river. There, it partakes in the long, long journey towards the ocean, with too many adventures to tell here… like the one where it got separated from the main current and was swept into a shallow eddy, where a cow drank it and it took days to work its way through all the cow's internal waterworks before ending up in a drain, from where it was washed back into the big river… it could have evaporated at any moment to start the whole cycle all over again. But it didn't, and eventually it ended up back in the huge ocean, from where it had started to rise up into the sky in the first place."

Lanya, with a contented smile, eyes on the road, drove along in silence. Eventually she said, "And the same unchanged, infinite, eternal spirit is taking form as the soul in the heart of the snowflake and all its subsequent forms – have I got that right?" And he nodded.

But then suddenly, she sat up in her driver's seat and said energetically, "Let me see whether I can summarise all this with regard to the soul: You are saying that what we experience as our individual souls are fragments – no, fractals – we learnt about fractals in school – of a transcendental, spiritual world, come here into this phenomenal world to learn something and then return to their origin. And all this phenomenal world, physical as well as mental, is like a university campus, provided for the souls' education. All right, I get all that! But what is it, that souls come here to learn?"

"Your summary is spot-on my dear – that is my picture in a nutshell! But as to what we come here to learn, I think everyone has to answer that for themselves. Some say that the over-arching subject or discipline is consciousness. Some call it self-realisation. Some say: 'to know thy Self!' is the basic lesson. But I think there are as many different answers as there are souls, and a lot will depend on the stage of evolution of a particular being. It seems to me that the experience you described earlier in the field of wheat has brought you very close to discovering the answer that is particular to yourself."

"Do you really think so?" she said thoughtfully. "Really? I shall ponder on that."

She glanced over to him questioningly, and he volunteered, "Perhaps I could now answer your earlier question about whether I can recall an instance when I found myself 'tuning-in' to my soul – a little story to give you a flavour of how this was for me – if you are still up for that?"

"You bet I am – you know how I love real stories," she replied happily.

Chapter Five

TUNING IN TO YOUR SOUL

Frederick took a moment to collect his thoughts. The occasion he had remembered was quite a long time ago but had left an indelible impression.

"It was when I was just about your age," he began. "On my way to my first meeting with Dr Albert Schweitzer at his hospital at Lambarene, I was being ferried in a dug-out canoe across the mile-wide river Ogowe in the Gabon, near the equator in Africa. We arrived at the shore and I stepped out of the wobbly canoe and stood, dishevelled as I was – having slept on a bus-shelter bench with my rucksack as a pillow the night before – facing the Doctor on the landing-stage. I accepted his outstretched hand. To this day I feel the touch of that surprisingly soft but firm, large hand. 'What are your plans young man?' he said. 'I… I don't have any plans right now,' I stammered. His eyes penetrated deep into mine, his grip tightened, and with a twinkle he said, 'Aha, a free man!' That was all he said. But at that instant it felt as if something awoke in me which knew what it meant to be free for aeons and infinite aeons of time and space. I think that was a moment when I 'tuned in' to my soul."

She threw a wide-eyed glance over to him and after a while said, "It must have been a wonderful time for you to be so close to such a personality."

"Oh it was," he said, "it was like being in the company of

someone who was fully in touch with his soul every moment of the day. It was truly life-changing – unforgettable! Such personalities are infectious. Something of what they are, inevitably rubs off if you spend time near them with an open mind. However, my most powerful lesson with regard to the soul as I have just remembered – was of a much humbler kind, and I really ought to tell you about that as well – to complete the picture."

She smiled across to him again and said, "I would love to hear it; I am honoured that you would want to share it with me."

"It concerns a lady who occupied the role of mother to me in England, after I left Austria at the age of fourteen and a half. She was an unpretentious lady in whom, for me, there was no malice or selfishness, only goodness and kindness. Helpfulness towards others filled her entire being. When she was ninety-three years old, lying in bed in the very cottage in which my wife and I now live, she said to me, 'It's been long enough; I want to move on now'. I asked her – with the naivety of youth 'What do you expect to happen when you move on?' and she replied simply, 'I will fall like a dewdrop into the ocean'. I did not know it then, but I realised later that her soul was indeed as pure as a dewdrop. And she was content, faced with the imminence of her departure from this world, to imagine herself falling, dissolving and merging harmoniously into the eternal, infinite expanse of the ocean of spirit and thus find her immortality.

"Two days later she died, alone, at night, in her bed – hopefully in her sleep. Concerned to be helpful to the very end, she had bequeathed her body to science."

Frederick lent back in his seat and looked vacantly into the far distance ahead. After a while he added, "That was the closest I have come to witnessing the reality of the immortality of

'*Soul*'."

They drove in silence for the remaining twenty minutes of this car journey – a silence full of awe and wonder – a silence which gently but indelibly coloured the remainder of their life's journey, each towards its own destination.

STORY THREE

OTHER SEARCHING QUESTIONS
On Garden Benches

Introduction

After the trip into the Midlands, Lanya did not see her grandfather for several months. They took the more cautious warnings from scientists to heart and throughout the summer continued to take voluntary self-isolation seriously. For Frederick, content with his own company, there was always plenty to do in his garden and workshop. Lanya's daily public contact in the shop attached to the bakery, where she worked, constituted a slight threat to her ageing grandparents in the thatched cottage.

But one fine autumn afternoon, Lanya could no longer resist a visit. Masked and with disinfected hands, strictly keeping the prescribed two-metre distance, she and Frederick took a gentle walk up the steeply inclined garden, stopping occasionally for Grandpa to catch his breath. Lanya talked enthusiastically about how she had dug over a bit of waste land behind the bakery and sowed an ancient strain of wheat in order to experimentally grow, harvest, mill and then bake bread with flour from her own home-grown grain. She so looked forward to experiencing the completeness of this whole process.

When they arrived at the bench at the top of the garden, they sat for a while admiring the view over the wide green valley, chatting merrily…

Chapter One

ON A BENCH AT THE TOP OF THE GARDEN

"Only a century and a half ago, this valley had still been a source of fuel in the form of dinosaurs' dung for open fireplaces in London's East End, which is why bits of narrow-gauge railway track can still be found here and there in the fields," Frederick was explaining, when Lanya could restrain herself no longer and asked:

"Do you remember the part of the conversation we had in the car going up into the Midlands, Grandpa, when you talked about receptors and how the noise of today's world – and especially the digital noise – drowns out and even obliterates the contact we have with our inner receptors? Well, I've been thinking a lot about that. I think we got side-tracked into other interesting avenues, and never really finished that subject. Anyway, I am left with this question: what can I do to help re-awaken contact with my own inner receptors and in particular, how I could tune in to what you call 'my inner voice'? Is there more that can be said about this? I know you meditate and pray sometimes. Can you tell me more about that? Like, for instance, can you explain what the difference is between these two activities?" Lanya paused, looking at him – at the other end of the bench – with wide, questioning eyes.

Frederick pulled himself up from his slouched posture into which he had slumped after the climb to the top of the garden, and slowly moved his gaze from her deeply sincere face to the distant horizon.

"You have quite a few good questions there, my dear," he began slowly, hesitantly, "and I think I understand what you are asking. I do remember that part of our conversation and I quite agree that we did get drawn away into other subjects. But let me try and answer your last question first: the difference between meditation and prayer? Of course, I can only speak of my own experience, which may be quite different from that of other people. Meditation – and, as you know, I practice a mantra-meditation which is only one of many methods – starts for me with a kind of cleaning-up process, you could call it mental filing or clearing the decks. Thoughts come up and are put away into memory, or into pending trays. Gradually, the desk clears; the internal chatter abates – there are so many ways of describing this, like: the muddy water in a glass clears as the sediment drops to the bottom; or, the dust settles and the shaft of sunlight through the window clears of dancing digits…

"In the language of my philosophy, it is Manas that settles and relaxes; inner silence begins to emerge; and that which hears the silence appears in the awareness. In the mantra meditation I have been taught, a short word called 'the mantra' which is devoid of meaning in our language, is constantly allowed to repeat, and the attention is encouraged to follow it wherever it leads. The mantra acts like a guide-dog leading a blind person. Eventually, if it goes well, the pair arrive at a threshold where the dog lies down and the blind person steps over into a completely silent space into which not even the mantra has access. If a thought comes along the dog immediately starts up and stops it from entering. It is blissfully silent, without movement or time. There are no words to describe this – it has to be experienced.

Anyone who gets there will know what it is to be with yourself alone – all-one! If you feel comfortable there, you will want to return.

"Eventually, the physical body makes itself known again. Your posture, the chair, the room, return to your awareness. Then I start to pray – mostly my adaptation of the Lord's Prayer. For me, this mainly consists of thoughts and emotions stating and affirming what IS.

"Usually, what is, is what should be, and prayer reminds me of that. There is no need to ask for anything. If after the Lord's Prayer there is an overwhelming problem, which sometimes does happen, then I ask for help in coming to a full understanding of the conditions surrounding that problem.

"Of course, that is a very personal interpretation of prayer, but for me, there has so far not been a better way of cleansing and tuning my inner receptivity, opening it up to my inner voice and differentiating this from the voice of my ego. Does any of that help you with these questions, do you think?"

Lanya took a while before replying, "The proof of that pudding will be in the eating of it. There remains the question of how or from whom one can learn to meditate?"

"That," he said, "is a matter of 'seek and ye shall find'… there are many different methods and there may have to be a bit of trial and error before you find the one that suits you best. I have found it helpful to trust to providence in these things and to accept and try out what comes my way – not forgetting due discrimination of course. But you have to really want it, in order to attract it – that's for sure!"

"So, you are not going to teach me then?" she asked, with a twinge of disappointment in her voice.

"No, Lanya, I'm not," he said softly, "for one thing, I don't think I'm qualified; but also, what I was taught all those years ago is very unlikely to be the right thing for you now. You need to find a group of younger people with whom to share this path, at least for a while, and see how you go. You are already well prepared. Of course, there are also many books on the subject and perhaps you can develop your own method. But method is secondary – the willingness and the inner determination are primary."

Chapter Two

MORE ABOUT THE LORD'S PRAYER

They sat in silence under the tall pine trees, enjoying the low evening sun on their backs. A green woodpecker shot across from the right in its swooping, wave-like flight, landed on a trunk above them and immediately started hammering. They listened for a little while until it moved to a tree further down the garden. Then the resident cock-pheasant came strutting proudly across the meadow in front of them, patrolling his patch. They watched him for a while.

Eventually, Lanya asked, "Incidentally, how are you getting on with your adaptation of the Lord's Prayer? It was still very much a work-in-progress when we last talked about it some years ago?"

"Ah yes, I have been working with it," he replied, adding after a short pause, "and in fact, I think I have arrived at some kind of a plateau. I think I'm pretty happy with where I've got to now and am just tinkering around the edges with rhythm and flow."

"Oh, do let me hear wherever it's at now!" she jumped in enthusiastically.

"All right then, I'll try. It comes out slightly differently each time, which keeps it fresh and alive. But the essentials now seem to stay the same. And I'm quite pleased with the overall structure. I often wonder what it is about the Lord's Prayer that still keeps my attention and still answers all I seem to need from a prayer. It must be very ancient and profound in its basic concept. The structure of four, four and three separate incremental thoughts fits very well into my study of harmonics. It is like a descending octave of eight notes followed by an ascending chord back up to the original DO – topped and tailed by 'eternal infinity'."

"You'll have to explain all that to me another time. For now, can I just hear the prayer?"

"Sure," he said, taking a deep breath, adjusting his posture to sit slightly more upright and gazing far into the distance.

"So I now address myself to the:

"Eternal Infinite:

1. –Who art the innermost centre of all your creatures, and in whom we all have our being;
2. –Hallowed be all the names we humans use when we turn to you in true sincerity;
3. –Thy kingdom awaits those who do so turn and offer
4. –Their willingness to merge harmoniously with your eternal will and purpose.
5. –Thou giv'st us this day our daily bread, nourishing both body and soul;
6. –And forgiv'st us our mistakes and failings, as we forgive those we deem to have failed us;
7. –And lead'st us in temptation, sharpening our faculties of discrimination;
8. –And deliverest us from the evil of separation and isolation caused by jealousy and greed.
9. –For thine are all the kingdoms,
10. –and all the powers, energies, and vibrations,
11. –and the glorious beauty of unconditional love;

in Infinite Eternity

Amen"

The sun was setting behind them, casting long shadows across the fields in the valley below and bathing the low hills opposite in the warm evening light of autumn.

It was several minutes before Lanya slowly turned towards him, her eyes still in a distant gaze and her instinctive movement to rest her head on his shoulder thwarted by the physical distance between them. For a few seconds, all her attention and energy were absorbed in resisting the urge to hug her grandfather. He remained motionless, seemingly absorbed in something beyond the far horizon. Eventually she said quietly, "Can you email this to me? There is a lot there for me to ponder."

"Yes of course," he replied, adding, "and then I can also send you all the sentences which contain the word 'soul' in the four Gospels. I have now read all four and made a note of each time the word 'soul' is mentioned. There are not that many instances – just eight in addition to the three in Mathew."

"Oh, all right," she said not over enthusiastically. "I hope you didn't do that just for me."

"Not at all. It's a long time since I have read the Gospels, and once I had started I was once again fascinated and couldn't stop. I find it so interesting – this relentlessly uncompromising height of ethical clarity spoken to – and re-told – by supposedly uneducated fishermen in Palestine, but written in Greek (so we are told) and translated from Latin into English – and no doubt nearly every other language on this globe – and preserved for two thousand and twenty years.

"The historical researchers tell us that what we now have as the Gospels is a selection from all sorts of material and an amalgam of various records, and that none of the four Evangelists had actually known Jesus when he was alive. Though I have recently discovered in G B Shaw's Preface to his play Androcles and the Lion – which by the way is a most fascinating exposition on what he calls the prospects of Christianity – that he was convinced that the gospels of Mathew and Mark were written within the lifetime of contemporaries of Jesus, and that Mark probably did know him. Albert Schweitzer also regarded these two gospels as the most authentic as far as the narrative goes.

"Be that as it may, we are told that all this was consolidated at the First Council of Nicaea in 325 AD. Is it not astonishing that these texts containing such radical ethical ideas and standards should be selected by a council of leaders at that time? Could you imagine anything like that happening these days?"

Lanya had been somewhat reluctant to be drawn out of the inner calm created by the prayer, only to be plunged into the generalities of Christian history; nevertheless she found a sufficiently pithy response to her Grandpa's far-reaching question.

"I'm not quite sure what you are implying, but I have recently come across people on the internet who say that we are in a time of transition from the age of Pisces – which is the astrological age you are talking about – into the age of Aquarius. Perhaps we should wait to see what depths of insight people come up with as this new age in human evolution develops, before we try to answer that question of yours?"

"Touché," he replied, "you have a point there. Perhaps we should pay some proper attention to this interpretation of the Earth's movements within our solar system. There was a lot of talk about this in the 1960s, and again more recently, as you say. I think it might have much to offer with regard to my Next Evolutionary Step Initiative, but I have never really looked at it with any serious intent."

"What about making that our next line of enquiry?" Lanya suggested enthusiastically, "But perhaps not today. I'm getting chilly, now the sun has set, and it's also time for me to go quite soon. But let's try and find a way of exploring this subject of Astrology and discovering its potential."

"I think that's a great idea," he said as they rose from the bench and began to make their way back down the garden.

Chapter Three

A NEW LINE OF ENQUIRY

Normally, they would have walked arm in arm, Lanya steading her grandpa as they went. As it was, they reluctantly kept their distance but continued chatting as they slowly and carefully descended the steeply sloping part of the garden.

"I probably never mentioned to you," Frederick was saying, "that my father thought of himself as an amateur astrologer. I know that he took this subject very seriously, although he never did anything professionally – not that I had much opportunity to learn about it from him, having left home before I was fifteen and returning only once a year during my school and college holidays."

"No, I had no idea," she replied. "I don't really know how I came to be looking at astrological websites. As children we used to mess about with astrological predictions in newspapers. But I soon realised what rubbish that all was. However, the idea that everything is somehow connected – that nothing happens in isolation and that in some way everything that happens sends out ripples affecting everything else, has always held a fascination for me. But I have only dabbled with the idea occasionally, superficially."

"Yes, my father had constructed horoscopes for all the members of the family," Frederick continued to reminisce, "and I remember very serious discussions amongst the grown-ups when I was a child, involving character traits and personality attributes as well as the qualities of certain situations and of various periods of time."

They had reached the top of the last set of steps leading down to the Cottage and had turned round to have a look back up the garden, now illuminated by the glow of the last rays of the sun in the tops of the trees in their glorious autumn colours. They just stood and looked for a while.

"Well, this will be an amazing new departure for us – a real 'quest' with an unknown destination," Frederick said, stroking his beard, as they turned to go down to street level. "In the meantime, I'll email you that list of quotes from the Gospels as I still think it's interesting. (To be found in Appendix 'A'). Come to think of it, with the COVID pandemic showing no real signs of abating as yet, or coming under control, perhaps we should make more use of email between us, because I think as we approach Christmas, there will be a second wave of infections following the inevitable shopping spree which the government is loathed to inhibit too much."

"Do you really think so?" replied Lanya hesitatingly, as they descended the steps. "I would miss our face-to-face conversations, and I don't know that we would spark each other off in the same way via email? But I suppose, if it needs to be, we can give it a try and see whether it would work." On the last step she hesitated. Walking behind her, he stopped as well, and she asked, "But actually, would you mind if I asked you another question – something completely different – before we go in. Something which has been weighing heavily on my mind?"

"But of course not, Lanya. Let me get a woolly jacket for you and we can sit on the bench in front of the Cottage, where we are sheltered from the evening breeze." Pointing at the bench just round the corner he said, "Why don't you sit down, I won't be a minute."

The bench stood in front of the seventeenth century door – no longer in use now – dating from the time when the building consisted of three separate single room cottages with haylofts under the roof, accessed by ladders. As late as the 1860s the end one of the three was home to a family of ten, as recorded by the local vicar at the time. Quite inconceivable now.

Lanya sat down somewhat nervously, hardly noticing the beautiful last blooms of the roses in front of her, absorbed in trying to frame the question on which she wanted Grandpa's opinion. He was back before long and carefully wrapped his favourite wooly jacket – knitted by her grandmother – over her shoulders before he sat down at the other end of the bench.

Chapter Four

7,874,965,825 HUMANS
The Total Global Population in 2021

Frederick sensed the slight tension. Easing into the next topic, whatever it was going to be, he opened with, "Isn't it amazing that we still have roses in bloom this late in the year. I don't think we ever had that before. Aren't they beautiful?"

"They are really lovely!" she said quietly, getting up to smell one. "They are probably still flowering because you look after them so well," she added, sitting down again.

"I think, at this stage, many of the plants are trying to make the best of things whilst they can, if you know what I mean: even climate change isn't all bad!" he responded, smiling.

"Well, in some way I suppose, that is vaguely connected to my question;" she began, "climate change, I mean – and whether it is right to bring children into a world that is heading towards a climate catastrophe. With the human population figure, globally, as high as it is – I read recently that there are now just under 7.875 billion of us on this earth – how can one decide to have children and add even more to this over-population? All these fears and worries about the future of our planet is making me question whether I will ever be able to decide to become a mother. This is what I wanted to ask you about. What do you think about this?"

He looked at her with wide eyes. That was not a question he had anticipated, but he sensed immediately that this was not any kind of theoretical question, but one that touched her life directly

– one that she was putting to herself in all seriousness.

"I suppose you are not asking this just as a general question, but one that is actually very close to your heart?" he asked, seeking confirmation of his intuition.

"Oh, very much the latter – you are quite right," she said, "but not just for me, but for my friends and many others of my generation as well. We are watching the scientists' reports on the climate and the statistics about the global population very carefully and talking about this a lot. Just the other day, when I was with my best friends Penny, Maggie and Clare – we were all at school together, so we are of the same age – we had a long, very serious conversation about this very subject. Penny is married and has a big beautiful house and they are all ready for children, but it turns out that she is not conceiving. So she is telling us not to wait too long, because it might never happen. Maggie has a partner and they want to get married, but they were debating which should have priority: a wedding or the down payment on a house – they can't afford both. They decided on a wedding. But then COVID prevented that from taking place for two years and she was worried by Penny's comment. Clare is a nursery school teacher, so she is surrounded by children all the time. She would feel ready and qualified to bring up a child, but she has not got a partner yet. For myself, I must say that I'm not at all sure that I am mentally ready to bring up a child. And my husband says he is not nearly ready and won't be for several years. He does not want to sacrifice his freedom yet."

She paused to catch her breath with a big sigh, so Frederick interjected, "Perhaps I should mention before we go much further with this subject, that we – your grandparents – are probably one of very few couples left alive who have never had to ask themselves this question, and I may therefore not be the right person to give you any advice on this. When we were your age the pill had not yet been invented. And it never occurred to us to exercise birth-control at that stage of our lives. When we decided to get married it was taken for granted that we would be starting a family. As you know, we had just come back from Africa, where we saw mothers bringing up babies in mud huts – ten or more to a hut. So being ready financially didn't come into it for us. I had saved one thousand pounds in Nigeria and that bought us a tiny two-up-two-down end of terrace cottage without water supply or drainage, and that is where we started our family. We furnished it with vegetable-boxes, a table top cooker and a sink outside the back door. Water had to be carried a hundred yards down a footpath. There was a bucket with chemicals in it called an Elson Toilet in a little shed in the garden – and this was in Essex not in Africa. Making it all work out was just part of the challenge of life."

"Yes I knew most of that," she said slightly impatiently, "but times have changed, expectations have changed, and it's just because you have experienced the time before birth-control, that I would value your opinion."

Frederick was silent for quite a while, trying to remember what it was like in the early days of their marriage. Eventually he said, "I can remember that I really did feel sorry for those slightly younger couples at that time, who were suddenly faced with having to make a decision about having a child. A child was suddenly no longer a gift – as it still was for us – it was something you would decide you were going to 'make'. This placed a huge new burden on young couples' shoulders! And this has now become part of the inescapable challenge of your married life, and everyone else's in your generation."

There was another pause. Both were aware of the enormity

and far-reaching relevance of the subject, but were unsure how to approach it; and they were searching for a commensurate way to address it. Lanya, with her clear and organisational way of thinking was the first to embark on a different tack. "So, what are the considerations to be borne in mind here?" she asked.

"Good question," he said, wanting to be enthusiastic and raising himself into a more upright posture on the bench. "Let's try and look at this systematically. Shall we start at the individual, personal level and work our way towards the general, global scale?"

"Agreed! I can think of a number of aspects straight away – things that people like myself worry about, as for instance: personal readiness: adequate maturity; financial readiness: shelter, two incomes, etc; loss of personal freedoms: women's career paths, etc; fear of bearing children later in life; complications of adoption and surrogacy."

Lanya took a deep breath and Grandpa chipped in with, "That's already a good list of individual concerns. I suppose uppermost on the global level must be people's concern about the growth of the total human population?"

"And the general anxiety about climate change," she added, "and maybe also the political instability of large parts of the globe – which climate change is only going to exacerbate."

"And just now the COVID-19 pandemic is not helping either," suggested Grandpa, rounding off the list. After a slight pause he asked, "So where shall we start?"

They looked at each other questioningly and Grandpa got up to stretch his legs. "I sometimes get a cramp, sitting on this bench," he said, and walked a little way along the path, looking up at the sky. Suddenly he turned and called back, "Oh come and have a look at this moon!"

She joined him and they both stood silently gazing at what the tall hedge behind the roses in front of the bench had hidden from their view: a nearly full, deep orange moon floating low in a most delicately coloured rose-pink, hazy sky above the dark, distant hills on the horizon.

Neither spoke – until, turning back towards the bench, Grandpa mumbled into his beard, "Did you know that there are people working on a draft declaration to protect the moon from human exploitation and conflict?"

Lanya just nodded. But the mood had changed and she began again more softly, "With regard to our list, most of these points came up in the conversation with my friends, which I mentioned earlier. The feelings of inadequacy and mental unpreparedness were big factors which Clare emphasised by pointing out that she was the only one of us with any training and experience with children. You might find this laughable, but it is a real concern for us – and we are all approaching thirty!"

"Not at all laughable!" he replied and she continued:

"I think I can understand how this feeling of uncertainty has arisen. I would hazard a guess that for the mothers of your generation this wasn't an issue, because in their mothers' minds – our great-grandmothers' minds – motherhood would still have been a very significant, if not the predominant, part of their life-expectations from an early age."

"And in their mothers and grandmothers," he added, reinforcing her point, "they would have had role models with considerable confidence and experience supported by a long tradition. Not for all, of course, but for very many. During the period of your mother's life, motherhood has been severely degraded in its relative importance to women's career potential. Your mother's generation was the first for whom financial life, by and large, had to be managed on the basis of two incomes per family, consuming huge parts of a woman's energies, which previously would have been available to managing the household – building and maintaining the 'nest', so to speak, and bearing children. I'm not saying that any of this could or should have been otherwise. It was part of a complex process of development within society involving many interdependent factors, but it explains why your generation very understandably might feel less prepared for motherhood than previous generations."

"So, we – our generation – just have to manage this as best we can," Lanya responded pensively, and then added after a slight pause, "But you can understand why this contributes to the feeling of many women nowadays, that it might be better not to have any children at all. And those who worry about the global population think that's a good thing."

"Shall we come back to that later and look at the financial readiness question next?" he asked.

"You've already touched on that with your comment about 'two-income' families," she responded, "and my friend Maggie's story speaks to that. The housing market has now become so bizarre, that even two young people with their combined incomes have great difficulty in saving enough money for a deposit on a house. So many of my generation don't even bother. They live with their parents or in temporary rented accommodation and having children barely enters their minds. And then accidents happen and you end up with single parent families. And again, those who fret about over-population aren't too worried about that."

Lanya was quite agitated now, and Grandpa agreed, adding, "Yes, it is a bizarre situation, and one that was quite knowingly created. The banks started offering such large mortgages that house prices shot up at an incredible rate needing two incomes to afford the repayments, and motherhood became a real nuisance. No – more than a nuisance – an impediment to a woman's career prospects and her, by now, essential earning capacity. So, obviously, motherhood became an inferior occupation – one that had to be 'fitted in' as and when, more as an irritation than a vocation, forcing itself into the equation through the pressure of a woman's natural feminine instinct to fulfil the role for which nature has equipped her. Of course, not all experience it this way, but I sense that this is how it is for many."

They both pondered this for a while. He worried that he might have gone too far. But then Lanya began again, "There are two points I can add to this: with regard to financial readiness, there is the other aspect – which my friend Penny highlighted – that you delay having children until you have everything perfectly in place, a large-enough house and garden in the right area for the best schools, the right kind of car, a fully furnished nursery and funds laid by for the school fees – and then you find you have left it too late and you can't conceive. What a lot of anguish lies down that road!… The IVF process, surrogacy, adoption… ?"

Grandpa interrupted with, "I'm not sure I would include adoption in that list myself. Although your grandmother and I never considered it for ourselves, with so many parentless and homeless children in the world at present, I think there are very strong arguments in its favour, particularly for people who cannot have children of their own. As long as the difficulties inherent in such arrangements are not underestimated – and there is strong protective legislation in place to prevent this in our societies – there is a lot to be said for adoption."

Lanya, nodding in agreement, responded with, "Yes, of

course, I don't disagree, but it is a complicated and difficult process to embark on. Anyway, the other point I wanted to add lies in the opposite direction. And I must admit I have considered this myself: children take up so much time and energy. In the present situation would that time not be better spent doing the things necessary to avoid the worst effects of climate change? Would the energy not be better spent devising ways of reducing our carbon-footprint? If I have children, I will need a bigger house, a bigger car, more food! And I won't be able to afford the more expensive organic food which I buy now. How much more could I do to help solve the world's problems without the distraction of having to bring up children?"

Again there was a pause.

Frederick was struggling to respond to these arguments. But eventually, he said, "There is another consideration which occurs to me, which we haven't got on our list: the value which is created in a healthy society by the love which arises between parents and their children? And, altogether, the role family plays within society? The human family structure is based, by and large, on the interaction of three generations rolling forward on a steady basis. This is entirely reliant on there being children in the process. When the children are small, their parents care for them and they in turn are helped by the grandparents. As these children grow up, the focus of care shifts to the ageing grandparents. This element of care seems to me to be a fundamental, indispensable element of a viable human society. As far as I know, all attempts at societal structures that try to eliminate this three-generational mutual care have failed. Think about your own life: what will your old age be like if there are no children and grandchildren around you?"

Lanya looked unconvinced and retorted, "But there are

plenty of instances where this continuity is interrupted for all sorts of reasons, and they manage somehow. Are we not in a fairly desperate situation at present, in which it may be necessary to forgo the luxury of this smooth flow, which you describe, in order to survive at all? May it not be the case that my generation has to focus all its energies on managing a transition to another way of operating and functioning in order for any of us to survive?"

She looked at him challengingly, and there was another pause before he said, "All right. We have looked at some of the personal, individual considerations and this last point leads us into the wider, global aspect. What are the other, more general, global arguments which we should consider?"

A little surprised that Grandpa did not respond directly to her challenge, Lanya replied, " I suppose for me the most worrying thought is that it might be cruel to bring children into a world in which they will have to face such disasters as are predicted; a world that appears to be walking so relentlessly towards apocalypse; a world in which it is clear – even with the most optimistic view – that huge unpredictable changes and upheavals are facing us. Such thoughts do sometimes overwhelm me and I think it might be irresponsible to ignore them."

"Yes, I quite understand that," he said softly, trying not to sound patronising, but she was in full flow now and continued:

"There are far too many people on this earth already and the numbers are growing all the time. How can I add to that problem? And so much conflict everywhere – all those migrants and displaced, starving people in camps, their homes destroyed, all their possessions lost, relatives lost, makeshift schooling for the children at best, no prospect of a better life, droughts and floods on the increase – making things worse. How can I bring myself into the right frame of mind to think about starting a family and be a good parent? Shouldn't I be using all my energies towards solving some of these problems?" She was close to tears now. The COVID mentality prevented her from throwing her head onto his shoulder, and he could barely restrain himself from taking her into his arms to console her.

The moon had climbed slowly up over the top of the hedge by now and had regained its usual silvery white luminosity in a clear, but not yet fully darkened, sky. The odd star had begun twinkling here and there. They sat in silence, looking at the moon. Grandpa was digging deep into his soul for answers. Who knows how long they sat there in the moonlit twilight, before Grandpa finally found his tongue, "Perhaps we need to step back a bit," he began, "and look at the situation from Mother Earth's point of view. The human species is one of the myriad of creatures she has evolved within her thin atmospheric mantel around her outer crust. As members of that species, we have no reason to assume that she does not want us to be here, even if it looks as if we might have gone off the rails a bit – lost our way, maybe – made mistakes – behaved badly. As a species as well as individually, we are evolving, we are on a learning curve. In her terms, she has not had us around yet for very long. For her perhaps, we are still toddlers learning to walk properly – or at least adolescents learning to cope with the responsibilities of life, as I have said before. Do you recall how, on our drive into the Midlands we talked about this earth being a *school for souls*? Seen in that light you might say that it is a privilege to be born on this earth. For all we know, souls are queuing up to be born here in order to learn the lessons which are on offer here. Learning hard lessons isn't necessarily pain-free, so all the complications, difficulties and challenges here may – in that sense – have their purpose? And for this process to function there have to be opportunities for children to be born. Do you see what I mean?"

Lanya had listened intently, nodding in agreement and recognition. Now, with her voice not yet quite steady, she said, "Oh, I do see what you mean! I had forgotten. It is so easy to forget the bigger picture – especially in this COVID-lockdown mentality."

"I am not saying;" he continued, "that it should be every woman's aim to have lots of children – don't get me wrong – but those who find that life has offered them the opportunity, might regard it as a gift and a privilege to play their part in nature's task to help Mother Earth to create places for the education and evolution of souls. And, in this scientific age, when childbirth has become so much safer and life-expectancy so much longer, it is not surprising that the control of numbers is brought within the orbit of conscious individual decision-making. This surely is part of the evolutionary process of the individual as well as of society."

Lanya's eyes had brightened and her voice was again full of enthusiasm when she responded, "Oh Grandpa, thank you so much for getting me out of the hole into which I had drifted over this, and broadening my outlook again. I can quite see what you're saying. Of course the idea of a society without children is a nonsense. There would only be old people left and the society would die out. The task is to find a way to bring up children who will help manage the transition which has to come all over the globe in order to avoid the apocalypse people talk about – or at least tame it and manage it.

"The challenge is to create a home – a human nest – in which children can thrive in a way that will make them proud of the lightness of the footprint they leave on the earth. My generation has to do its bit, for sure, but there is no way we will turn things around before any children I might have are grown. We will need their help and they will be our hope. And if we can learn to be less greedy and less wasteful, there will be plenty to go round – for everybody!" Her eyes sparkled in the moonlight – not with tears now, but with excitement.

Grandpa was breathing a sigh of relief, and felt encouraged to make another point, "And – you know – there is another aspect we don't value highly enough about human existence on this earth: the transmission of spiritual energy. We humans act as transformers and transmitters of spiritual energy. That is part of our role, our function, on this planet. If only this was better understood! That is what empathy, compassion, kindness and love is really all about. We have the capacity to allow that energy to flow through us into all the other entities living on this earth. Mother Nature needs us for that. We have that responsibility. And it is through our children that the evolutionary refinement of this capacity can take place. We, and Mother Nature needs our children for that."

They sat for a while just looking at the moon, which had climbed higher into the night sky, now weaving in and out of little wispy, white clouds, and Sirius was twinkling brightly just above the black hedge. Lanya pointed out the constellation of Orion looking down at them.

Eventually, she said, "It's getting very late. I'm really going to have to go. But it seems to me, that we have set the scene perfectly for our next enquiry – our new quest! I can now see that the question is not whether or not to become a mother, but how to raise children who are awake to the needs of Mother Earth and aware of the contribution they can make to her wellbeing so that they will feel properly 'at home' and proud of their footprint. What do you think? Is that a reasonable basis from which to start a quest?"

"Well, I think we are in a much better frame of mind now for embarking on this new quest than we were at the top of the steps earlier on this evening," he said with a big smile and pointing over his shoulder.

They got up from the bench and started moving towards the loggia doors whilst she handed back his jacket, and he continued, "But your original idea of starting with an investigation into what the idea of a new astrological age might have to offer us, seems a very good starting point to get us going."

She went indoors to say good bye to her grandmother, who came back out with her and all three walked along the moonlit path, the full length of the extended cottage to the car park.

They stood for a moment two metres apart, holding out their arms in imagined hugs and she jumped into her car and was gone. The old couple stood waving until her car was out of sight and the village high street lay deserted in utter silence bathed in gentle moonlight.

STORY FOUR

QUESTING VIA EMAIL

Introduction

How can we Humans best co-operate with Mother Earth?
(Explored via Email during a pandemic)

The balmy summer, during which Lanya had had those searching conversations with her grandfather on garden benches at his cottage, gave way to a very wet and increasingly wintery and cold autumn. In the charts on our TV screens the curve of national COVID-19 infection numbers began to rise steeply. The government was at a loss to know what to do. Hope that things would be sufficiently safe for a few days of Christmas festivities began to dwindle. Tiers of restrictions of greater stringency for more heavily infected areas were introduced, but nothing seemed to stem the increase of infections and deaths. Then a new and more virulent strain of the virus was discovered, causing even more panic.

    Frederick had undertaken to make a few Christmas presents in his workshop, causing him to spend much time there on his own, keeping his head down and out of sight and distracting his mind during this period of 'Lock Down', from his usual thoughts about the realms of human destiny and the fate of life on this planet.

    Not so Lanya. She had been inspired by their conversation on the bench at the top of the cottage garden, and by her idea of researching what people were saying about the Age of Aquarius. A past master at surfing the internet, she soon found a wealth of information and interesting data. As face to face meetings with octogenarians, such as her grandfather, were now quite out of the question, email communication it would have to be and by the middle of December she was ready to attempt a first salvo on the subject.

Chapter One

NESt AND THE AGE OF AQUARIUS

14/12/2020

Hello Grandpa,

Hopefully you are keeping well and I'm sure Grandma is looking after you splendidly.

I'm sure you won't have forgotten our last conversation up in your garden, and my idea of looking into what the Age of Aquarius can offer our general 'search for answers'. But I expect you've been busy with other things. I, on the other hand, have been surfing the internet and have come across all sorts of interesting stuff.

One website particularly appeals to me and whilst of course you can look at it yourself, I thought I would extract and summarise some of what I found especially relevant to our discussion. I like its name as well: 'Astro-Butterfly' <https://astrobutterfly.com/> They have a blog called *'The Age Of Aquarius – The Next Chapter'*, which I thought might appeal to you with your interest in the 'Next Evolutionary Step'… :-)

Anyway, they trace these astrological Ages back to some ten thousand years BC, like this:

The Age of LEO 10,800 - 8,600 BC
CANCER 8,600 - 6,500 BC
GEMINI 6,500 - 4,000 BC

TAURUS 4,000 - 2,000 BC
ARIES 2,000 - 0 BC
PISCES 0 - 2020 AD

Don't you think that's amazing?

And they say that these Ages are caused by a 'wobble' of the Earth's axis. Apparently, it's only a very slight wobble, and it takes about twenty-six thousand years to complete one gyration. When that gyration is divided into twelve equal periods – one for each *Sign of the Zodiac*, each Sign has a duration of two thousand one hundred and fifty years.

I visualise it like a spinning top which doesn't only spin around its axis, but its axis also gyrates; only with a top the gyrations become bigger and bigger as its energy runs out and eventually it topples over and stops. Though I expect the earth is not going to do that... well, not in our lifetime anyway!... :-)

So, according to this website, the Age of Aquarius is taking us into the second half of this particular gyration. This, they say, means that Aquarius will have similar qualities to Leo, but on a higher level – at the start of this second half of the gyration. I suppose we are going to have to learn what these qualities are all about, if we are going to make any sense of this. But I have to say, my appetite is truly wetted.

Enough for one day – I await your response, if you are still up for pursuing this course of research?

Oh, one more thing. Did you know that on the 21st of December – the Winter Equinox – there is a conjunction – apparently practically an eclipse of the two biggest planets in our solar system – Jupiter and Saturn? We are supposed to be able to see this quite clearly with the naked eye in the early evening – weather permitting of course. So, you better keep a look-out! Apparently, some say that future centuries are likely to designate this day as the official beginning of the Age of Aquarius, though they say the transition period is in the region of two to three centuries.

Anyway, I give you a big 'virtual' hug and look forward to your reply, with lots of love
Lanya

17/12/2020

Hello Lanya,

What a splendid start to our investigation – you set the scene beautifully! And of course I have looked at the Astro-Butterfly website straight away. I quite agree – it's a beautiful website. How good to be reminded at the outset, that we are looking at a cyclical journey, which could be spiralling upwards or downwards, depending on our viewpoint and our behaviour.

You have prompted me to look up 'Hindu' cosmic timescales on the internet, because I vaguely remembered coming across references in my youth to such cyclical concepts of time in my readings of some of their literature. And sure enough, there is lots of information to be found, but it is highly complex and would need intense study to properly comprehend.

The most stunning first impression is the vastness of their concepts. They talk about cycles of three hundred and eleven trillion years at the macro or Brahma level, coming down through a series of intermediate levels to arrive at the Human level with an age lasting four hundred and thirty-two thousand years as the last and shortest one of four ages – rather like the four seasons of an earth year, but of unequal lengths.

In their calculation we are now five thousand one hundred and twenty-two years into this last season of four hundred and thirty-two thousand years, called the age of Kali-Yuga. The whole cycle of the four million three hundred and twenty thousand years is called the Maha-Yuga. As I say, it is complex – and I hope I've got this roughly right.

My search has by no means been exhaustive, but unfortunately, I could not find any easy correlation in this Hindu system with the twenty-six thousand year gyration of the earth's axis leading to the ca. two thousand one hundred and fifty year period for each of the twelve signs of the Zodiac. That is a bit disappointing. Perhaps we can find an astrologer who can help us here? Wouldn't it be nice if the two systems could somehow be interconnected?

With regard to huge timescales, I used to think myself so cool and 'with-it' when I quoted global and universal timescales – as I frequently did in lectures to university students – about the next step in our evolutionary process, or in the little booklets I self-published on similar themes. The timescales I then quoted came from Peter Russell's book *The Awakening Earth* (1991 edition by Arkana), which I must have first read shortly after its publication. This sets the supposed Big Bang at 13.8 billion years ago. To help us grasp the length of such an expanse of time it was suggested that we imagine these 13.8 billion years as being equivalent to the height of the Empire State Building. The period during which we humans have walked upright as bipeds is then proportionately equivalent to the amount by which a layer of paint on the roof of that building increases its height. Or, to use another analogy: if the 13.8 billion years are taken as being equivalent to one earth year, then our species began to walk upright one hour before midnight on the very last day of that year;

we developed language one and a half minutes before midnight on that last day, and the Buddha attained enlightenment five and a half seconds before the end of that year – which was in fact about two thousand five hundred years ago, and very close to one gyration of the Earth's axis.

I suppose the point of all this is to make us realise that in terms of universal timescales, we humans have not been around for very long – just a blink of a universal eye, really – so that, as a species, we are still very young and there should be plenty of scope for further evolution.

Be that as it may, and fascinating as these various concepts of dividing up time into different cycles may be, it will – as you say – be an understanding of the specific qualities of the time in which we live and the era we are moving towards, which will help us throw some light on how to prepare for – and assist in – the process of helping humanity take the next step in its evolution.

I suppose that is why astrology may be able to make a contribution to our quest, because it has things to say about the qualities and specific characteristics of different times. At least, that is what I remember my father talking about.

Well, we'll see what turns up. I certainly agree that learning about what qualities astrologers ascribe to the sign of Aquarius should be our next focus.

What do you think? How shall we go about this?

Do take care and keep yourself well protected when you are out and about.

Big hugs (virtually of course)
Grandpa

27/12/2020

Hi Grandpa,

Goodness me, we have been ever so busy at the bakery in the run-up to Christmas. Luckily, we were allowed to continue to remain open – of course people always need bread. But it was still very gratifying that people liked ours, especially all the Christmas biscuits and goodies we produced went like hot cakes – :-).

I'm afraid in all that rushing around, I missed the conjunction of the two planets. Did you see it? But we had a lovely Christmas in spite of everything. I do hope you both have had a good time too.

Since then, I've managed to have a brief second look at some of these astrological websites, searching specifically for Aquarian characteristics; and this is what I have found out:

His image is that of a Water-bearer – he pours water from a jug over the world below his feet.

It is thought that the age of Aquarius will work towards increasing individual freedoms and liberation from many forms of constraints and that the extraordinary advances in science, technology and the advent of the internet are already part of this Aquarian influence.

The culmination of the age of Pisces – now ending – is the realisation, according to Astro-Butterfly, that liberation comes as a result of the harmonious unification of the ego with the soul, or to use Chinese terms: the yin with the yang. This results from the recognition that separation is an illusion, created in our psyche by the confrontational duality or opposition – the either/or syndrome – between the ego and the soul. Their unification, leading to a new renaissance of feelings of wholeness and liberation is thought to be the aspiration of the age of Aquarius, but this will not come easily and whilst the battle between ego and soul rages, machines, such as weapons, robots, the internet, etc. will be used to justify one side against the other in both directions.

Don't you think it is amazing that this juxtaposition of the ego and the soul should now turn up to confront us like this, in the light of my fascination with the word soul ever since my wedding. I am very excited and have the feeling we might have stumbled onto something very significant. What do you think?

Anyway, other 'key words' associated with Aquarius in the websites I have looked at are:

• Amongst the elements, he is associated with *Air,* though depicted as the 'Bringer of Water'. (I suppose the air does bring the all-nourishing rain).

• Amongst the planets, the discovery of *Uranus* is regarded as heralding in the Aquarian age.

• Amongst concepts: free-spirited open-mindedness and egalitarian, humanitarian liberation are qualities which are mentioned in connection with his radiation.

• The discovery of new energies (such as electricity), new technologies (such as artificial intelligence), and connections with other forms of life (space travel) are all said to be the result of Aquarian influences.

• New forms of egalitarian, democratic operating systems, which have not been seen before, are expected to come to the fore, in which the concept of *me* acting in the service of *we* without losing the dignity, liberty and respect for each individual's contribution to the whole will be the norm.

• In the Age of Aquarius, (says another website), power within society will shift from oppressive top-down regimes to systems of governance which allow individuals the freedom to choose her/his own reality based on what aligns with the individual's soul, but within a strong awareness of the whole.

• Wellness for all is the very spirit of the Age of Aquarius, meaning that even with dark days still ahead, there is something magnificent on the horizon.

• It seems to me, that for our quest, the significant indicator to investigate further and delve into deeply is the relationship between *ego* and *soul* and the transition from *me* to *we*.

What might these really point towards?

Anyway, plenty to get our teeth into in the New Year, don't you think?

Have a good slide across that threshold into 2021 – and good riddance to 2020 :-) …though it was not all bad by any means!

Love you lots
Lanya

02/01/2021

Hello Lanya,

Yes, I did see the conjunction, but not very well – in and out of the clouds – but spectacular nevertheless! And all the more poignant because of what we are already into with our *quest*.

Did *you* see the light show over London's skyline in the first ten minutes of this New Year?

If not, try and find a recording of it – it's well worth watching. Definitely the best yet in my view!

They kept it a secret to avoid crowds gathering in the streets, and apparently, they largely succeeded. But isn't it interesting how constraints bring out the best in people? The show was much less expansive and grand, but so much the better for that – so much more inventive!

But to return to our 'quest':

Thank you so much for painting such a vivid picture for us of what astrologers expect from this New Age into which our planet is taking us. I find it an awe-inspiring image to contemplate that we are traveling on this planet – spinning (at the surface of its equator) at one thousand miles per hour and around the sun at a speed of sixty-six thousand six hundred miles per hour. Whilst we feel nothing of either of these speeds – not to mention the wobble of its axis – it is carrying us into new influences and presenting us humans with new challenges and opportunities for our own growth and development. I must say, I am surprised at how hopeful and full of promise the astronomers' vision of the Aquarian attributes sound in your description of them. But I suppose it is only natural that on the threshold of such a new adventure, those whose field of study this is, should flag up the aspirations and positive aspects of what they see coming? After all, that is what I have been doing with my 'Next Evolutionary Step' (NESt) Initiative: flagging up what – in my view – we humans are destined to evolve towards.

I now feel the need for a definition of our quest. If you agree, let's both have a go at formulating one, so that each of us has a chance of finding what we really need. But before we launch into that, let me say a few things about the ego, because it looks as if it might play a significant role in our research.

For most of my life this word has signified something derogatory, something to curb, to dismantle, to constrain. But about a decade ago, at a group session at the Schumacher College, where the ego was getting a particularly strong hammering, I found myself defending it – quite against my expectations. From then on I had to examine in depth what I really thought about it, and to my surprise a quite different view emerged:

I began to see it as a legitimate aspect of our psychological makeup, which is in the process of development, and constitutes an essential aspect of the evolution of our species. I began to equate it to what the Hindus call Ahamkara – the feeling of 'I'. This is not the individual Self – or Atman (as the Hindus call it), but the feeling of individuality – you could call it a reflection of the Atman when incarnated in matter. I began to regard it as being at a stage in the evolution of our species comparable to that of adolescence in the development of an individual – experiencing all sorts of new feelings: swinging from excessive confidence to great uncertainties; reckless bravado and hunger for adventure, but also a shyness and reticence at other times; high idealism and motivation to do the right thing, but also a tendency to feel that everything revolves around its own needs and desires.

This then led me to see the next phase in the evolution of our species as revolving around the growing up of the ego into full and responsible maturity – the adulthood of humankind – in which the proper role we are to play in the totality of life on earth is fully appreciated and acted out consciously, responsibly and caringly.

So you see, with these ideas floating around in the back of my mind, I could not agree with you more, that this new concept of working towards transforming the opposition between the ego and the soul into a unification – a harmonious union and cooperation – would for me be a most welcome aim for our quest.

Now, since this email is already long, and the little inescapable tasks at this time of the year, like thanking for

Christmas presents and tidying the house, are waiting to be tackled, I shall send this off as it is. Perhaps you would like to go first in formulating a definition of what this 'quest' really means to you?

Let's not be intimidated by this virus pandemic and put our best foot forward into 2021 – and the third decade of this millennium. Much needs to be accomplished… but: whatever will be will be!

    your loving Grandpa.

Chapter Two

THE QUEST IS DEFINED

05/01/2021

Hi Grandpa,

    Happy New Year!

    I did find a recording of the London New Year's Drone Show. It was lovely to watch. It must have been wonderful to see live on the night.

    But what a way to start a New Year – with a complete national lockdown!

    We'll make the best of it though, won't we? I'm certainly not going to sit around whinging. As you say: there's much to be done! And how better to start than by trying to spell out what it is that – deep down – I hope to learn, discover, appreciate and understand next, on my journey through life.

    I'm not sure what to make of what you say about your Damascus Experience with regard to the Ego… clearly one of the things I need to learn more about… :-)

    But to be serious: what did I really have in mind when I suggested this enquiry?

    I think I am trying to get to a place from which I can see the good in our present situation. I wish to see a positive purpose in the hardships which I feel certain are to come; to see a constructive direction of travel for the whole of life on Earth. I want to be able to contribute my energies towards a constructive picture of the future, rather than mope about and bemoan our plight.

I can't believe what many people – and that includes you – seem now to be hinting at or even threatening: that we are possibly facing the end of the road as far as the human species is concerned; that we have gone too far in the pursuit of our own interests, endangering the balance of life on Earth and that 'Mother Earth' is taking action to restore its equilibrium by putting a stop to our reckless behaviour. I want to believe that we can turn this around – manage the bend in the serpentine ascending path – as you once put it, and stride out in the new direction.

Mind you, when I listen to the daily news reports, it does seem as if this virus is several steps ahead of us in its ability to disrupt our status quo. So part of my question – my quest – revolves around finding some clarity about how to accept our present situation – as a serious warning, certainly – but also as a launch pad into a positive future.

I suspect that we need to ask ourselves – as individuals and as communities – '*how we can best cooperate with Mother Earth in helping her to restore balance and equilibrium in her garden*'. We need a '*vision of the role we humans are to play in this phase of Earth's journey, as part of a balanced, thriving community of life*'.

Does that seem a reasonable definition of a quest for us at this time?

You have said before that this place is a school for souls, who come here to learn specific lessons as part of their own growth and development; and that the opportunities for learning are largely presented as challenges which arise in our relationship to the environment into which we are placed. I agree with this proposition. So I expect my quest to play itself out on two levels: that of my own personal development, and that of my role as a member of my species and of the whole community of life.

A tall order, you will say. But is that not what the present situation demands from all of us: – that we find some clarity about how – in full recognition of the upheavals we have been causing – we can at least lay the foundations for a new, more harmonious and balanced way of living together?

I think that sums it up from my side. Your turn now... :-) ...! How does it look to you?

Big hugs – if only!
Lanya

06/01/2021

My dear Lanya,

You have excelled yourself!

There is nothing I would like to add to your beautiful definition of our 'quest'! Except perhaps, to show how I come to the same point from a slightly different direction.

For several decades now – ever since I began to think seriously about my response to the epoch-ending situation, into which we humans are sleepwalking – I became convinced that only a step in our own evolution as a species could lead us through this. Thus I felt challenged to come up with some kind of vision – however vague – of what such an evolutionary step might entail.

So this is the direction from which I come to this quest of

ours.

As you know, I am no scientist and I do not subscribe to the Darwinian concepts of evolution of the 'survival of the fittest'. But the fundamental concept of evolution makes sense to me, however dubious the criteria by which its progress as applied to our species during the last few centuries may seem.

Since Darwin's time, we expect animals and plants over millennia to adapt themselves to changing environmental conditions as part of their evolution. Whilst this has also been applied to homo sapiens in the far distant past, more recently we humans have been busy adapting environmental conditions to our needs, whims and fancies, regardless of the effect on other global inhabitants, now driving alarming numbers to extinction. Thus, it appears, that we humans now regard ourselves as *having arrived* – requiring no further evolution in ourselves. If a change is thought necessary it is achieved by what is called a revolution, i.e. – an upheaval in circumstances external to ourselves. But as we have seen, these revolutions prove to live up to their literal name, in that the upheaval they cause is simply a turning on the spot, with a return to the original, but more intensified condition. Thus, the French revolution ended up with an emperor instead of a king; the Russian revolution ended up with a vicious despot instead of a tzar; and the industrial revolution has resulted in a disparity between rich and poor more than a hundred times greater than the feudal aristocratic system it supplanted.

This realisation made me draw the conclusion that the human species has not yet arrived at its evolutionary destination – as some may have thought – and that only a further evolutionary step will now enable us to adapt to – and survive – the quite drastic environmental conditions brought about by our own actions. And since humankind is a species which has developed a certain degree of consciousness and the beginnings of self-consciousness, it seems reasonable to expect its next evolutionary step to be consciously generated.

This then is where I find myself now: it seems to me that our task at this juncture is to generate a step forward in our evolution, in order to cope with the conditions we have created. My quest therefore is to learn how to do that.

What you have described in your last email will surely take us in that same direction: namely that we find clarity about how to find a way to establish a new, harmonious equilibrium, not only for our own relationship with Mother Earth but with all of her creatures.

This is indeed a tall order! – as you said I would say. But what do we have to lose? And think of what there is to gain?

However: – How to actually begin? Over to you!... :-) ... Let your youthful enthusiasm carry you forward.

    Yes – HUGS! – alas, not yet...
    Grandpa

Chapter Three

HONING THE PARAMETERS OF THE QUEST

07/01/2021

Hello Grandpa,

May I remind you, that I'm not that young any more either... :-) ...youthfulness feels like a memory, but I'm still less than a third of your age – I grant you that!

Did you by any chance see the BBC film about Greta Thunberg, screened last night? Now there's a youthful person who seems to have worked things out for herself with extraordinary clarity and is determined to 'walk her talk'.

I found it a really hard film to watch though. Apart from the fact that the background music was far too loud – as it so often is these days, I get very irritated in documentaries such as this, by the pretence that there isn't a person with a camera standing there recording what is going on. Nevertheless, as the film progressed, I really began to feel for her. When she speaks to these assemblies of politicians and business leaders, and in a very few words tells it to them just as it is, quietly accusing them of messing things up for her generation, and then they clap and give her a standing ovation, you just know that she is thinking: 'Stop clapping, you idiots – DO something! You think clapping me is going to absolve your consciences?'

And when, after that ordeal of crossing the Atlantic in a yacht, she lambasts the United Nations General Assembly with: *How dare you…!* …she must have felt so deflated and helpless.

But seriously, Grandpa, watching this film has made me realise more clearly than ever before, that going on strike, protesting, marching, haranguing politicians, and even recycling, reducing waste, eating less meat, saving energy, shopping more carefully etc. – whatever all the necessary little adjustments to our life-style have to be – essential as these all are – they will not be enough for us to help Mother Earth in her efforts to restore equilibrium amongst her creatures. We will have to learn to visualise – as individuals and as communities – what role we humans are expected to play in this phase of Earth's journey, in order to re-establish a balanced, thriving community of life on her surface! – as I wrote before.

It seems to me that this is where we have to start: we have to first imagine, and then work towards building this vision. It will have to be broad enough, to allow most people to share in it and identify with it. All the activism and life-style adjustments I mention above will be part of it, but it will also have to guide us towards that inner evolution of our psyche which you speak of; that merging together and unification of ego and soul, – of yin and yang – which the Astro-Butterfly speaks of. It will incorporate the Aquarian characteristics, as best as we can visualise them at this stage, but all under the umbrella of the idea of working in unison with Mother Earth.

Is that not an inspiring basis on which to start?

We just have to trust in the power of our imagination. I can't wait to hear what you think…

Love you
Lanya

11/01/2021

Hello Lanya,

Sorry for the delay in replying. I had to have a few days to allow all this to sink in and to settle.

Despite the cold weather, I decided to work a few hours each day in the garden, pruning, trimming, cutting back, reacquainting myself with my old friends the apple and pear trees, the bilberry and current bushes. The ground is too wet and sticky to do any weeding. Anyway, it's not even mid-January! – and already some primroses and snowdrops are flowering, and some of the roses still have buds which are trying to open… where have our winters gone?

Not that I am now ready with any kind of adequate response to your inspiring and enthusiastic salvo. But as you say: we have to trust in our imagination, which also means mustering the necessary patience.

However, in the meantime I want to tell you about a book I have just finished reading, which, in its own way, makes a significant contribution to our search. I would say that its author is undoubtedly a fellow traveller on the same journey you and I are undertaking. He is a German neurobiologist called Gerald Hüther and the title of his book is '*Würde: Was uns stark macht – als Einzelne und als Gesellschaft*' (Dignity: What makes us strong – as individuals and as a society). It was sent to me for Christmas by one of my brothers and I have already finished it. I don't think I have ever read a book that quickly.

Hüther – who, according to his BIO on the cover is one of Germany's most renowned brain-researchers – suggests that much of what is going wrong in our world today is due to the loss of dignity – or what I would prefer to call self-respect. He makes out a convincing case that this quality, this *inner compass,* as he calls it, is a biological given, well anchored in the human brain. But for reasons he describes in great detail, our society has drifted into ways which systematically impede its development in infants and even largely destroys it during the formal education to which every child is subjected. A significant factor in this debilitating process, he says, is the nearly universal legitimisation of the mental stance of objectivising others and thereby treating them as means to our own ends. He illustrates this by examples from many different walks of life and shows how the erosion of our inner sense of dignity or self-respect is the inevitable consequence. To quote just one of his examples: viewing children not as individuals but as a future workforce, drives the educational establishment to pitch them against each other in constant competition, and to shape them into certain preconceived formats deemed useful to those in charge of the economy. This destroys not only the dignity of the child but also the self-respect of the teacher.

The second half of the book is devoted to describing ways in which we can help each other regain and nourish our self-respect. He shows how we can re-awaken our sensitivity to its function as our inner compass and guide, helping to shape our lives. He explains why this is not only natural but also essential to our survival.

Let me translate a passage near the end of the book to give you a flavour:

'… I began to appreciate for the first time that whilst we will be able to continue to live and to organise ourselves as we have done hitherto, this will not now be possible for very much longer… As human beings we cannot continue to live without developing not only our technologies, but also ourselves… We cannot now emigrate to somewhere else in order to continue to pursue the same aims elsewhere, causing the same problems we have created here; (unless it be to the Moon or Mars – my comment). Instead of constantly wanting to change the world in order to make it fit our will, purpose, concept and image, we are today left with no option but to change the hitherto held concept and image of ourselves. We will not find this easy, because... the question arises as to the direction in which we want to develop ourselves further? And to answer that question we need that inner compass as never before – we need a concept, a conscious vision of what it is that makes us *human*?'

Is that not very close to my NESt concept and to your question: what is humanity's role meant to be in the life of our Mother Earth? And, like you, he calls for this concept and image – your 'vision' – to arise out of our imagination.

He suggests that people who become fully conscious of their dignity and self-respect are no longer corruptible. Their thoughts and actions are guided by their inner compass and so they take care to preserve their dignity. For instance, they no longer have any use for all that advertising machinery, finding that its products insult their intelligence; etc. etc. (...music to my ears – I can tell you!).

Whilst I'm not entirely convinced that the concepts of dignity or self-respect would in themselves be sufficient to turn things around, as he seems to think, they may be more accessible to many people than phrases like 'listening to your inner voice' or 'heeding your conscience' or 'striving for self-perfection' (as Schweitzer puts it). What do you think?

Your grandmother and I have now both been invited to book our appointments for the first corona virus vaccination and we managed this afternoon to get both bookings before the end of

January – isn't that good?

As ever
Grandpa

P.S. Interestingly: I have just received an email from a member of an internet group which discusses the role of *wisdom* in our time, (to which I am an occasional contributor), in which he shares his wish-list for what life could be like in 2035, and this includes the following human values: dignity, well-being, flourishing, fairness, compassion, human rights, empathy, symmetry, the golden rule, and solving grand challenges. He also has *dignity* as the first item on his list.

P.P.S. Because I commented on the above email, I have just received another email from someone in the same group attaching a blog, in which he talks about finding his moral compass in the following three values: dignity, well-being and integrity. Obviously, the concept of dignity is rated highly.

Chapter Four

CASTING ABOUT FOR INSPIRATION

13/01/2021

Would you believe it, Grandpa:

Someone at the bakery now has the virus and we have all had to self-isolate, so the bakery is shut. I'm at home, enjoying myself doing lots of drawing and sketching and studying. It's so great that you have your vaccination appointments now – that must be the beginning of things looking up again for you both and for all of us to be able to come and visit you again. I know it's still a few weeks before we can relax a little with each other – but still, it's a beginning to look forward to!

I must say, that does sound like an interesting book, which you describe in your last email – it must have been, for you to finish it in such a short time... :-)

Is it not amazing – despite all the trash that is about – how many people are writing and working in the same direction as we are? A break-through to a critical mass can't be that far off!

And, you know, what you have written about dignity and self-respect has helped me put my finger on something that has been in the back of my mind as a nebulous feeling for a while. A book I have read recently touched on it.

It is a little book by Charlotte Brontë called 'The Professor'. I really enjoyed it. I love her language and her descriptive passages. You may not know the book. I don't think they have made a film of it. The beginning and ending of the story play out in England but the main part is located in Belgium, which gives an interesting insight into relationships between the UK and continental Europe at that time. No mention of visas or passports or controls on currencies – the impression given is of free travel and movement between countries and a readiness to speak each other's languages with relative ease. All of which surprised me, with so much about 'Brexit' in my ears for the last few years.

Another thing that surprised me was the general impression that is given in this book concerning trust. You and I have often talked about the importance of trust and trustworthiness in all aspects of society and have bemoaned its disappearance from so many areas of our lives, especially with the arrival of the term *fake news*, and all the lies and falsehoods peddled on social media. I keep being told that I exaggerate when I go on about this topic. People say that there have always been liars and cheats and robbers and criminals; that deceit and falsehood has always been the stock-in-trade of the ruling classes etc. etc.

So it surprised me, that on several occasions in the book, Brontë quite casually describes situations where doors to private dwellings in towns were not locked at night – not as something unusual, but as a matter of course. Her story tells of a parcel being delivered secretly at night into a flat via its unlocked front door. Clearly this incident could not have been planned, had it not been taken for granted that the door in question would have been left unlocked. Another time, also in the town of Brussels, one of the characters arrives at the same flat, where his then girlfriend lives alone. He knocks, and without waiting for the door to be opened or even to hear the invitation to come in, he just walks straight in. So this girl lives on her own in a flat in town and the door to her dwelling is not locked. Several similar incidents are described. The fear of being burgled, or for any harm to befall a young woman living alone was clearly substantially lower then, than it is now. I think this is proof that trust in our time is very much lower than it was then. That was one point.

But there is something else I really wanted to mention about this book:

It is – in our terms – a fairly undramatic story of two people's efforts to make their way in the world whilst remaining honest and straightforward, true to their feelings and convictions, and indeed, concerned to preserve their dignity in the face of various temptations. They encounter a series of humiliations and challenging situations in which, each time, they choose to respond in a way which preserves their self-respect whilst being financially disadvantageous and risky.

Brontë does not really spell this out in so many words, but she is describing a heightened sense of personal dignity and self-respect which these two people are very carefully guarding and which they are quite unwilling to have compromised. It is exactly this that sets them apart from nearly all the other characters in the book. And I think your Mr Hüther is quite right: it is a quality far too neglected and even trampled underfoot these days. Obviously, Brontë thought it worthwhile highlighting and demonstrating this in the narrative of her book. And perhaps in earlier centuries they would have called this *a question of honour*. But I agree that these are core sensitivities which need to be re-awakened and nurtured in any vision or plan for the future.

Incidentally, another aspect of that book gave me pause for thought: these two people, who find each other and get married in utter poverty, then make a prosperous life for themselves out of their innate abilities and diligence. After ten years of intense and concentrated work in Brussels, they are able to retire with enough capital to buy a country house in England outright and live a life of leisure for the rest of their days. Although this might have been optimistic, it must have been a sufficiently realistic expectation for Brontë to make it the quite 'normal' framework of her story.

To compare that to my own expectations today, I need only look at my uncle, your son, who made it to the top of his profession as a very young man and has now, after twenty-five years, been able to buy a roughly equivalent house to the one they bought in Brontë's story, but with a mortgage for which he will have to work at least another twenty-five years to pay it off. Such is the 'economic miracle' which the '1% nouveau-riche' have created for the rest of the population in this post aristocratic, modern, advanced and highly developed age, in which we have been told: 'you have never had it so good!'

Enough of this – it makes me angry. Tell me something uplifting and creative... :-)

Love you lots
Lanya

14/01/2021

Hello Lanya,

Today is Schweitzer's birthday. Your Grandma and I are always a little nostalgic on this day. After all, we met at his hospital and got engaged with his blessing. And if that hadn't happened, you and I would not be talking to each other now... :-) ...isn't that worth celebrating?

Because it is a day of celebration, I shall resist commenting on the '1%' syndrome – you know how I get carried away on that subject! But I was very intrigued by what you say about Charlotte Brontë's 'Professor'. I looked her up on the internet – did you know that you look rather like the images of her which they show there? I have already ordered the book from Amazon and look forward very much to reading it when I get a chance.

I say, 'When I get a chance' because I'm now halfway into another book, which we have to talk about:

Your sentence: *...to help Mother Earth in her efforts to restore balance and equilibrium amongst her creatures*, triggered a vague memory in me, that years ago I had read a book which spoke about a similar thought. And when we were thinking about universal timescales – as I mentioned in my earlier email (17/12/2020), I got out Peter Russell's book which has that very useful chart in it; I happened to look at its contents pages and realised that this was the book of which I was reminded by your sentence, and I started re-reading it. (*'The Awakening Earth – The Global Brain'* by Peter Russell. It was first published in 1982, but I have the 1991 revised edition). When I first read it in the mid-1990s, I was still fully engrossed in my professional career and in the study of harmonics and the relationship of musical and visual proportions.

The book obviously made a deep impression on me then because I have thoroughly absorbed its ideas into my subconscious and have treated many of them as my own. Re-reading it now, it is clear to me that, as part of this quest, I have to ask you to read it too. It contains amazing information and ideas affecting everything we are thinking about at present. I imagine you will quickly catch up and overtake me, since I am such a slow reader, and I also think that we can start to discuss certain aspects even before we have finished the book. In fact I am going to plunge straight in and tackle something which you know bothers me a lot – namely: the question of the 'Big Bang'. I think I can say my piece about that without undermining the credibility and pertinence of everything that follows.

Russell starts with a 'Prologue', in which he very thoroughly and very carefully describes the basis and origin of the Gaia Theory which postulates that earth is a self-regulating living entity. He then examines criteria which could define 'life', and explains the 'General Living Systems Theory'. Then, in Chapter two, he turns his attention to the concept of evolution and I quote the paragraph in which he responds to the question of how the Universe began, as follows:

'…Many theories have been put forward at different times, some based on physical science, others on spiritual, metaphysical or philosophical frameworks. At present the most widely accepted theory in the West is the scientific model based on the notion that the Universe started with a 'Big Bang' some fifteen billion or so years ago. According to this view, the whole Universe as we know it, was born from a gigantic superheat fireball… Of what happened before the Big Bang, physical science knows nothing and may forever know nothing. Time and space only came into being once the process began – hard as that may be for us to grasp…'

Having read this far, I expected him to at least put this into some context and consider other theories. But he doesn't. Throughout the book, this – to me a quite impossible idea – is taken as the basis for all calculations and speculations which follow – insightful and inspiring as these are.

To my mind this notion of a big explosion as the beginning of everything has no more credibility than the story of Adam and Eve, which at least has some poetic potential and all sorts of allegorical and mythological overtones. This Big Bang Theory is for me just a reflection of our obsession with explosions, bombs and bright lights as opposed to trees, apples and snakes.

For something to go BANG, there first has to be a SOMETHING to go bang – not to mention the space and time in which to go bang; and what about a cause to make it go bang? This is being said in the language of science, and in that language the whole proposition is impossible. So why not admit that we do not know how it all started? Why pretend that we know something so unrealistic?

OR: why not acknowledge that this universe is most likely one of many and began like any other life-form we know, with an act of fertilisation which caused a rapid expansion of energy, creating and dissipating heat. Experienced from inside an unfertilised egg, fertilisation may well be experienced as a sudden *new beginning.*

As you can sense, I feel strongly about this. But I don't want you to be put off by this issue, because in what follows Russell addresses the very questions we are asking ourselves, and he does so in great depth and detail.

I'm very anxious to know what you are going to say to all this?

Reading this book will be like a BIG BANG for you – I promise… :-)

Lots of love
Grandpa

18/01/2021

Good evening Grandpa,
Oh for the wonders of technology: I was able to get the book

onto my kindle instantly and have been reading it these last three days.

Russell seems to have received some of his inspiration from Teilhard de Chardin. Have you come across him before?

As you say, reading this feels like a 'déjà-vu' experience, but through a magnifying glass under a very strong light: what we were searching for – tentatively, groping about as if in a fog – is described here in great detail and sharp focus. Quite astonishing! But it does raise the question as to why, if this was written forty years ago, are we struggling to rediscover it anew? Why has this not become common knowledge by now? Why, when I wrote the sentence: '...*We will have to learn to visualise – as individuals and as communities – what role we humans are expected to play in this phase of Earth's journey...?*' did this feel as if I was expressing a new idea, when forty years ago, Peter Russell, who seems to be quite famous, wrote the following – right at the beginning of his book:

'...*Humanity could be on the threshold of an evolutionary leap, a leap which could occur in a flash of evolutionary time, and a leap such as occurs only once in a billion years...*' and on the next page: '...*Rather than humanity suffering major setbacks, the dramatic changes could be a growing-up and maturing of our species'.* These are phrases and ideas I have heard you express many times in conversation, but also in your book My Path with Albert Schweitzer.

I must say however, that what is going on just now does not feel like a growing up and maturing of our species. But I suppose these current events could be seen as birth pains? Or perhaps death throws in the sense of 'the old order changing, making way for new'.

I love the way he deals with the increasing tempo of

evolution. That feels so very true: everything seems to be speeding up and gathering momentum so dramatically. And he finishes the first paragraph of Chapter 5, 'Our evolving society', with the sentence: '...*The three principal aspects of complexity appear to be once again reaching the point where a new order of existence could emerge, and the area for this next evolutionary breakthrough is humanity itself*'. And then he finishes that chapter with: '...*No longer will we perceive ourselves as isolated individuals; we will know ourselves to be part of a rapidly integrating global network, the nerve cells of an awakening global brain*'. Does that not have the flavour of 'merging *me* into *we*', as the astronomers put it?

I think that's a very useful image for our endeavour of finding the role for humanity in Mother Earth's scheme of things. And I also like the term self-reflective consciousness. It circumvents the slightly negative connotations of being self-conscious.

But I should read on and catch up with you... :-)

By the way, isn't it time for your vaccination soon? I can't wait to meet up again!

Love you
Lanya

21/01/2021

Hello Lanya,

Well, the USA has a new president! Perhaps that also signifies the start of a new era?

Your grandmother and I watched the whole of the

inauguration on TV yesterday, and I read Joe Biden's speech again today. Would you believe: dignity and respect are mentioned four times! I thought it was a very good speech, full of soul, promise and hope – hope to re-establish unity and truthfulness in his country: '*We must reject a culture in which facts themselves are manipulated and even manufactured*' he said. – Much to live up to!

There is still a long way to go before we can think about transcending nationalism, but his pleas for a more benign and even loving society in America seemed to come from the heart. I was struck though, by the way the reporters, summarising and commenting on the speech immediately afterwards, totally ignored that aspect of it.

But enough of this chat! I have now finished Russell's book.

I don't think it will spoil the ending for you when I tell you that when I read the Epilogue, I felt that my outburst earlier about the idea of the Big Bang was fully justified. He makes the reader contemplate the minuteness of our earth, our solar system and even our galaxy within other possible formations in the universe, comparing the size of our solar system within our galaxy to an apple within the continent of North America. Then he postulates – as I have done – that each entity might be capable of being a living organism. He says that these stars, solar systems, galaxies and clusters of galaxies could evolve into living super-organisms and asks: 'Could the Universe as a whole become a living system?'

But here, I think, his speculation is inhibited by the concept of a beginning in the form of this Big Bang. For some reason he assumes Earth to be in the privileged position of having had a head start with regard to becoming a living and conscious entity, with other entities having the potential of following our lead sometime in the future.

This is where I perceive our work could take this whole exploration a stage further, in that I see all this not as something in the future but a reality NOW. For me, our universe already is a conscious being! Just as our human bodies, its cell-structures, individual cells, molecules, atoms, electrons and protons are all living entities. Living entities are born, have a life with the potential for evolving towards greater unity and consciousness, and they decline and die. And new ones are born. But to know the beginning and the end of the whole process – and whether indeed there is a beginning and an end – lies beyond our capacity to comprehend. These reside within the concepts of infinity and eternity – whose existence our minds can grasp, but whose being remains a mystery; like parallel lines approaching each other but never meeting; or beginnings, infinitely far in the past, and endings receding eternally into the future and therefore never happening… these are the ultimate mysteries!

But good luck, Lanya, with getting to the end of the book yourself; and then let's consider where we are and where we can go from there.

Are we not living at a most exciting time? – at the beginning of a new era – a new astrological age – on the threshold of a next evolutionary step for humankind!

Incidentally, your grandmother and I have had our first jabs. It was a very uplifting experience. It took place in a community centre and was extremely well managed. There were many volunteers around, organising us in very calm and efficient ways and you could sense how glad they all were to be able to do something to help.

Keep taking great care of yourself, remembering the triple COVID protection armoury - Distance, Mask and Wash – DMW

– at all times… :-)

> Big HUG
> Grandpa

24/01/2021

> Oh Grandpa,
>
> It's Sunday! And it's snowing! Big flakes are falling gently and dancing in eddies, settling on leaves and paving slabs – a sprinkling of sugar on the whole picture seen from my window. I watch, mesmerised, soaking in the peaceful, gentle stillness of the scene. The birds are busy around the feeder and all things seem to be just as they should, right now!
>
> I had a quiet afternoon and evening yesterday and was able to finish reading Russell's book.
>
> As you say, he ends it in a rousing and challenging flourish. I don't know whether I would have picked up on the point you make, but having had my attention drawn to it, I quite see what you are saying about the beginning of it all. As you say, there seems no other way to make sense of this question but to assume that something – which is no *thing* at all – and which some call consciousness, is a pre-existing condition whose beginning – if it has one – remains a mystery which we cannot penetrate.
>
> Now, what I wanted to do today is to summarise the gist of Russell's book as it affects our quest:
>
> I shall try and do this on the assumption that what is referred to as the Big Bang is in fact the birth of this particular universe as one of many in a still bigger picture. And I think we can, for our present purposes, safely ignore the presumptions scientists

make about the early seconds, minutes and even millennia of the baby-stage of this universe of ours. We can even leave to one side the stages of growth and evolution before the advent of human history – interesting as these are of course. I shall try and extract what I think is pertinent to our present quest.

Basically, the proposition is this:

Earth is a self-regulating living entity. (Russell calls it a living system; I prefer the word entity). Following eons of evolution, this entity has reached a stage when its nervous system, spearheaded by the agency of humankind, has expanded its reach, speed of connectivity and handling of information to a point when its individual components – we humans – are poised to acquire the ability, through the development of increased synergy, to expand our skin-encapsulated egos into an inclusive self-awareness which encompasses the needs and aspirations of the earth and all its creatures. If successful, this newly evolved self-reflective consciousness will act as earth's vastly expanded and sophisticated brain, or more accurately, its cortex, (analogous, in evolutionary terms, to the relatively recent expansion of the human brain).

If unsuccessful, humankind's unruly and exploitative activities will accelerate, and their cancerous effect on earth's wellbeing is likely to arouse her self-regulating mechanisms in order to rid herself of this disruptive element as a failed experiment.

To escape this failure, Russell postulates the evolution of human society into a super-organism. He describes how evolution has moved through the physical and biological levels into the evolution of consciousness and self-reflective consciousness, and is now on its way to moving even beyond that to a further fifth level which Russell calls the Gaiafield: planet

Earth's equivalent to human consciousness, (which he sees as akin to Teilhard's Noosphere and Aurobindo's Supermind).

These new evolutionary levels are to be achieved through the 'progressive integration of human minds into a single living system'. Successfully functioning living systems such as the human body – or that of any other living creature – work because there is synergy between the constituent parts and the whole. 'Each individual element of the system works towards its own goals, yet they function in ways that are spontaneously mutually supportive'. Since the current level of synergy in human society is still very low, a crucial factor in accomplishing the next evolutionary step is to understand how this level of synergy can be increased.

Here Russell suggests that this can only be achieved by changing the image we have of ourselves, namely: the concept of who we think we are and what gives us our identity. He calls this predominantly held image the skin-encapsulated self; (sometimes also called the ego). This is the image of an individual 'I' or *self* as an entity, which sees itself restricted – some would say imprisoned – within the skin of each individual physical body and separated from other bodies around it. This image is fostered, encouraged, reinforced and perpetuated from infancy onwards, through earliest parental attitudes, through the system of education and through social norms and institutions of all kinds. Yet it is the cause of most of the difficulties experienced by societies nearly everywhere, and results in the very low level of synergy prevalent in the vast majority of the human race.

However, this is not the only model of *self*... A radically different yet complementary model is possible: that of a universal self, not bounded by the skin; a self, whose essential quality is connectedness and unity with the rest of creation, rather than separation from it. By way of numerous examples from the past, and a trawl through what is called perennial philosophy, Russell describes and substantiates this other model of *self*. Then he suggests that '*one of the most crucial tasks now facing humanity*' lies in answering the questions: '*How do we wake up? How do we de-hypnotise ourselves*' from the dominance of the skin-encapsulated self. He says that this challenge requires a paradigm-shift towards inner self-development; a shift from evolution being an external process to being an inner development of consciousness towards self-realisation. The emergent social super-organism acting as Earth's cortex or Gaia's self-awareness, cannot be something that is imposed. It must arise spontaneously from an inner shift in orientation within each individual component, until a critical mass of the global population partakes in the evolutionary flow towards higher degrees of unity (what Russell calls synergy) within the living entity that is Mother Earth and all her creatures.

He asks – just halfway through the book: '*…how can we facilitate this inner evolution, and even more important, can we do it in time?*' (written in 1982).

The chapter headings of the second half of the book give a good overview of his response to this question: from Chapter 10 to the end:

The Spiritual Renaissance;
On The Threshold;
Towards a High Synergy Society;
Choosing The Future.

I found it all extremely interesting to read, but whether it conjures up a credible picture for me of how this inner evolution would be accomplished in a critical mass of humankind in time? – I'm not sure – especially within the timeframe in which we are now looking at this, forty years later. He himself seems to have drawn inspiration from transcendental meditation which he studied directly with the Maharishi in the Himalayas in the 1960s; and whilst he does not push this specific meditation too hard, he thinks that some kind of meditation is essential to this process.

At one point Russell gives a list of external issues which were receiving the attention of interest groups during the New Age movement of the 1960s, and I find it astonishing how little that list has changed since then; I quote:

'...*There are ecologically orientated groups concerned with the protection of endangered species, organic farming, communal living, alternative technology, voluntary simplicity, energy and resource conservation, nuclear disarmament and other ways in which we can live more in tune with the planet*'.

Forty years before I was even born, they – or should I say you, Grandpa, – were already talking about all these things...! And I was amazed how well informed he was about technological developments and he predicts pretty accurately what is now happening in this field. But I find his optimism on that score unconvincing. His expectation that real help towards an inner evolution, such as he predicts, will come from that direction seems to me not to be borne out – at least not so far. There is indeed hugely increased connectivity and capacity for the storage and accessibility of information, but can you see a marked increase in orientation towards inwardness? You were there at the time, Grandpa, you should be able to tell?

In the Epilogue he paints a fascinating picture of how space exploration can be seen as an indication, or early symptom, of Gaia's developing self-reflecting consciousness and her evolving awareness of her place in the larger scale of galactic formations, as well as her curiosity and longing to make connection with other potential life-forms – out there.

In a Postscript, written some ten years later (1992), he looks back and evaluates the progress made during that decade. The Berlin Wall was then being demolished, ending half a century of Cold War in Europe and greatly reducing the Nuclear Threat. We can now see how that raised positive expectations during the last decade of the century leading to big *End of the Millennium* celebrations.

Interconnectedness across the globe had vastly increased. Satellite communication had started, video cameras were communicating live news in pictures from around the world onto people's TV screens, the Live Aid Concert made people feel compassionate and raised enthusiasm about helping globally. News programmes proliferated exponentially and began to include reports about the climate crisis. All this could be seen as Gaia developing her nervous system.

An awareness started to dawn on some, that the environmental threat was for real and could not be ignored for much longer – or else the millennium celebrations might be in doubt.

'*The global brain was beginning to be aware of its body's wellbeing,*' – as he puts it.

Whilst Russell remains cautiously optimistic, he acknowledges that '*the fight between the egoic mode of thinking that lies at the root of these problems, and the inner knowing that there is more to life than that which meets the senses…*' is not going all that well, and that there are grounds for pessimism. But he concludes with a hopeful belief in '*the unexpected*'.

I'm sorry, Grandpa, this has turned out to be rather longer than I had anticipated, and it took me until now (28th Jan) to finish it. But hopefully it will give us a firm basis from which to move forward into our own journey of discovery as to what is necessary today. There is so much to discuss and I look forward to your response to this summary.

I found this book really fascinating and I think it makes a significant contribution to our quest. Thank you so much for drawing it to my attention.

    Love you lots.
    Lanya

Chapter Five

TAKING STOCK

30/01/2021

My dear Lanya!
What a valuable and helpful summary! It sets the scene beautifully for us to start our real work.

And in the meantime events are racing forward and hotting up at a breakneck speed:

A few days ago, I was sent a link giving access to the write-up of an interview on Davos Radio with Mark Carney, the previous governor of the Bank of England and now the Prime Minister's advisor during the run-up to Cop 26 in Glasgow in November. The interview was part of the Davos Agenda for day three: 'The Great Reset'. Carney is strongly pushing the global financial sector to move assets into climate-friendly activities, pointing out that the risks posed by climate change will drive big changes in financial markets; and he predicts that companies will increasingly be required to disclose their climate impacts and their plans to reduce emissions in their annual reports.

Also on the same day, the weekly update which I receive from the WWF (World Wildlife Fund) reported that the World Economic Forum (in Davos) last week published its 2021 global risk assessment report, which highlights that environmental concerns such as climate change and nature loss – linked to the rise in global pandemics – are the top risks humanity faces in the next ten years.

Thus, I was presented with what must be some of the best news for those of us concerned about the climate crisis since the Paris Agreement. My first thought was: 'Thank you Greta Thunberg! Your courage and determination has helped bring this about. There is now real hope that COP 26 will be a watershed!'

Exciting and hopeful events in the external world!

Towards the end of your last email you ask me... '*Can you see a marked increase in orientation towards inwardness?*' That's a very good question. Inwardness is an utterly private thing. How can you tell about people's orientation towards inwardness other than by external signs? Let me list some external manifestations from my own experience, which may give an indication:

- In the late 1960s, when Peter Russell was in India with the Maharishi, my wife and I were also being initiated into that same transcendental meditation, and in the 1980s, when he was working on the book we are discussing, we were practising this meditation twice a day, but very much in secret. It would not have done, for me, as a partner in an architectural practice to let it be known then, that I was into this sort of thing. It would have been regarded as distinctly weird.

- The same goes for the yoga training which we were receiving then and practicing in evening classes.

- Nowadays, both these activities are openly discussed and their practice is widespread amongst the general population in Europe, and in the USA.

- Friends of mine are devotees of Thich Nath Hanh, a Buddhist Monk. I have read several books by him. He is the author of the movement towards mindfulness, which is now practised by millions including executives of global companies as well as top flight actors and performers of all kinds. A few years ago these friends gave me the chance to attend a public meeting which had been organised for this monk at the Royal Festival Hall. There was not a spare seat in the whole two thousand five hundred seat auditorium. For a full two hours, with very little activity taking place on the stage, there was no restlessness in the Hall. Thich Nath Hanh spoke occasionally about mindfulness; some monks chanted and sang at intervals; there was a little dancing. The audience was totally silent – you could hear a pin drop. This was mid-week. I heard later that on the following Saturday he had a similar gathering in Trafalgar Square attended by five thousand people.

For me, these examples give some measure of inwardness amongst the population of London, and I would say they undoubtedly show an increase since the 1960s. However, this is deceptive, because at the other end of the spectrum, the gross absurdity of external events makes so much more noise – dominating the news, the media and our superficial distractions.

But there are also numerous other similar indicators, such as the popularity of the Resurgence and Ecologist magazine, the seminars of the Schumacher Society, the continuous thriving of the Findhorn Community and countless similar communities around the globe participating in the Global Eco-Village Movement... to mention but a few I happen to know about.

That is not to say that there are not plenty of counter-indications as well. But is there as yet any evidence of a discernible increase in the kind of synergy Russell talks about, i.e. energy moving towards a spontaneous and mutually supportive synergy amongst individuals with global aspirations to promote the common good, integrated into a single living system acting as a global brain? I would say that amongst individual members of the general public: yes there are the beginnings of such a movement, but politicians, leaders of commerce and industry and the media are as yet going in the opposite direction. And a critical mass? Well, that seems still a very long way off to me. Synergy at a global scale still seems like a distant dream.

Does this bring us to another possible formulation of the essence of our quest?

As for instance: *How can we contribute – today – to an increase in synergy among human populations and between us and Gaia, hastening the evolution of humankind into a single living entity?*

Or do you think that this is altogether too ambitious and out of reach? What do you think? Has Russell's book really helped us? Or has it taken us into a 'never-never-land'?

If only I could give you a real hug – soon!

But our second 'jab' looks like being guaranteed after all, as of today – though we don't have a date as yet – so there is light at the end of this particular tunnel…!

Love you
Grandpa

31/01/2021

Hello Grandpa,
One twelfth of the year already gone – how time flies!
I do feel strongly motivated to further explore Russell's idea, and

to try and find a way of working towards the kind of synergy he describes – towards a humanity merged into a single living system – or entity. Aquarius will help us, as we have now learnt. And even technology will help us, potentially. I don't know whether you engage with any of the on-line campaigning sites like AVAAZ, 38 degrees, 350.org, Friends of the Earth, Greenpeace, change.org, and I'm sure there are many more? But I think these are expressions of a desire amongst the general public to move in the direction Russell has indicated. And some of these campaigns get huge numbers of supporters – like hundreds of thousands – and they are beginning to have successes.

The problem with technology, especially now we are in the digital era, is that our inner evolution is not keeping up with the challenges, and has actually fallen so far behind that our ability to manage unintended consequences is eluding us. In fact, I am inclined to think that this race between our inner growth towards a fully responsible maturity and the advances in digital mechanisms presenting us with seductive temptations luring in the wrong direction, is every bit as critical for us as the race to reduce CO_2 emissions in time to stop the permafrost from tipping into speed-melt.

Russell's vision however, is for the long-term – for the distant horizon. And he relied on the unexpected to get us there. I think you and I are searching for the immediate next step… and at the moment I haven't a clue where to start looking for that. But it seems to me that if we don't get a move-on, the machines being invented will get there first – as in the incredible progress in the development of AI (Artificial Intelligence). Not that I think there would be anything intrinsically wrong in that – it just seems impossible to trust the designers and more especially the financiers. It would all be so much simpler, if people didn't always want more than they actually need, with the cunning and more ruthless ones taking most of it for themselves and leaving many with far less than they need. I suppose Russell set out the psychology of this scenario pretty clearly with the description of how the skin-encapsulated ego constantly seeks reassurance of its identity and thinks it can secure that through having more and more possessions. And he suggests that if we can only escape from this ego, everything else will naturally fall into place. Have I got this right?

If I have, it looks as if tackling this 'skin-encapsulated ego' should indeed be our priority and should constitute the 'next step' in the human evolutionary process. So, how do we do that?

Easy enough to throw down the gauntlet – not so easy to pick it up… :-)

At least the row over the export/import regulations of vaccines is dying down again and more people are coming forward to call for a globally coordinated approach to distributing the vaccines.

Looking forward to your next salvo…
With lots of love
Lanya

31/01/2021

Hello Lanya,

I've got an hour or so left before supper, so I might as well make a start.

I don't think you are wrong about working on the skin-encapsulated ego being a priority. And I wonder whether Gaia is actually helping us by attacking on several fronts at once. I have had the thought playing around in my head that the Trump phenomenon and the COVID-19 pandemic are both acting as allies in disguise in support of our quest.

I know that you know the Narnia books by C S Lewis, but I'm not sure how well you know the one in the series called 'The Horse and His Boy'. There is a passage in that story, which made a deep impression on me when I first read these books – your mother was still a child then – and I have often thought of it since. I mean, the part of the story where the usually serene and god-like lion, Aslan, acts ferociously to scare the main characters of the story away from danger and in the direction of their safe destiny. I think it perfectly illustrates what I mean by… 'disguised allies in our quest'.

It is well worth reading the story again as I have done earlier today. I don't know a better illustration of the phenomenon I so often experience, particularly when already in a stressful situation. Something even scarier happens unexpectedly, which causes a doubling of effort and/or a sudden change of direction. Then later it turns out to have been instrumental in avoiding total disaster.

Let's take the Trump phenomenon first: don't you think that people will look back on this period of history and say that Trump did everyone a service by scaring the various establishments out of their complacency and self-satisfied arrogance, hubris and conceit – certainly in those parts of the globe which are in thrall to what we call Western Civilisation. By showing how easily the very foundations of trust, respect, dignity and honesty can be destabilised and rocked to breaking point, he pushed the inhabitants of the USA – only by a whisker, mind you – to bring back a more sane and – at least on the surface – a more committed and responsible group of people to govern for a while, under the banner of build back better. We have yet to see what that better will be like, but initial signs are encouraging and the world is breathing a cautious sigh of relief. The news from Davos and the prospects for COP 26, mentioned in my last email, speak to that.

(I'm called to supper – more tomorrow).

01/02/2021

And what about this pandemic? How could that be doing us a service?

Well, for one thing, it is helping the concept of one humanity to become an acknowledged reality by making it self-evident that it affects us all, since it won't be beaten until it is beaten everywhere. If the moon landings and other space adventures have helped bring the image of earth as our beautiful, blue home vividly into focus for many of us, then this pandemic can be seen as helping to make the image of us as a single human family more real. Nothing like having a common enemy for bringing people together. In terms of Russell's idea of humankind being Gaia's evolving brain and the vehicle for its evolving nervous system, the image and feeling of togetherness, of sharing in a common destiny, is of crucial importance. A few individuals throughout history have held this image for themselves and have spoken about it. This number has greatly increased in recent years, and now it has a good chance of becoming accessible to all of us as an image shared by everybody as a common birthright.

And I'm sure you agree, Lanya, that the pandemic has demonstrated, how easily and quickly the complex apparatus that keeps our economic systems functioning can be completely disrupted and even brought to a near standstill. There had been the hope that the 2007/08 financial crisis would shake the captains of the global economy out of their complacency. But that was not to be. Governments across the globe came to their rescue by bailing them out with taxpayers' money, and within months everything was very nearly back to what it was before. Now, even top management and government are suggesting that 'we cannot go back to how it was before'. However, the IMF is forecasting a quick recovery and even increased growth for the next two years, and there is no guarantee that the 'elite' – our proverbial one percent – will not try and use the situation as an opportunity to strengthen its grip. The populations of many economies have been severely shaken out of their comfort zones and I fully anticipate, or at least hope, that as soon as the worst panic is over, strong voices will be heard putting forward models of how to go forward in new and better ways; and perhaps this time these will not fall on deaf ears. But who knows: this wake-up-call may still not be loud enough for humankind to come to its senses.

For this very reason, this is a good time for us to be having this conversation. It certainly is a time for taking stock, for re-evaluating and for setting new goalposts.

It seems essential at this juncture, not to look at the world through rose coloured spectacles and to be aware of the dangers lurking – not only in the shadows – but also in the new developments and innovations which are being pushed quite openly at us all the time. However, if our warnings and criticisms cannot also point to better ways of doing things, if we cannot show a better direction in which to go or offer some protection against the dangers we flag up, our contribution will remain a half-baked affair of little practical value.

During recent decades, I have certainly been guilty of that fault. I thought that I was doing the world a great service by drawing attention to all the things that appeared to be going wrong and to be flagging up dangers and pointing the finger at the supposed villains. But more recently I have realised that a far greater challenge lies in finding ways to circumvent the dangers and to extract the poison from the new innovations which come our way, rendering them not only harmless but truly useful.

I have been going on for quite long enough… :-)

I hope you are keeping warm and managing to stay cheerful in this grey and wet season!

We are approaching the completion of the fortnight after our first jab, so we should then be ninety-five percent protected. It will be interesting to see what difference that will make to our lives… :-)

With lots of love
Grandpa

07/02/2021

Hello Grandpa,

You have given me so much to think about. I don't really know where to start.

Let's start with technology and our relationship with it – I have thought a lot about that – on and off:

I think the exponential acceleration of its development during the last two centuries will inescapably continue. The advent of 5G networks, the rapid advancement of robotics and artificial intelligence are but symptoms of that process. Whether these will turn out to be game-changers, I couldn't say – probably just a continuation of what you have coped with during your life time but at even greater speed.

The fundamental problem, in my view, has not changed since the harnessing of gunpowder for the projection of missiles, but its intensity has increased with each milestone along its path. These milestones are well known. To mention just a few: the harnessing of steam, of electricity, of oil and of nuclear power; the invention of synthetic materials; and most recently, the harnessing of the means of gathering, storing and transmitting information. This last marks the beginning of the digital age, which some call the second industrial revolution, and which I think is still in its infancy.

The problem is, that this development has not been accompanied by an adequate evolution of human psychology and the human spirit. There has been some, I think, but it has not kept pace with the speed of technological innovation, so that now – as we have said before – humankind's capacity to control the powers which these technologies have placed in our hands, is lagging far behind. As a result, the collateral damage which is being caused by the indiscriminate use – and abuse – of these powers, goes unchecked and is out of control. The danger does not lie in the innovations themselves, but in our inability to put them to good use and prevent their abuse, and in the lack of care and attention paid to the control or prevention of their unintended harmful consequences. All that, I think, lies quite within achievable realms of possibility, but as a species we have so far lacked the will, insight and ethical character to manage it. The disparity has now become so serious that the viability of all life on this planet is endangered. This situation has become obvious at least since Hiroshima, but what was then a single-issue syndrome has now become a multi-headed hydra thrashing about out of control. And we two – with many others, it has to be said – are going in search of ways to tame the beast and bring her under control.

At the moment, I see humankind as being like a hoard of unsupervised children playing with real and loaded guns as if they were toys. We need to grow up really fast and recognise the danger.

There – that's my take on the issue of technological innovation... and there is me throwing down the gauntlet – once again!

Incidentally, I have been watching some of the very fascinating YouTube interviews and presentations which Peter Russell has recorded during the last decade. You really should watch them. You will be pleasantly surprised. After one presentation he was asked by a member of the audience about the Big Bang and he dismisses it as just some made-up concept and admits that we really have no idea what happened and how. It seems that he has gone along a very similar path to yourself. In one presentation he explains – very convincingly, to me – that consciousness must be a pre-existing condition before any appearance of what we perceive as physical matter could take place... and further, that physics have now conclusively demonstrated, that what we experience as solid matter is no such thing. But, he says, that whilst this can now be demonstrated, we – as a community living in this scientific age – are not prepared to take this seriously and are too afraid of the consequences of what he calls this mega-paradigm shift. All that is right up your street... :-) ...you must watch it. He is still giving talks and takes part in seminars organised by a group called 'Science and Non

Duality' (SAND). He says the only reality is *being* or 'aming' as he calls it, (derived from '*being: I am*'), and that instead of living in fear of what is coming towards us we should celebrate and rejoice in the fact that we are living in such an exciting time with such amazing opportunities... You can see that he got me quite excited!

Oh, and I did take down The horse and His Boy from the shelf and much enjoyed re-reading the passage to which you refer. I remembered exactly where it was – and anyway, the drawings help you find it; they are such lovely books these Narnia stories! But I'm not so sure about Trump and the 'Virus' being allies of our cause. Well, Trump maybe; he is such a strange phenomenon, and perhaps ruling elites will heed the warning he represents, though I doubt it. But this pandemic? When you consider the squabbling and in-fighting that is already going on about the supply of vaccination vials? Do you really think that the spirit of sharing in a common cause, which was evident at the outset, will prevail? I do oscillate so much between optimism and pessimism as far as the human condition is concerned. However, I do agree that this is a very good time to be having this conversation.

Anyway, don't you think it is time to get down to the nitty gritty and spell out how we think this next step in human evolution is going to come about? ...and what it will entail? Have we not done enough beating about the bush and flushed out enough of the relevant issues?

Come on Grandad – you are the 'wise one'!... :-)
Love you lots
Lanya

Chapter Six

SHARPENING THE FOCUS

08/02/2021

My dearest and cheeky Lanya!

Of course you are quite right: we have to stop beating about the bush – fun as that is – and get down to finding some real answers. But we have been honing the question – very important in any search – doing your re-search. There is no answer without a question; and the better the question, the more helpful the answer! Isn't it interesting though, that in scientific language we call it 're-search'? But no more diversions…! Shall I try to recap and summarise where we are with the honing of the question?

Yesterday, I wrote the following to my sister in Austria in an attempt to explain to her what you and I are doing. (I wrote in German and this is my translation):

'In essence, it is a question of clarifying and fully describing what the words 'The Next Evolutionary Step' (NESt) are truly intended to convey? What do I really have in mind when I use this phrase? What is the role of humankind in the evolutionary story of the earth? What is the task into which we humans are to grow, or for which we are being prepared, in order for us to fully play our intended part? – I say 'intended' because I cannot believe that we are fulfilling this role at the moment. And since the basic living conditions, not only for us humans, but for all living creatures on earth, are changing very fast, Lanya and I are trying to understand where all this is leading?...

'Aiming far too high' I hear you say... :-) ...but we can't help ourselves. The questions are there, in front of us: we have to stop shirking them and learn to confront them!'

This is what I wrote. Isn't that what we're about?

So what steps have we taken so far:

1) Astrologically, the globe is said to be transitioning into the 'Age of Aquarius', and we have learnt that he stands for qualities like free-spirited open-mindedness and egalitarian, humanitarian liberation. Wellness for all is thought to be the essence of the spirit of the coming age and this will be achieved through the harmonisation of the ego and the soul – the yin and the yang. Technology is expected to help. Space travel, the advent of the internet and artificial intelligence are thought to be early manifestations of the tools which are being placed at our disposal.

2) The research into astrology caused us to think about universal and global timescales which put the present era during which we are expecting this 'next evolutionary step' to happen, into a wide perspective, one in which the whole history of the human species is but a blink of a universal eye, (or is it 'I' ?). Our globe is but a speck of dust – (hopefully not the speck causing the irritation and that blink) – within one of uncounted numbers of galaxies. No cause to take ourselves too seriously then!... :-) ...?

3) You have suggested that our quest consists of going in search of a deep understanding of what would be necessary for us to cooperate with Mother Earth with a view to restoring health and equilibrium amongst her creatures; in other words, understanding what role we humans are expected to play in this

phase of our common journey towards the restoration of a balanced, thriving community of life?

4) I added to your definition of our quest, the search for a way of expanding the concept of evolution from being a physical adaptation to external conditions, to including the inner development of human consciousness and self-consciousness, as a critical next step, generated by ourselves on behalf of all life on earth.

5) We then started discussing various films and books which happened to have turned up, in order to help us in our search: Greta Thunberg on fearlessly calling it out as it is; Gerald Hüther on dignity and self-respect; Charlotte Bronte's *Professor* on trust, character and integrity; and especially, Peter Russell on nearly everything else we have been considering.

6) An interview with Mark Carney, recorded at Davos, thrust us back into the present, and face to face with your original question (your email of the fifth January): '...*trying to get to a place from which I see the good in our present situation... see a positive purpose in the hardships which I feel certain are to come... see a constructive direction of travel for the whole of life on earth...*'

7) This has brought us to the realisation that our fundamental problems arise from the disparity between the accelerating speed of technical innovation and our inability – in our present state of spiritual immaturity – to keep up and cope with the resultant responsibilities; and we came to realise that the matters which will hopefully be dealt with at the forthcoming COP26, essential as these are, will not tackle this disparity. Therefore, it is here that the outcome of our quest may make an important contribution.

Please add anything else you think should be included in this summary and let me know whether you think we are now ready to narrow the focus down to specifics and work towards an answer: a conclusive definition of the Next Evolutionary Step.

With much love
Grandpa

09/02/2021

Well, Grandpa, that's splendid!

I can't think of anything that I would want to add to that. But I do have one further comment and one further question:

Comment: During several conversations in the past, we have talked about the idea of seeing life on earth as a school for souls, and in your book My Path with Albert Schweitzer you write about this in some detail. I quote some of what you write there about it: '*This world into which we are born… is a school for something that might be called 'the soul'. Whatever else the function of this world may be, it is a place to which souls come in order to learn some specific things… In my view, souls are at different stages of maturity and have different learning schedules… Soul is present in all living creatures, from rocks to microbes, to elephants, to planets and stars… and is capable of crystallisation, also often referred to as growing in consciousness towards self-consciousness and finally to self-realisation.*' [pages 53/54; section no. B 106].

I have been thinking about how this view of life impacts upon what we are discussing here about the role we humans are expected to play in this phase of Earth's journey? Is there a contradiction here?

Question: What is it that we actually expect to find on this quest? Do we expect to come up with something that will transform people's behaviour? Something that will make us all unselfish, caring, empathetic, and generally 'good people'? If so, isn't that rather unrealistic? I think it would be helpful at this juncture to have some idea of what we are expecting to find, if only to ensure we stay within the bounds of what is possible and avoid disappointment, but also to help us recognise it, if we *do* find it.

Of course, I do realise that we are in a creative process in which we should engage without prejudging the outcome and be open to receiving the unexpected. I think it was me who said somewhere near the beginning of this journey that we *just have to trust our imagination*. But are we not also in danger of *tilting at windmills*?

As to where we go from here: I somehow still feel that the key issue lies hidden in the astrologer's phrase describing the essence of the age of Aquarius as *liberation resulting from the unification of ego and soul*. I would very much like to explore this further to see whether it would yield up its inner meaning to us. My instinct tells me that it might lead us to the threshold of the gate leading to our quest's destination.

Please excuse the flowery language. I've just been reading up on the phrase *tilting at windmills* and some of the flavour has spilled over into my thinking, so I had better call it a night... :-)

But I have a feeling we are getting close...

Big hug
Lanya

10/02/2021

My dear Lanya,

I hope you are keeping warm. We are having a fire burning in the snug all day to keep cosy in this taster of a real winter we are having just now… minus 10 degrees C is forecast for tonight! Mind you, I like this dry cold much better than the muggy dampness we have been having.

So – let me respond to your comment first:

Life on earth seen as a school for souls: is there a conflict between this view and the aims we are formulating for our quest?

This view of life here on earth – or indeed in the whole of the created universe – is one aspect of a much much larger picture of which I have only the merest inkling. However, that makes it no less real for me. I assume your comment is probing whether humankind messing things up here on Earth by its reckless behaviour affects the efficacy (such a popular word just now) of Mother Earth's ability to play her role of being a school. I would not have thought so. And indeed, in another part of the book from which you quote, I address this directly: on page 101, section no. B 410 I write:

'One aspect of the analogy which is particularly important but difficult to grasp, concerns the relationship of the pupils to the facilities of the school… The way in which the pupils treat the facilities – i.e. their environment – forms a major ingredient of all aspects of the curriculum. Learning to care for, appreciate, value and understand the facilities into which a pupil is placed, constitutes one of the basic lessons that have to be mastered…'

Therefore, as seen from the point of view of this school analogy, I would say that our quest is part of our attempt to master this part of our personal learning program. I would say –

in this context – that the extent to which we individually are able to set an example and actually influence the effect we as a species have on the school facilities, has now become a measure of how well we are doing at our *lessons*. How our massive failure as a species to master this lesson up to now will actually affect the school's ability to continue to function within this bigger picture is, I think, not for us to speculate. I would prefer to keep what you and I are up to here within the scope of us doing our homework.

And now to your question, Lanya: what are we actually hoping to find and are we tilting at windmills? Such a very real question!

If we were setting out – as it were single-handedly (or should I say double-handedly...?) to turn this whole mess around, solve all the problems, and by some magic formula turn everybody into saints, I think we would definitely be tilting at windmills. And not only that: within the school analogy discussed above, we would be setting out to deliberately jeopardise the efficacy of the school. But if we are trying to properly understand the real fundamental issues and allow that understanding to guide our actions and our behaviour within our own field of influence, I think we would be quite properly doing our homework, don't you think?

What we are hoping to find on this quest, I think, is understanding, with a view to allowing this to infuse our every action. But for action to be truly appropriate, it must spontaneously fit into the particular situation in which it takes place, and can therefore never be wholly predicted or prescribed. For there to be – what has been called – *right action*, it must come out of right understanding and that is what I think we are seeking.

Will that do?

If you agree, let's start examining what the *unification* – or I might prefer to say *harmonisation of ego and soul* might truly mean?

With so much love
Grandpa

Chapter Seven

FINAL PREPARATIONS

11/02/2021

Hello Grandpa,

Right then – let's look at these two fellows: *ego and soul,* and see what we know about them, what keeps them apart or at odds with each other, and what they have in common?

We have talked quite a bit about the soul during our conversation on the trip to the Midlands. I feel that for me it is important that we adhere as closely as we can to our own personal experience. Of course, we have to take note of what other people have written and said, and we can draw inspiration from that, but I feel, that for me, in the end, it will be what I can actually experience myself that will count towards my understanding and influence my actions.

So it is that day in the field, with the farmer, harvesting the wheat, that has left the strongest impression on me. On that day I felt connected to something I had not felt before, and I call that feeling the connection to my soul. In good moments I can remember it well enough to re-connect strongly with that feeling, at will. So let me take that as my 'soul connection'.

What then do I know about the ego?

Quite a lot, I suppose; although I just take it for granted and don't think about it much. It must be what I take to be myself most of the time. It is that which responds when my name is called. I used to think that it actually was my body, but I don't think that any longer. I have taught myself to think that I am not my body – it is an instrument for my use. Now I would say that it is the ego which worries about what my body looks like and whether people like it or not? My ego obviously wants to be thought of as clever and attractive and wants to be liked by others. But it often worries me that it is none of these things and that it is alone and cut off from the rest of the world and even that the world is against it and that it has to fight for its rights and not allow itself to be trampled on by others. But as long as others like it, and they think I am clever – it is happy.

That's what I would say about my ego. I can observe in others that their ego may need power or wealth or any number of other things to feel happy. I expect there are as many different egos as there are people. But one common, basic attribute of the ego seems to be, that it wants things in order to feel happy. One of its basic functions – it seems to me is self-protection – looking after the interests of number one. And in a world fraught with danger and competition, that is a very important function, is it not? However, the question now arises: how large is the circle drawn around that number one? The larger and more inclusive the circle, perhaps, the more synergy between ego and soul – do you think?

So what keeps these two apart?

Now that I think about it, I wonder whether that is the right way of looking at it? I suppose, the reason why I am thinking about what separates them is because we are talking about the unification of ego and soul. But it feels more like a question of domination rather than separation. Which one attracts all the attention? Which one dominates the situation and influences the decision-making process? And as you said, perhaps *harmonisation* is a better word to use than unification?

Also, I must say that I have difficulty with equating the ego – soul relationship with that of yin and yang, as the astrological website does. The ideal yin – yang relationship for me, is one of intimate equilibrium and balance – as between the sexes. Whilst I visualise the ideal ego – soul relationship as being one of servant and master.

In this context the problem could be expressed in terms of the ego usurping the role of master and pushing the soul into a subservient position. In fact, in my experience of this relationship, it is the ego that wins out most of the time. But to be fair, it is the ego that has received nearly all the attention in my upbringing. It has been encouraged, supported and nurtured by nearly everything that has happened to me since I was a very small child. Whatever activity I was engaged in – as far back as I can remember – I was encouraged to compete against everyone else around me: to be the best; to come first; to be the prettiest; to win out over all others; to be assertive; to aspire to have the most... the list is endless.

To be honest, the times I can remember receiving encouragement towards the feeling I had that day in the field of wheat are very few and far between. Occasionally I felt that something similar was at play in fairytales – perhaps that is why I used to be so interested in fairies – and some children's books – like the Narnia Stories – had some of that quality; and of course music had it; and especially, when I was dancing I felt it most strongly. Sometimes, when walking in nature, especially in the mountains, there was a similar feeling in the air, but never before was the experience as vivid as in that field. And, of course, our conversation on the train to Vienna and back, and some of our other conversations had a very similar quality about them. On these occasions, basically, the ego just recedes into the background. It is still there but just not so prominently; it is not so important; not so dominant. I suppose, it doesn't feel threatened, but feels secure and can relax.

And finally: what might the two have in common that would contribute to their unity?

They are, of course, both part of what I really *am* – part of my *aming* as Russell would say. And thinking about it just now, it doesn't seem to be so much a question of unity between them as of equity. It would seem to be a question of finding the appropriate balance; each in its proper place, don't you think, Grandpa? Normally, the ego is getting all the attention and the soul is not getting nearly enough. Isn't it a shift of emphasis that is required, and an acknowledgement that they are both part of something much bigger? Perhaps, if that awareness of being part of a bigger entity could become more permanent, that would remove the competition between them and eliminate the either/or syndrome – once and for all?

What do you think? Am I anywhere near what the astrologers have in mind? Or, more importantly what we are looking for?

Do please reply soon, because I feel I'm really into this now!

Big Hugs
Lanya

11/02/2021

Well Lanya,
What a start to our quest proper…?

I have also, these last few days, been trying to leave other people's thoughts about all this behind me, and search within myself for a framework which might help me to come to grips with our questions. And – you know me: after a lifetime of architectural thinking about three-dimensional form in space... a diagram began to construct itself in my mind – a model or framework that might help us to navigate within our 'inner landscape'. To be more precise: when I woke up a couple of mornings ago – there it was, in my mind – clear as anything! If we were now sitting on a bench together, I would draw it for you, but I'm sure you'll be able to visualise it from my description. It is very simple.

You will need six sticks of equal length and a flat wooden board a bit longer and wider than the sticks – in your imagination of course:

You start by laying down one stick near the bottom of the board. At the left end of this stick you attach a label which says EGO.

At the other end you attach a label saying SOUL.

For future reference I will call the ego-end – *end 1*, and the soul-end – *end 2*.

At this one-dimensional – linear – stage of the construction, ego and soul oppose each other and vie for attention, as you have described so beautifully. You are either looking at one or the other, and they seem to pull in opposite directions. That is the state in which most of us find ourselves most of the time. Many reside predominantly – some exclusively – at the left end, – *end 1* – and rarely ever venture towards *end 2*. *End 2* of course is there all the time, though rather neglected. Scientists have told us that our brains have a left and a right side and that each side has its particular function and emphasis. From what we are told about these functions, they seem to me to be not dissimilar to the two ends of the stick I am describing.

Now, some people, often at a point in their lives when they least expect it – have an experience similar to the one in your lovely description of harvesting with the farmer in his field of wheat. In the model I am describing, this would be a trip to *end 2* of the stick. Because it is often very beautiful there, as you so eloquently describe – this experience develops a taste for more. Thus, these people begin to seek out opportunities to go there more and more often. Gradually, they become more familiar with what goes on at *end 2* of the stick and they also begin, at certain moments, to experience a vague feeling – just an inkling at first – that there actually is an awareness inside themselves which can see both ends of the stick at the same time, and even seems to be able to be at both ends simultaneously – which you also describe. At this stage these are occasional vague feelings. But gradually it dawns on them that this awareness may indeed be who they really are, and that when they are at *end 2* of the stick they can actually feel that awareness quite strongly and they begin to feel at home, experiencing that awareness as their new self – often referred to as their second birth, or being re-born.

Thus, an interest in the nature of this new self develops, and a desire grows to explore that nature more thoroughly. For the sake of our conversation I shall from now on call this self '*you*'.

So *you* now take the next step in the construction of my model. *You* take another stick and place it carefully on the board, so that its right end touches *end 2* of your first stick and its left end is located near the top of the board exactly above the middle of the first stick. Now you write the word OVERSOUL on a label and attach it to this new point which we will call *end 3*. (People have used the term oversoul in various ways; it will become clear what I mean by it).

Something quite momentous has now happened, because we have moved from a one-dimensional world into a two-dimensional one, which is quite a breathtaking step. By taking this step towards *end 3* you are moving into an entirely new dimension – the second dimension. Having done this once or twice and become familiar with that experience, you can now look from *end 3* at the first stick and clearly see both of its ends at the same time. From this vantage point you can see that both *end 1* and *end 2* have different and complementary rolls to play in your life, but that neither of them are the real you.

Now, to continue with the construction of our diagram or model, you take another stick and place it so as to connect *end 3* directly to *end 1*. You have now created an equilateral triangle which is completely in balance with itself within the realm of two dimensions. And you now begin to live your life from *end 3*. As you had already learnt that you are not your body, so you now see that you are also not what you thought was your soul, nor your ego. You see that *end 2* is all about your emotions and feelings and memories and experiences of beauty and friendship and love, but you are now able to observe all these experiences and feelings from another place which we have called *oversoul*.

After a while, when you have become quite comfortable and feel at home in this second dimension, you begin to gradually realise that you are part of something yet much bigger. At first this is again just a vague and elusive feeling which sometimes comes over you in sudden moments of heightened lucidity when a very special quality of light surrounds you. And in those moments, you are also vaguely aware that in that light you are connected to every other living being that is within the realm of your consciousness. You feel a great sharing in which all sense of loneliness and separation disappears. Then, one day, this light will feel unusually bright and you find yourself receiving it with open arms, looking up, and opening yourself to yet another new dimension – the third dimension!

You will now take the remaining three sticks and place one end of each on each of the three corners of the triangle we already have. Then very carefully you bring their other ends together exactly over the middle of that triangle and you hold them together with a little pointed hat on which you write the word SPIRIT and we shall call this *end 4*.

This is huge! You have now created three further equilateral triangles in the third dimension. Leaving the two-dimensional world below you, you have created space and entered the three-dimensional realm in which our lives play out their allotted time, though few are fully conscious of it. The resulting form is called a tetrahedron, which is the simplest of the five Platonic solids, of which only five are possible in a three-dimensional world. The ancient Greeks associated this with the element of fire and with energy, light and vision.

You now have a glimpse of the world of spirit. Standing at *end 3*, where you had thought you had found your true identity, your awareness has opened up to yet another entirely new world – the world of spirit. But here you find that you cannot go straight up to *end 4*. The sticks here are on a steep incline and they are hard to climb. Many lessons are to be learnt and skills to be mastered. It is a climb which requires much application, patience and endurance to make even slow progress towards the top. I myself cannot speak with personal experience of what it is like up there at *end 4*. I am still climbing. Only very few human individuals, during millennia of history, have left legacies indicating that they had reached the top and what it was like there.

Some are known to us, because their advice has been handed down – albeit in somewhat distorted fragments – in the religious movements which have been inspired by them. You know their names.

This then is the model which was there when I woke up the other morning. You can see that within its context, the concepts of ego and soul are not fixed but can change quite considerably depending on where you are standing. Obviously, this model is nearly as new to me as it is to you. Whilst I saw the form of the tetrahedron early that morning in my imagination, and knew it was connected to our quest, the actual description of its construction has evolved just now, as I was writing this. So as to its interpretation and application we are both as 'green' as each other (in the green-horn sense).

But we can already appreciate, that if you climb but a little way towards *end 4*, as I believe you surely will, you can see that everything becomes quite naturally more and more connected and that separations begin to fall away.

One advantage of this diagram over others I have seen, is, that it keeps the spiritual world fully grounded in our three-dimensional reality and does not export it to some other-worldly heaven. It is here, in this space-time continuum that we can experience and share in the world of SPIRIT.

I wonder what you think about all this?

Anyway, let me know how you get on with it. As I say: it's nearly as new to me as it is to you, so don't hold back. We need to get to grips with this together and see whether it helps us to move towards a conclusion.

Hoping you are managing to keep warm in this cold spell, and that you are not yet running out of patience with this Corona predicament – I get the sense that some people are getting near to breaking point…

With lots of love
Grandpa

13/02/2021

Good Evening Grandpa,

Yes, I'm nice and snug in our little flat. Luckily, life at the bakery is again in full swing, so I'm not nearly as badly affected by the pandemic as some. And when I'm at home I have drawing projects to keep me occupied, when you and our quest are not distracting me… :-) …and, boy, was Thursday's email a distraction! That's going to take some figuring out! I think by my third reading I did get the picture about right, in my mind. And it's true – it's simple enough to visualise once you have got it mentally set up. And once I have got the analogy straightened out, it will be a splendid aide memoire and reference model.

I'm not even going to begin to comment on the model itself. It is obviously an inspired insight and we need to test it by working with it to see where it takes us.

But I have a suggestion which might be a slight improvement: I visualised the sticks to be bamboo-sticks like the ones we use in the garden, and more or less straight away those rubber balls came to mind which one can buy to connect bamboo sticks to make up frameworks for garden netting. Could we visualise using these to connect the ends of our sticks, with predrilled holes at sixty degree angles to each other to receive the sticks as our tetrahedron builds. And could we call the corners *nodes* rather than ends, so that they conjure up locations where things can happen. Thus we would have *node 1*, *node 2* etc. These nodes would already contain within themselves the imprint – in the form of the holes – of the future direction in which the construction proceeds. What do you think?

Now let me see whether I can fit the pieces of information, or attributes, about the ego and the soul, which we have already gathered in our discussion so far, into this model, and whether I have therefore understood you correctly.

For instance, I suppose that all I say about the ego in my email of the 11th February takes place at *node 1*, whilst what we have said about the soul so far takes place at *node 2*. So that all of this discussion and our thoughts about the ego and the soul being separate entities which are in need of harmonising with each other during the age of Aquarius applies to the realm of one-dimensional thinking. When I then question whether that is the right way of thinking about this, I am presumably beginning to move into the second dimension.

You will remember that on our trip to the Midlands, when we explored the meaning of soul, you explained that there are four identifiable worlds: the physical or gross; the energetic or subtle; the creative or causal; and the eternal, infinite or spiritual. Presumably, these four worlds correspond to the four nodes in this diagram.

And in the Hindu terminology of Advaita, which you also explained at that time, Manas, which you called the office boy, or the ordinary, perpetual chatter in our heads, and who is also referred to as 'the messenger' would straddle *nodes 1* and *2*, but remains within the first dimension. But Buddhi – the creative mind, Citta – the space for memory, insight and understanding, and Ahamkara – the feeling of 'I' or ego, all belong to the realm of the second dimension and to *node 3*. If this is right, then I find it interesting, that for Hindus, the ego as the feeling of 'I' persists all the way through the second dimension, but presumably in a more rarified form.

Do you think there is a way of fitting what are normally referred to as the various kingdoms of the natural world into this model? As for instance: the mineral, microbial and plant kingdoms being at *node 1*; the animal kingdom, including humankind at *node 2*; a kingdom as yet un-named and still at an embryonic stage, at *node 3*. Maybe first inklings of this are starting to emerge with the Age of Aquarius and with what you call the next evolutionary step; and a kingdom of higher intelligences of which we know practically nothing as yet – at *node 4*?

I think it is salutary, but to my mind quite right, that in this analogy most of what we have been talking about feels as if it has been within the realm of the first dimension, between *nodes 1* and *2*, with just a few glimpses into the second dimension. If this is indeed so, then the threshold at which we are standing with the intention of taking the 'Next Evolutionary Step' is much lower in the hierarchy than I had imagined and therefore much more likely to be doable, much less fantastical! Don't you think? Less ambitious and more achievable!

Whilst my husband and I were talking at breakfast this morning about the COVID vaccinations, and the 'stuff' we are all allowing to be pumped into our bodies with very little idea of what it does to us… there appeared the image in my mind of the vast majority of the human population being affected first by the virus and then by the vaccinations; and I suddenly saw this in the context of your idea of Aslan chasing us! – Stampeding us into a certain direction! And – if this is possible with chemicals and viruses, should it not also be possible with a shift in consciousness – an explosion of awareness as implied by the idea of NESt?...Don't they talk about certain images or tweets going viral?... why not something that actually affects our awareness in a positive way?

Do you think I have understood your model as intended, and am I interpreting and applying it in the right way? I think we have got something very useful and helpful here, and your muse, inspiring you in the early hours, is due a big vote of thanks!

Any news about your second jab? I can't wait to talk all this over face to face... :-)

Lots of love
Lanya

14/02/2021

Hello Lanya on Valentine's Day!

Sorry that I haven't sent you a card. I have actually only ever sent one Valentine's Card. I asked your mother to post it for me to my wife. Its arrival at our home then induced your grandmother to reveal all the men from whom she hoped/guessed that it might have been sent. It was interesting, but I've never sent another card since... :-)

Back to work!

What you say certainly makes me feel that you are reading the model as it is intended, and your idea about the rubber balls at the corners, and calling them nodes is brilliant! I was struggling with how to visualise these and your suggestion does it perfectly.

The way you fit the four identifiable worlds of our previous conversations into the image is a little more complicated, I think, as is the integration of the Advaita terminology.

I think the model or diagram applies to the world of thought, i.e. the subtle, energetic world.

The gross, material world – refers to the realm of physical objects. The ego at *node 1* however, is not a physical object, but a mental concept. You are right though, to the extent that at *node 1* the feeling of 'I' – which we call the ego – is fully identified with the physical body. It thinks it is the physical body and it thinks that everything that exists is physical in the sense that it can be weighed and measured. You and I think that this is a deluded way of seeing things, but nevertheless, for many, that is the reality in which they think they live.

The roll that Advaita assigns to Manas, if I remember it correctly, would indeed extend somewhat into the second dimension and, in some interpretations, the feeling of 'I' – the ego seen as Ahamkara – would survive right through to *node 3*. But there are many subtly different interpretations even within India, let alone by us over here. We Westerners seem to think that we can confine the ego to the first dimension. Those of us who think about this at all, tend to demonise the ego and think that by getting rid of it, all its destructive influences can be made to disappear, and all will be well. But in my view we are all deluding ourselves on this, and such an attempt is doomed, because we fail to recognise the essential function the ego has and the valuable contribution it makes to our growth and development. Therefore, in practice, this way of trying to deal with it goes horribly wrong.

The East sees the ego – I think rightly – as persisting all the way through the second dimension right up to the threshold of the third. Beyond this however, it cannot survive and falls away quite naturally. The East, on the other hand, with its concept of Maya, demonises the whole of the second dimension along with the first, calling all of it a delusion. By rejecting and denying the reality of the whole of that part of creation – calling it a mirage – they imply that all of it can be left behind and we can escape from it. I think this is an equally false premise. I would interpret our diagram to indicate that, when our awareness starts to open up to the third dimension, and we start the ascent towards *node 4*, the first and second dimensions are seen correctly for what they are and lose their grip on our attention quite naturally without having to be demonised or rejected.

I really like your attempt to fit the notion of 'kingdoms' within nature into our model, especially your quite original idea of a yet unnamed kingdom at *node 3*, and your inspirational idea of a 'kingdom of higher intelligences' at *node 4*, of which we know practically nothing. It prompted my mind to expand the model a step further: the tetrahedron can be inscribed into a sphere, which can represent a fourth dimension in which the notions of infinity and eternity hold sway, uniting the four nodes without actually creating a fifth node, but still implying a yet further state of Being which pervades all the other dimensions via the space in which they have their existence.

I like that a lot and thank you heartily for it! I think it completes the model nicely.

Finally, I thank you also for pointing out, that within this model our postulated evolutionary next step will occur far closer to our normal everyday level of existence than it had appeared to us up to now, and is therefore more accessible.

As you say, we have created a context in which this next step is not quite so implausible, and the current goings-on with this pandemic are showing us that happenings, which affect the whole of the human race, are already an undeniable reality and that there is no reason why we should not contemplate such happenings being instigated for positive evolutionary purposes.

You ask about our second vaccination: no news as yet – but it can't be that far off now. They are doing so well with these vaccinations and we should hear more of the government's immediate plans for the next period in one week's time.

Big virtual hugs – soon to be converted and cashed in for real!

Grandpa

15/02/2021

Hello Grandpa,

Right! We seem to be on the same page. So how does this lead us to a conclusion of our quest?

I think we can agree that my question about '*what role we humans are expected to play in this phase of Earth's journey, in order to re-establish a balanced, thriving community of life*' and your NESt Initiative have the same aim in mind.

And I think we have established that bringing ego and soul into their rightful relationship, is going to be the way of unlocking the gate to the path which leads towards our aim. And we also now have an image of a framework within which this rightful relationship between ego and soul can be seen, at least theoretically, not only in their relationship to each other but also within a much larger picture of the created world in which we find ourselves.

Our rucksacks are packed; our walking boots are ready; all we need now is the map which will show us the way: and we're off!

Let's draw this map.

You are the architect. I think you have got to set out the grid and the overall framework. I am getting to be quite good at drawing cartoons, so I will be able to illustrate the odd corner here and there.

How about it Grandpa – let's go!

Chapter Eight

AT THE THRESHOLD

17/02/2021

Oh – the impetuosity of youth!

During a telephone conversation with my sister in Austria yesterday, I was reminded of something that might help us at this point: *self-remembering*.

Many many years ago, I attended group sessions at a school of philosophy where the term SELF-REMEMBERING was written large as a key ingredient of every practice that was taught. It was based on the premise that at our arrival here on earth – at this school for souls – we forget who we really are. It is therefore a central part of the curriculum to learn and practice remembering – to remember at all times who it is that has come here and will leave again at the end of our stay! And along with all kinds of other tools which are placed at our disposal, we are given a feeling of 'I' – the ego – in order to help us to see clearly all that we are NOT.

This self-remembering could be our lamp to help us read our map and see our path ahead. The three wise men who arrived at Bethlehem at Christmas time had a star which they followed. Let this be our bright star lighting our way.

Let me tell you a little story from the East, which is told for those who are in danger of being over-awed by the enormity of the task ahead of them – it is quite short:

It is late at night. Ahmed, a man in a mountain village, gets a message to urgently visit a friend many miles away over treacherous terrain. It is a matter of life and death; he must leave immediately. But it is pitch dark and Ahmed only has a small lantern which casts its little light barely a few yards ahead of him. He stands in front of his house, afraid, hesitating, thinking of the long path ahead and not knowing how he will find his way. As he stands there, a wise man happens to be passing. Seeing Ahmed's hesitation, he enquires after his problem. Ahmed tells him that he has to go a long way and that he must start right away, in the dark, but his little lamp is not up to the task. How is he to find his way?

The wise man pats him on the shoulder and tells him to be of good cheer. "Because the little lantern will be travelling with you," he says, "It will always be throwing light on the few yards of path just ahead of you, enabling you to take the next few steps in safety. And before too long, the sun will rise and you will see your path clearly for a long way ahead and you will reach your destination in good time." And so it did indeed prove to be.

I have to admit, Lanya, that for the last few days I have felt rather like Ahmed: hesitating, fearful that all this 'quest' of ours is leading us nowhere. I felt unable to see even a few yards ahead, let alone draw a whole map of the 'way'; unable to even focus properly on the question. Every time I tried, which was nearly all the time, it seemed quite impossible that we would ever be able to come up with a scenario that would wake up a majority of the human population to remember who they really are, and consciously merge their ego into its rightful relationship with their soul, starting to live in tune with the needs of 'Mother Earth'... how?... Is it not a hubristic pipe-dream?

Then, last night, I woke up at three thirty in the morning –

which by the way, is not at all unusual – and I started walking up and down our hallway, as I often do. And there, all of a sudden, was the 'wise man' whispering in my ear, saying, "This evolution you have in mind is already well under way! It had already started before you were born; Albert Schweitzer, Manfred Kyber and Peter Russell, amongst many others, were its heralds. What your son is doing within the company he now works with is amongst today's evidence of it. What Lanya is doing in her bakery is evidence of it. What you did during your career in architecture is evidence of it. There are boardrooms all over the globe where preparations are being made for it. Must I remind you of the difference between re-volution and e-volution. The revolutions of past centuries set out to destroy the then current forms and structures in the hope that something new and better would suddenly emerge. As we now know, they begot more of the same, only worse.

"But this evolution, which is already under way, is quietly constructing new forms and ways of doing things within the old frameworks – in small ways to start with here and there, without having to destroy anything and without a huge fanfare or upheaval. The success of its methods will be seen and followed by others and the old forms will fall away and be superseded."

I was stunned and elated, as you can imagine. This is a totally new way of looking at this for me. What we are searching for has already started – is already well under way! We just need to recognise it for what it is. It's just a case of getting on board! I went back to bed and slept like a log.

And I think now I am ready for the 'off'… :-)

How about you? Can you buy into this new view of things? We haven't looked at it like this before.

What an adventure we're on!

Looking forward to your response.
Love and hugs
Grandpa

19/02/2021

Whaou, Grandpa, now you're talking!

What your wise man was whispering in your ear at four o'clock in the morning is music to my ears! It makes total sense to me. I was wondering how we were going to make any real headway when I threw down the gauntlet – yet again – a few days ago. But now I can see an uninhibited sprint to the end of our quest straight in front of us.

I am thinking of what is happening in the motor vehicle industry, for instance. Just yesterday we heard on the news that Jaguar are planning to go all-electric in the next few years. It caused me to google the subject. Apparently at least fifty brands are already selling all electric cars, and by 2030 the sale of all new petrol and diesel cars will be banned – so they say. Of course, they've been talking about this for several decades, and how worried were we that it would never happen? But once the penny drops, so to speak, and they see that it is actually happening, the entrepreneurs can't switch over fast enough.

I'm not saying that switching to electric cars is such a significantly important step. Of course in terms of CO_2 output it will be, but in other areas it will cause other problems. However, as an example of how global change can take place and at what speed, is it not a salutary indicator of what could very well apply to the things *we* are talking about?

Incidentally, who is Manfred Kyber, who suddenly turns up between Schweitzer and Russell in your nocturnal revelation?

So how are we going to proceed? What about us taking it in turns to describe an aspect of our culture and society in which we can see signs of this 'evolution' already being under way? And you could start with 'animal welfare', I would suggest – knowing how close that is to your heart, what with Schweitzer's 'Reverence for Life' and all that? And that will give me time to think about which subject or 'theme' I will tackle first.

How about it?

Wasn't it lovely to have some sunshine today - at last - though the wind is still chilly… :-)

Love you lots
Lanya

19/02/2021

OK – little bossy-boots… :-)

It's a perfect plan for our finale, and I'm very happy to start with animal welfare, which is indeed close to my heart – as you say.

But first let me tell you about Manfred Kyber, who did seem to 'slip in' unannounced. He is someone for whom I have a great regard.

I first came across him many years ago, when I was given a copy of what I think is his only full-scale novel: '*The Three Candles of Little Veronica – A Story of a Child's Soul in This World and the Other*'; (published in English by Florisbooks). It is said to be for teenage children, but there is plenty in it for adults

– as I found out when I recently re-read it. If you haven't read it yet, I can thoroughly recommend it in the context of what we are talking about.

Kyber was born in 1880 in Riga, the capital of Latvia, north-east of Poland. He regarded himself as a product of the 'East' but ended up in Germany and wrote mostly in German. He made his name as a writer of animal stories, myths and fairy tales, and became a leading light of the animal welfare movement in Germany between the wars. But I came to love him especially because of a little booklet of poems, which I found here at the Cottage – left by the previous owners – as well as a little book which I ordered for myself just a few years ago called *'Neues Menschsein – Betrachtungen in zwölfter Stunde'* (A New Humanity – Reflections in the Twelfth Hour). The poems for me are a lantern like no other I know for illuminating the climb from *node 3* to *node 4* in our model. Alas, they are in German and are, I suspect, untranslatable. The *'Reflections in the Twelfth Hour'* is an amazing essay, written in the 1920s, looking at society and humankind as a whole against the background of a premonition of imminent catastrophe – hence the *twelfth hour*. He sees humankind – but particularly Western civilisation – faced with the challenge of: *evolve or disappear*! – Yes, already then, in the years between the Wars! You can imagine how that went down with me? I still can't get over the fact that this was written a century ago. It is actually such strong confirmation of what *my wise visitor* of the early morning hours whispered into my ear! I don't think it has been translated into English and I have often thought that this is something I have yet to accomplish. Who knows… I'll translate a few extracts from the first chapter for you here, to give you a flavour, starting at the very beginning:

'What is said here is for the few or the many, who would still

like to be truly human. And it is said in the twelfth hour. The world, especially Europe, is faced with decisions which mean evolution or demise and destruction... Many people today harbour the vague longing for an existence which is more worthy of humanity and more dignified than a civilisation of technology and capital... The undoing of European society lies in the inhumanity of its thought, resulting in this situation, in which capital and technology and all the powers of materialism have enslaved us and have led us to the edge of the abyss which we now face... The basic errors of Western civilisation are on the one hand, blind and nearly total materialism, and on the other, estrangement from nature. When I speak of Western society, I mean the Europeans and the Americans as well as the globally scattered groups which have been infected by these Western thought-structures... This inhumanity is far from the work of spirit and far from nature, far from being truly human and from the animal world. It is intellect without feeling and spirit; speculation without intuition; an ego without spirituality... materialism... is a corruption of thought; the other – the estrangement from nature – is a corruption of feeling and emotion...'

You get the drift? Does it not chime amazingly with what we are talking about? I will have to translate the whole book when we have concluded this quest of ours.

And I have just seen – a little further on in this book – that there could hardly be a better introduction to the subject of **'animal welfare'** than this next passage (on page 22). So I shall continue to translate a little further:

'*...We Westerners take the assumption for granted that we have to feed ourselves by eating animal corpses, and our materialistic scientists are busy supporting this myth although* *this theory has long been disproved... Even assuming it were impossible to live without eating meat, how can we find this slaughterhouse culture acceptable, with its horribly cruel transportation and killing mechanisms perpetrated on millions of feeling creatures every day? And not only this. Nature has suffered our profligate and ruthless exploitation: whole species of animals have been exterminated; millions of creatures are caught in agonisingly painful traps to be clubbed to death in order to sell their fur... into an insatiable marketplace; countless highly evolved animals are tortured for pseudo-scientific reasons in vivisection-laboratories;... the most horrendous hunting practices go unabated;... in Spain and South America bullfights are vigorously applauded;... draught-animals are cruelly abused not only in less developed countries, but also in those claiming to be at the forefront of civilisation in Europe. For citizens in the 'West', animals are just objects because they no longer feel themselves as part of nature... and they think that all of it exists purely to satisfy their exploitative purposes. The state says nothing to all that cruelty... neither do schools, nor the church... only humans are seen as having any rights... Every individual, who has preserved a modicum of uninhibited thinking, has to agree, that something here is not right, that this constitutes a terrible disturbance of our moral balance which must destabilise our world today...'*

Strong stuff! – written all those years ago! The little book of 116 pages was first published in 1931, eight years after Albert Schweitzer's first two volumes of his Philosophy of Civilisation, in which he first presents his ethical vision of 'Reverence for Life' (Ehrfurcht vor dem Leben), but I have not found any indication that the two men ever met or even knew of each other. Yet they express such very similar views.

There is clear evidence here that on the subject of animal welfare strong clarion-calls for an evolutionary step went out well over a century ago.

In the following summary on this subject, I will confine myself broadly to Central Europe and in particular to the UK. There are of course wide variations in different parts of the world.

In Europe it was St Francis of Assisi, a mystic Italian Catholic friar, who, in the early 1200s cultivated a close and loving relationship with the world of creatures, pronouncing himself a brother to the animals and birds around him. Though founder of the still important order of St Francis and canonised in 1228 – only two years after his death – his attitude towards animals did not seem to have had much influence either on the Church or on the population at large, because in the early 1600s the influential French philosopher Rene Descartes (1596 – 1650), a devout defender of the Catholic faith, declared that animals had no soul, no feelings and were insensitive to pain.

In 1915, Albert Schweitzer, struggling with the whole question of ethics in his time, had his inspirational realisation, leading to his philosophy of Reverence for all Life, in which he expanded the parameters of ethical behaviour to include the treatment of animals. My translation from Kyber's booklet (above) gives a vivid impression of how things stood in the 1920s which caused Kyber and some friends to launch a vigorous animal welfare campaign in Germany.

Things, however, were not quite so bleak in the UK, where the RSPCA (Royal Society for the Prevention of Cruelty to Animals) was founded in 1824, the RSPB (Royal Society for the Protection of Birds) in 1889 and the Blue Cross in 1897. The latter aims to provide support for pet owners who cannot afford private veterinary treatment, helps to find homes for unwanted animals and educates the public in the responsibilities of animal ownership. This shows that hand in hand with the abolition of slavery in parts of the British Empire in the 1830s, the feelings of empathy which had brought that campaign to fruition expanded to include the animal world, at least in some sections of society, during the second half of the 19th century.

This, however, was not enough to prevent the horrendous cruelties and insults to animal dignity, resulting from the proliferation of industrialised food production and increased meat consumption during the second half of the 20th century, leading to the destruction of habitats and the decimation of numbers of all kinds of wildlife and even an escalation of extinctions.

This has now, by the beginning of the third decade of the 21st century, been met by an upsurge of public protest and an increasing commitment to preventative and remedial action. Google lists thirty-nine animal welfare organisations in the UK alone and who knows how many rescue centres, small research initiatives and animal charities are not included in that list. Public awareness of the dysfunctional relationship of the human species to the rest of the natural world has expanded exponentially during the first decades of this millennium. This is in part due to the broadening of interest amongst wildlife photographers to go beyond the previous two obsession: predators' hunting exploits and sexual rivalry, to now include the full range of animal behaviours and relationships. With their films and programs having become a significant proportion of available television viewing, supported in no small measure by the hugely popular and influential work of David Attenborough, and with the exposure on television and other media of some of the worst excesses in cruelty perpetrated by the farming and slaughtering of beef, chickens pigs and salmon, the general public is much better informed than ever before, resulting in more engagement in both protesting against these atrocities and supporting preventative action.

The widespread global public support for recent arrivals on the scene such as Extinction Rebellion and Animal Rebellion is evidence of this. But of no less significance is the invaluable but less conspicuous work of charities like the Durrell Wildlife Conservation Trust, the Born Free Foundation, and countless other charities, who work tirelessly and with great skill and care to combat the numerous threats, including poaching and trophy hunting, to which the ever-shrinking areas of wild habitats left on this globe are exposed.

To what extent is any of the above evidence of a step forward in the evolutionary process of the human species?

I do think that there is real evidence of a genuine desire in a growing proportion of the population, for a more harmonious relationship between our species and the whole of nature. Calls for human needs to be more respectfully re-integrated into the overall workings of nature are widely and increasingly acknowledged. If that growth is sustained, it would, in my view, unquestionably constitute an evolutionary step forward. As I believe the most essential role we humans are here to play on this earth is to help bring conscious awareness into created form, we are not only looking to cultivate such awareness within ourselves, but also to encourage this in other creatures through our relationship with them. Careful observation of communication between domestic animals such as cats, dogs and horses with their owners, demonstrates how this works. From January 2020, in England and in seventeen other countries, the use of wild animals in circuses is banned; there is growing support for the abolition of all blood sports; there is considerable interest and research into the high levels of intelligence observable in whales and dolphins, amongst others; vegetarianism and veganism are expanding exponentially and ever more evidence is coming to light and finding support, that animal experiments are neither necessary nor desirable for medical and cosmetic research. All these are surely evidence that a new empathetic relationship between the human and animal kingdoms is gathering pace – even though it still has a long way to go.

With regard to the wider, more general environmental movement, I'm not so sure. I would say that, although a vast majority are now finally convinced that there is a serious issue to consider, and that something has to be done to avert calamity, really effective action on a meaningful scale has yet to gather momentum. Where there are signs of small beginnings, they are driven by fear of what might happen to us humans and to our accustomed lifestyle, rather than a recognition that we ourselves need to change inwardly – need to reorientate our inner stance towards our surroundings and to what we want to take from and give back to life.

On the other hand, the fact that the book '*A New Earth*' by Eckhart Tolle is a global best seller, – to give but one example of many – and that the shelves in bookshops – and online – are full of books on spiritual renewal and human development, surely means that a significant start in this field is also under way and that many people are open to the possibility of a fundamental reprioritising of their primary purposes.

What do you think, Lanya? Have I convinced you that in the field of animal welfare and even in the sphere of a spiritual awakening, a step across an evolutionary threshold is under way?

Did you listen to the PM today, announcing the roadmap to

our irreversible COVID-recovery? It seems as if – in this, at least – the precautionary principle has won through. Is there hope that this might leak out into other spheres as well, do you think?

Now *I* can say: Over to you...! Have you chosen your subject yet?

Big hugs...
Grandpa

24/02/2021

Yes Grandpa, I've chosen my subject.

I want to write about **FOOD**, because it follows on nicely from your animal welfare. But you have set the bar pretty high and I'll be hard pressed to follow that. Never mind – here goes... :-)

You may ask, "What has food got to do with the next step in human evolution?"

Then I would reply, "That you will see how the production, transport, marketing and consumption of food, and the disposal of the associated waste is highly indicative of our relationship to nature and the planet, and of our inability to manage our common household sustainably. It is responsible for many of the problems we are having to deal with and these will only get worse as more and more of us, globally, will live in mega-cities in the vain hope of raising standards of living."

So, let me deal with these five aspects of the industrial food mechanism in the order in which I have just listed them at the beginning of the previous sentence:

FOOD PRODUCTION

Within your and your parents' lifespan, food production in Europe, America and what we call the *developed* countries has moved from being a life-style for families and village communities, to being a predominantly industrial, commercialised industry in the hands of a small number of global corporations. In what we call the *developing* nations, those in power are trying to cajole their populations to play catch-up in this game.

The trump cards in the game are: i) consolidation of land holdings; ii) specialisation into monocultures; iii) mechanisation of work-processes; iv) chemical fertilisation and pest control; v) global marketing strategies, and vi) industrial food processing.

The claimed benefits are: i) the release of large numbers of the population from agriculture into the industrial labour market in huge cities; ii) temporarily increased production per hectare; iii) cheaper food, releasing more purchasing power for manufactured products; iv) larger quantities of food, supporting the increased populations; and v) huge profits for a small number of people.

The unintended but unavoidable losers in the game are: i) long term loss of soil fertility and erosion of topsoil; ii) loss of wildlife habitat replaced by vast areas of monoculture, causing widespread extinction of species and resulting in the decimation of insect life; iii) the creation of shanty-towns and slums for a landless, jobless, migratory population; iv) reliance on expensive, oil-powered machinery; v) pollution of the land, waterways and oceans with poisonous chemicals; vi) cheap, processed food causing obesity and health deterioration in the general population; vii) separation and alienation from nature for large sectors of the population.

Ever since Rachel Carson blew the whistle on this agricultural game and exposed these losses in her book *Silent Spring* in 1962, a growing number of people have become aware of the downsides of this ruthless and unnatural way of producing our food and have begun to appreciate the heavy price it will bestow on future generations. Whilst in the aftermath of the *Silent Spring,* some chemicals like DDT where discontinued and eventually banned from use as agricultural pesticides, the momentum of industrialised agriculture continued unabated with very little public recognition of its downsides and dangers at government levels or by legislators, who are still not fully behind the protection of bees and other insects, including in the UK, even though their drastic decline in numbers seriously threatens the fertilisation of our crops.

However, I would suggest that with the advent of the Permaculture Movement, the small pockets of resistance to this juggernaut received a significant boost, and is now fuelling a new approach to food production appropriate for the third millennium. Its founder, the Tasmanian, Bill Mollison, whom, as I remember you saying, Grandpa, you met in South Africa in the early 1970s, introduced a design system and a philosophy which advocates agricultural ecosystems that are sustainable and self-sufficient. Whilst re-instating much of the tried and tested wisdom and experience of past generations, the movement is adapting these and incorporating them into a philosophy that redresses the imbalance in our relationship to nature, but in the context of today's possibilities and taking on board the basic requirements of urban and mega-city living. I would say this surely indicates the beginnings of a next evolutionary step.

Awareness of the dangers of current industrial agriculture is now growing – slowly but surely – helped greatly by organisations such as The Soil Association and the Centre for Alternative Technology (CAT) in North Wales – to name but two of many – offering real hope that a decisive shift is not too far off. Though we must recognise that pressure in the opposite direction is still very strong and powerful.

The astonishing increase in commitment to vegetarianism and even veganism, as you have already mentioned – which has happened quietly without much fanfare or propaganda, is evidenced in the fact that within just a few years, all kinds of products – not only food – on supermarket shelves are including the statement *'suitable for vegetarians'* on their packaging, and the variety and availability of these products has increased substantially. Also, you would now be hard pressed to find a restaurant menu – certainly in Europe – that does not include vegetarian and vegan options. In some European countries as much as ten percent of the population admits to adhering strictly to a vegetarian diet (five percent in the USA – 2020 figures) whilst polls in Germany have revealed that up to three times that number commit to what is called a 'flexitarian' diet, describing a person who occasionally mixes small quantities of meat and fish into a primarily vegetarian diet.

You must admit, surely, that we are seeing a genuine change of heart here, beginning to gain momentum.

25/02/2021 (It got rather late last night)

TRANSPORTATION AND MARKETING

Some years ago, I remember – as you will, Grandpa, it became a family joke for a while, when we discovered that a piece of cheese called 'Emmentaler' – after a valley in Switzerland – declared on its packaging that it was 'made' in Austria, packed in Canada, and imported from there into the UK. I was still a little girl then and remember it just as being funny. I don't think the 'carbon footprint' of food transport and plastic waste pollution had yet risen up the agenda of issues we worried about then.

So I can say that even in my life-time there has been an awakening in awareness of the damage being caused by so many aspects of our life-style. There is a real willingness by many people to accept the need for change and many efforts are being made. How real, significant change is going to come about is not yet clear, but the necessity for it is now widely accepted – I would say – by a majority of the population.

Whilst the pollution of our beaches with plastic food packaging and individual efforts at cleaning them up are making headlines, headway is being made with supermarkets co-operating in the encouragement to *buy local*, to eliminate plastic shopping bags and even with experiments of offering unwrapped vegetables. An increasing number of shoppers now pay careful attention to where things come from and whether they are grown or reared organically.

Public outrage at conditions in which animals are being transported long distances to slaughterhouses – even across continents – has led to legislation ensuring some improvement.

I know all this is barely scratching the surface of what needs to be achieved, but nevertheless, we are trying to show that *a start has been made*, and that momentum is gathering in the right direction, are we not?

CONSUMPTION

Here too, attitudes are changing in many sectors of society. Tables are returning to kitchens and dining rooms, and mealtimes at home are being re-instated as significant and enjoyable family events. Of course COVID restrictions are impacting on this at the moment, but following last Monday's announcement by the Prime Minister, there is hope that in a few months' time both going out to eat and family dinner parties at home will be back on the agenda.

Of course I could go on at length about obesity problems, junk food, fast food, processed food, fat-free, sugar-free, reduced salt content, etc. etc. – but all I will say here is, that the fact we are discussing all these things is surely a sign that many people are aware that there are problems and are worrying about them.

Numerous television programs are reviving home cooking as an art-form – even to be shared equally between the genders – and eating well prepared, healthy food is becoming a high priority in very many people's minds.

Of course there is still a long way to go before Tich Nhat Hanh's *mindful eating practice* becomes widely adopted, but I read somewhere that he was invited to teach and demonstrate the practice to all the staff at the Apple Headquarters in Silicon Valley and that apparently many said afterwards that this was the most enjoyable meal they had ever had. So, hope may blossom even there?

DISPOSING OF WASTE

This is a very sad chapter: an astonishing and devastating by-product of the affluent society!

We are told that globally one third of all the food produced goes to waste, and of course the lion's share of that happens in or because of the so-called *developed* world. I won't cite the shocking statistics here – they can easily be read up on line – but in the very fact that these statistics are readily accessible, lies our hope with regards to this subject. That people have started to monitor this atrocious waste and to calculate its effects and consequences is a sign that people have started to care. And very recently, some very honest and revealing documentary films have helped raise public awareness to a level that allows us to hope that significant improvement must come – though there are no real signs of it as yet.

The real culprit here is a lack of respect for the gifts that nature offers us. This is aided and abetted by the short-term success of industrial agriculture in making food so cheap and in some parts of the world so plentiful that all sense of its real value and its real cost has been lost. In a way, I think that it is here, that the full tragedy of industrial agriculture comes into focus. And it is from here that the energy and motivation must come to shift both the inner attitude and the external mechanisms to turn us back onto a dignified and humane path in our relationship to humanity as a whole, to all of nature's creatures and to Mother Earth.

But we cannot think of Mother Earth in this context and ignore food packaging. Because of all the unintended consequences, this is perhaps the most devastating and mind-blowing subject.

Information is gradually accumulating and can be read and seen online. It is hard to believe. I just give a glimpse of it here:

There are now five garbage islands in our oceans, two in the Atlantic, two in the Pacific and one in the Indian Ocean. The one called the GPGP – the Great Pacific Garbage Patch – is now said to be three times the size of France. These islands – which are not solid islands, but areas of plastic filled *soup* – consist ninety-nine percent of plastic, accumulated by ocean currents carrying the floating pieces from all the coastal cities and river estuaries.

Add to that the mountains of waste surrounding nearly every major city and the conditions of the rivers flowing through them – we have all seen these pictures by now… The mind boggles at the thought of what is to happen to all this stuff which does not decay but only disintegrates into ever smaller fragments before penetrating everything, everywhere. Some of what is deposited in the oceans contaminates marine life and ends up on our plates and in our stomachs.

But even here there is good news. Technologies are well on the way to being finalised in test-installations, both for the collection of plastic in the oceans and for recycling all types of plastic back to their original reusable substance. Both are on the brink of being ready for commercial *roll-out*. In addition, the financial strategy exists, to increase the cost of producing plastic from crude oil obtained from below ground to just above the cost of oil obtained from recycled plastic. This will give recycled plastic enough *value* to make its collection financially worthwhile everywhere and it will produce a global fund to kick-start the necessary shift within the less than one hundred firms involved globally, and to finance further research and environmental reparation. Only the willingness to make the change is still lacking.

Enough! This email is too long already. But don't you think the point has been made? I don't know how many other subjects or 'themes' you have in mind to tackle, but I have the feeling that we have achieved what we set out to do, and have convinced ourselves that at least the lifting of a foot in order to *take the next step in human evolution* has indeed begun?

I hope you are taking full advantage of this lovely spring weather we are having, now the wind has dropped and the sunshine is getting really warm in the mild air. Your garden must be lovely now. I wish I could come and enjoy it with you… and after the eighth of March, I will be allowed… :-)

Love you
Lanya

28/02/2021

Good morning Lanya,

Yes, I've been spending time in the garden and the workshop – hence my delay in replying. Whilst the snowdrops are nearly over, other early spring flowers are in full swing now and the ground has dried out quite a bit – it is glorious! I have started weeding and mending things and getting back into the swing of an outdoor life… hurray! Unfortunately your grandmother has not been too well – in fact she has been in bed all week – so she has been missing out. But, yesterday and today she is showing signs of getting better and hopefully she will be able to get out a little bit today.

Do I think we have convinced ourselves… ?

I think you have covered the theme of 'Food' as it impacts on our quest extremely thoroughly and convincingly. Who would have thought that there is so much to say about food?

You have brought back very vivid memories of my childhood in Austria in the late 1940s, after the war, when food was really scarce and every cooking and eating utensil was fought over and thoroughly scraped and licked clean by us children. Throwing away anything edible was simply not an option. I think that for people who have never experienced such times, it is hard to fully appreciate the significance of what you say about the dignity and true value of food. And yet, how many people are there still today, in faraway places – yet not so far in our digitally connected world – whose circumstances are far worse than those I experienced then? And we seem unable to find adequate ways to help them, even though there has never been a bigger charitable sector than we have now. Yet it is nowhere near enough.

And I agree with you: we have sufficiently proved the point.

When we started this 'finale' – on the 18th Feb. – I did make a list for myself of possible themes for us to consider. In addition to the two we have now covered, it included: the corporates, climate change, education and the digital world. But as you say, we have now shown convincingly enough that the shift which we call a 'next evolutionary step' is already under way, and that this could be demonstrated in any aspect of our lives.

I could very briefly summarise what was in my mind when I made that list. For instance:

i) Under the *corporates* I was going to show how the global company, Therme Group, with whom my son now works, is dedicated to solving fundamental issues of wellbeing posed by current mega-city-life. They build facilities that nurture and encourage healthy living, combining physical exercise, cultural activities, food and nutrition, mental regeneration and much more in carbon neutral ways, at a cost that's affordable by the majority of the population and in widely accessible locations. Proving that it is possible to operate successfully within the current corporate world in ethically responsible ways and for the common good.

ii) Under *climate change*... well, I don't even need to start to list the countless initiatives which are already underway to tackle this subject; and now finally – hopefully – it will be faced head-on at the upcoming COP 26.

iii) Under education I was going to encourage you to talk about your mother's initiatives in her career as a head teacher; explaining how she was able, successfully, to base the ethos in her schools and her curricula on sets of values voluntarily and enthusiastically adopted by the children and the teachers, as well as being supported by the school governors – alas only reluctantly tolerated by the national education authorities

iv) Under the digital world I was similarly going to encourage you to talk about the original intention for the world wide web as conceived by Tim Berners-Lee in 1989, and its expression, amongst others, in Wikipedia, as a voluntary, free information system with minimal governance, totally reliant on the honesty of its participants, growing and surviving successfully since 2001. And I was sure you would have many other examples to show how the internet – in spite of all its teething-problems – has many aspects which support our contention.

Of course, you may have had your own list. But the point is, that these are just typical, representative examples of what is happening in all fields of life, and details of all of them can be read up on the internet.

However, what will be harder to find on the internet is evidence of the inner transformation and the reorientation of internal, subtle energies below the surface, which has also begun, and of which these are outward expressions. I think to end our quest and bring it to a fruitful conclusion we ought to talk once more about these inner aspects of our lives.

How does that sound to you?

Hope you are able to enjoy this glorious Sunday to the full.
With much love
Grandpa

28/02/2021

Hello Grandpa,

That sounds great!

I take it that you mean we should go back to your model of our *inner landscape* and see how all of this fits in there?

Absolutely! But you will have to navigate. I don't yet feel confident enough in that sphere to know where to start. I can see though, that any real answer to our quest must have its roots there.

So please, start us off?

Hugs
Lanya

P.S. There are two documents that come to mind, which I think might bridge the outer and inner landscapes we have talked about. I know you are familiar with both of them: *The Earth Charter* and the *Laudato Si* by Pope Francis. Are they not both evidence that the transformation is under way on both the inner and outer levels? Are they not signposts along this path? Or, perhaps I see them as Ahmed's lanterns – both. The Laudato Si is even sub-titled: '*On Care for our Common Home*'.

01/03/2021

Dearest Lanya, (in the early morning)

I'll gladly make a start.

First though, the two documents mentioned in your P.S.:

The Earth Charter, as you know, is a document very close to my heart. I had a draft copy of it even before it was finalised and formally launched in the Hague in June 2000, because just then I happened to be in touch with the secretary of Prof. Steven Rockefeller, the chairman of the drafting committee which coordinated the responses to the – until then – widest international consultation ever conducted. I wrote numerous papers about it at the time of the launch... well, I won't go into all that now. Suffice it to say that I think it is a splendid document and certainly a milestone on the road towards global governance. Sadly it has never really made the headlines in the UK or received much official or even media support here. I think it is receiving widespread endorsement elsewhere and particularly in the Spanish speaking world of South America. That is helped by the fact that its headquarters are located in Costa Rica. It is proving to be a popular teaching aid in schools, which is great! I think its potential is huge and its time has not yet come.

The Laudato Si was an enormous surprise for me when I first read it in 2016. That the head of the Roman Catholic Church could produce such a document, and that the Catholic Church could elect such a person as their Pope, seemed to me like a highly significant milestone for the whole of humanity on its path towards the goal we are both exploring in this conversation. I am so glad you brought it up at this point. Everyone should read it – really, everyone, not just Catholics!

Thinking about these two documents now, I can't help

feeling that their fate seems to underline what we touched on earlier: that on this journey, real, lasting, evolutionary change has to be the result of an inner compulsion experienced by individuals. Top down influence is of limited significance and must be content to inspire and to give encouragement. In this area prescription is useless. I have no insight into the extent to which the Laudato Si may still be playing a role within the Catholic Church, or – more likely – whether it has found its place on the bookshelves to be preserved for posterity. But I do know that in the very early days of the millennium the expectation was for the Earth Charter to be adopted by the United Nations as a document to directly influence decisions at that level. Outwardly, that has not happened, but perhaps, in the background, it is doing that work in the hearts and minds of the individuals sitting at the conference tables; and perhaps that applies equally to the Laudato Si. That would be entirely in line with what we have learnt of astrologers' predictions about the age of Aquarius, don't you think?

Thank you so much for remembering these two documents in this context.

Now – about *the inner aspects of our lives* I mentioned:

As you say, our tetrahedron model provides us with an image of our inner landscape; and the themes we have spoken about above, illustrating our claim that a next evolutionary step is already under way, are manifestations in the outer world. What is the relationship between these two?

As I see it, changes can happen in both worlds independently of each other. Since the inner world is personal to each individual, developments there can remain hidden and un-manifested for a long time, or may never manifest directly as a change in the outer world at all, only changing the quality of other outer manifestations. Changes made in the outer world which have no roots in the inner world are only like superficially rearranged deckchairs on the Titanic with little real value. They do not change the substance of things. Like the revolutions we talked about earlier, they are but movements on the same spot and cannot be called evolutionary.

Obviously, in our quest we are trying to detect evolutionary change – that is: change that takes place in both worlds more or less simultaneously. That means it must take place in the inner life of individuals, and if it is to affect a whole society it must take place in a sufficient number of individuals to constitute a critical mass. As Schweitzer described it: *'when the meadows turn green in Springtime, it is because each individual blade of grass is turning green by its own inner compulsion'*; and I would add, 'because the time and the outer conditions are conducive'. Everything is connected and when the time is right the change will happen. The willingness is all. The necessary energy comes through inspiration – *in-spirit-action*. Then the *inner* and the *outer* are in harmony and evolution takes place.

By setting in motion a gradual process of remembering increasingly clearly who we really are, we raise our consciousness into what – in the language of our tetrahedron model – we call the *second dimension,* from where the illusory opposition of ego and soul becomes clearly visible, unification and harmonious balance becomes possible; and natural feelings of inner peace and harmony begin to emerge. The noise of inner conflict begins to subside and the still small voice which speaks to us in our hearts begins to be heard. With this, the voice of conscience makes itself felt ever more strongly and the possibility of all this being experienced consciously becomes a reality.

Thus, by working in the core of people's hearts, this conscious evolutionary process develops the energy for its journey, and, as we have now realised, this process has been on the move for well over a century and a half.

Yes, there is no doubt that this process, this awakening of a new evolutionary initiative within the human psyche is already in full swing, and I have a feeling that very soon it will no longer rely on outstanding personalities to keep it going and give it impetus, but that quite ordinary people like you and me will carry it along in great numbers.

How does this sound to you? Is it coming together? Do you feel the *inner* and the *outer* merging together into a unity?

Enjoy the sunshine when it comes!
Much love
Grandpa

01/03/2021

Oh Grandpa, (in the early evening)

I read your email of this morning on my phone, sitting on a bench in my little town garden, drenched by warm spring sunshine. You know, a baker's life has its drawbacks, like starting the day at three o'clock in the morning, but one of its perks is, that you can sit in the garden and enjoy the sun at three o'clock in the afternoon.

Anyway, having finished reading, I just sat there. Everything was so quiet and I just sat – at peace. Birds were quietly twittering in the distance; a huge bumblebee was struggling to balance on the delicate blossom of a little blue wood anemone. Eventually it gave up and moved on to a sturdy primrose where it was much happier. A robin came and sat on the wall opposite and literally sang for me. I just sat there and was part of it all. And whilst these things were happening, inside me time seemed to stand still – everything was still – and safe, and all was as it should be; everything belonged together; and something in me knew that if anything needed to be done, I would know what to do and it would be done.

I must have sat like that for at least twenty minutes before going in to make myself a drink. I brought it out munching a biscuit and sat back on my bench, soaking in the sunshine. What a wonder it all is? Living on this planet – circling around the sun, receiving its light and heat and all sorts of other radiation which we particularly appreciate after a long winter. And we are all part of this huge solar system, which on the other hand is such a tiny part of our galaxy and all is connected and hangs together just like the cells in our bodies. Something in me was aware of all this but was also part of it – an integral part – tiny, yet important – above all: not separate, not alone, but all one!

Gradually, my mind went back to our quest, and it seemed that here was the answer: right here! In the letting go of all the complicated stuff and being resigned to the simplicity of this moment! A feeling that *it is all really quite simple* emerged in this stillness. There was the certainty that it is possible in all the hurly burly of life to remember this stillness, which is always there, behind it all. I suppose that is what you mean by the *self-remembering* you mentioned a few days ago?

Is this then the evolutionary step you talk about? That we all experience this awareness from time to time but carry the memory of it with us all the time? Then we know what has to be done! There is no need for long lists, big programs, elaborate prescriptions, complicated solutions and systems... we just go back to the stillness inside us, where ego and soul are in harmony, where all of humanity is united with all life on earth, the sun with all her planets, and all the stars in our galaxy are united, – and from here we know – each moment – what to do.

I feel I have arrived. For me this quest is at an end. There will no doubt be other quests, but for the moment, I am content.

And I thank you from the bottom of my heart for making this journey with me. I hope it has been as rewarding for you as it is for me!

your loving Lanya

P.S. Nevertheless, the question still arises: How can this whole quest of ours resolve itself into sitting on a garden bench for half an hour?

03/03/2021

My dear Lanya,

What you describe seems indeed to be exactly what we have been searching for – the experience of the reality of ego and soul in harmony with each other in stillness and in peace, giving rise to the conviction of knowing what needs to be done from moment to moment.

In this, our quest has indeed found its target – for me also.

You ask: '…how can it all resolve itself into sitting still for half an hour on a garden bench'?

I would say: because the answer lies in the experience – and not in any words; and the experience is instantaneous: once tasted, it cannot be undone – as I know – and you now know.

Nevertheless, words help to digest what has been tasted.

Thus, in the context of our tetrahedron model: on that bench in the sunshine, your awareness actually began to rise up into the third dimension from *node 3* towards *node 4*; and your view encompassed the whole of the base triangle and its connection to the world of spirit at *node 4* flowed through you. This felt like the answer to our quest because – as it seems to me – this is indeed the role assigned to us as human beings: to act as a channel, a transmitter, for the energy of spirit to fill and be experienced consciously throughout the whole of the tetrahedron – i.e. the whole of creation within our sphere of influence – which is all of life on earth.

And I think, this is indeed the answer to your very original question posed at the outset of our quest: *this is how we can co-operate with Mother Earth. It is what we can do for her!* And that is why it felt like the destination of our quest.

Making this experience of stillness and inner peace accessible to all of us is 'the next evolutionary step' which humankind will accomplish by all of us finding a path to this destination in the privacy of our own hearts.

Much work has already been done to make this possible, as our quest has shown.

Which is why you and I can conceive of the possibility, that experiences similar to the one you describe, can become regular occurrences for many ordinary people. They can become the bedrock of a new attitude to life for the majority of the population. Of course, such experiences cannot be forced or manufactured or induced. They must arise freely as a result of inspiration. But there is work that can be done to prepare the willingness to receive them, to allow them, recognise them and to treasure them.

What we have been doing on this quest, I would say, has been concerned with just this kind of preparatory work, which

Albert Schweitzer calls *self-perfecting*. We tend to over-complicate our expectations of where this work should lead. But you have clearly demonstrated, by the simplicity of the *experience* you describe, that a simple surrender to the present moment is all it takes...! But as we know from so many spheres of life: the simplest is often the most difficult.

When society has finally overcome its fear and prejudice against the world of spirit, and people find the courage to surrender their egos into the arms of their soul, then the ground work to prepare for the 'willingness' of which we have spoken, will be done by many. And it will be taught in primary schools where children are still naturally receptive without intellectual complication. This will then better prepare them for the real work which they have come here to accomplish, filling their lives with meaning and purpose and a deep happiness. A happiness that is nourished by *caring and giving* rather than by *coveting and receiving* and there will be no need for *grasping*.

As you say, Lanya, let us leave it there. It is the work of the age of Aquarius to take it further and bring it to fruition. His reign spans some two thousand six hundred years, and I think we have shown that the springtime of this new age had begun about a century and a half ago. Its fragrance of hope, anticipation and new adventure fills the air. We can sense it and welcome it, and we can embrace the emerging vision of a full flowering of a mature humanity. Let us look forward to a long summer for our children's children in future generations.

My dear Lanya, I thank you for inviting me to join you in this quest and embrace you heartily – hopefully, very soon, no longer virtually,

Your Grandpa

Epilogue

12/05/2021

Dear Reader

Since Frederick and I have decided to share this account of our joint quest with all who might come across it and might be interested, let me conclude with an invitation:

The evolutionary train is 'on the move'; it is climbing up the tetrahedron pyramid we have created. So, wherever you are: be it on the terrace outside your sitting room, or in a forest, on the high seas, on a balcony on the 27th floor of a mega-city skyscraper, or high up in one of earth's majestic mountain ranges, or in the back garden of your little cottage or bungalow, why not come on board, let nature speak to you through the buzz of one of her tiny insects, or the fragrance of her colourful flowers, or the robin singing on the garden wall… and in Grandpa's words:

> **Why not give a thought each day**
> **To the role we humans**
> **are here to play**
> **In the life of our evolving planet.**
>
> **As our adolescent ego comes of-age**
> **We'll play our proper part**
> **upon this stage.**
> **As consciousness matures among us.**

**Our common cause with Nature
will come clear:
Instead of raping Mother Earth,
we'll hold her dear.
And learn to care for all her creatures.**

But as he also said: words can only take us so far. They are only symbols carrying ideas, not the ideas themselves. These have to be experienced and lived to become real. In that sense the conclusion of this 'quest' is only just a beginning…

So let's continue this journey together!

– Lanya

THE END

APPENDIX 'A'

THE LIST OF QUOTATIONS FROM THE FOUR GOSPELS

(Scripture taken from the New King James Version®. Copyright © 1982 by Thomas Nelson. Used by permission. All rights reserved.)

- Mathew 16, 26 – '*For what profit is it to a man if he gains the whole world, and loses his own **soul**? or what will a man give in exchange for his **soul***'.

- Mathew 22, 37 – '*Jesus said to him, "You shall love the Lord your God with all your heart, with all your **soul**, and with all your mind."*'

- Mathew 26, 38 – '*Then he said to them, "My **soul** is exceedingly sorrowful, even unto death. Stay here and watch with Me."*'

- Mark 8, 36 – '*For what will it profit a man if he gains the whole world, and loses his **soul**?*'

- *37 'Or what will a man give in exchange for his **soul**?'*

- Mark 12, 30 – '*And you shall love the Lord your God with all your heart, with all your **soul**, with all your mind and with all your strength. This is the first commandment'.

– **Mark 14, 34** – *'Then He said to them, "My **soul** is exceedingly sorrowful, even to death. Stay here and watch."'*.

– **Luke 1, 46** – *'And Mary said, "My **soul** magnifies the Lord."'*.

– **Luke 10, 27** – *'So he answered and said: "You shall love the Lord your God with all your heart, with all your **soul**, with all your strength, and with all your mind and your neighbour as yourself."'*.

– **Luke 12, 19** – *'And I will say to myself: "**Soul**, you have many goods laid up for many years, take your ease, eat, drink, and be merry."'*

– **20** – *'But God said to him, "Fool! This night your **soul** will be required of you; then whose will those things be which you have provided?"'*.

– **Luke 21, 19** – *'In your patience possess ye your **souls**'*

– **John 12, 27** – *'Now my **soul** is troubled, and what shall I say? "Father, save me from this hour"? But for this purpose I came to this hour'*.

Comments by interested readers

Predrag Cicovacki,

Professor of Philosophy and Director of Peace and Conflict Studies at the College of the Holy Cross, Massachusetts, USA. Author of twelve books and editor of eight:

"Percy Mark's book 'Lanya' is not easy to classify. It is certainly not an academic book of any kind, nor is it a work of fiction, as we usually understand this term. One of the first associations may be with Jostein Gaarder's bestselling book, 'Sophie's World'; it contains the same concern for wisdom and love, unfolded through various narratives covering the history of Western philosophy. But 'Lanya' is broader in its vision, by opening itself up for the entire wealth of human wisdom, that of the non-European traditions included. This book also has an advantage insofar as it does not present things in terms of puzzles that can and should be resolved. 'Lanya' is a story of questions to be asked at all ages and by all individuals; the story of the world-wonders and life-wonders narrated through the dialogues of an eighty-year-old man and his fifteen-year-old granddaughter. And what a magical narrative it is! It takes us to the world of the Vedas and the performance of Mozart's 'Magic Flute'. It makes us recall the poetry of Goethe and the unorthodox wisdom of the former Vietnamese monk Thich Nath Hanh. It immerses us in 'The Chronicles of Narnia' by C.S. Lewis and in the 'Laudato Si' by Pope Francis. In its main tenor, this is surely a book of wisdom and love. At its deepest level, however, it may be even more precise to describe it as a book of trust- and connection-building in our disoriented and disconnected world. This is a book inviting us on a magical journey, and everyone who undertakes it will come out of it with a nourished soul and a happy smile."

Patricia Morris PG Dip.Couns., MA (Couns.Psychol.), Dip.Online Couns.(Distinction), Dip. Online Supervision (Distinction).

Therapist, Counsellor and Counselling Supervisor; Author of ten published books:

"The sage and the ingenue are the protagonists of a pedagogical genre that goes back to Plato's Socratic dialogues. In the 1990s there was Jostein Gaarder's blockbuster novel 'Sophie's World' in which a father covertly directs his young daughter towards uncovering the mysteries of classical philosophy. Percy Mark's 'Lanya' is of the same literary family but his intent is to use western and eastern philosophy to find the means to rescue us from the threats of the future.

By engaging her in dialogue, a kindly grandfather answers his schoolgirl granddaughter's intelligent questions. The complexity of their affectionate conversations increases as she gets older and as they cover more territory, including literally, for whenever we meet them they are travelling, first by train, then in a car, and at last virtually via email during the COVID pandemic.

Their dialogue explores diverse subjects such as climate change (from Rachel Carson to Greta Thunberg), religion ('we are but a speck in the finger of God'), astrology (we are entering 'the Age of Aquarius'), prayer, meditation, free will, artificial intelligence, our purpose on earth, and more. In time the teacher and student become intellectual peers developing further the grandfather's theory of the 'next evolutionary step' that we are moving towards and that will save us from our own destructiveness. They hold that human beings are 'transmitters of spiritual energy'. Our survival depends on individuals separately unifying the ego and the soul which will effect collective, global change.

'Lanya' is a carefully argued, endearingly optimistic work, wide-ranging in its philosophical and historical reach. It is structured to lead the reader on a journey from worried paralysis to a necessary, comforting solution."

Catherine Howell,

Twenty-eight-year-old lawyer, commenting on 'Lanya's Jouney', as available on Amazon, now Part One of 'Lanya' the MS included here.

"This book makes you think for yourself and gives you things for your mind to mull over. It is a book that contains a lot of deep and meaningful information which isn't imposed on you but rather warmly invites you to think for yourself whilst teaching you valuable insights. It is a very open-minded book and easy for any age to read and understand. A great book on life."